GHOST QUEEN

A BOOK FROM ELSEWHERE
BY
BRITT WILSON

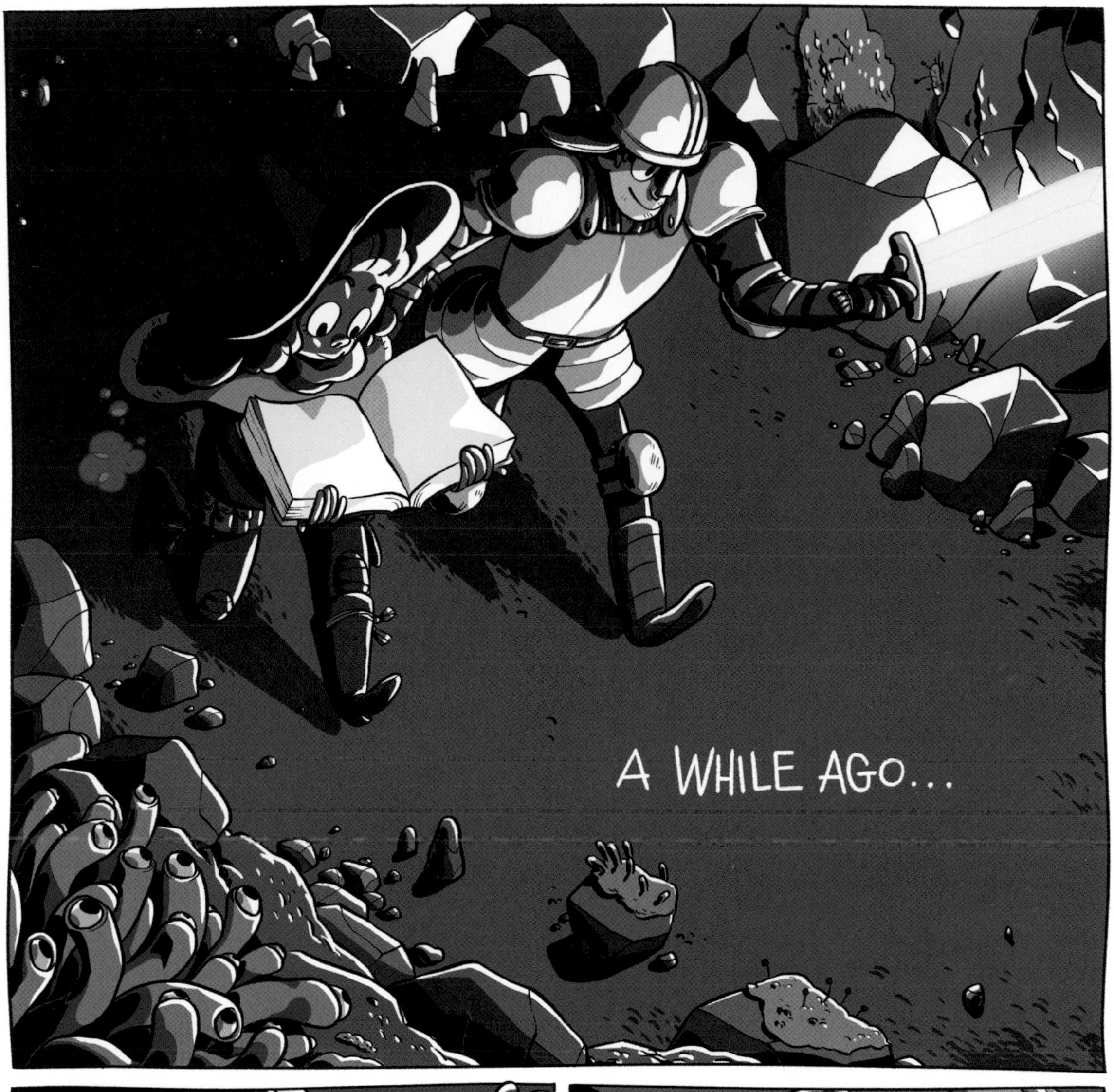
A WHILE AGO...

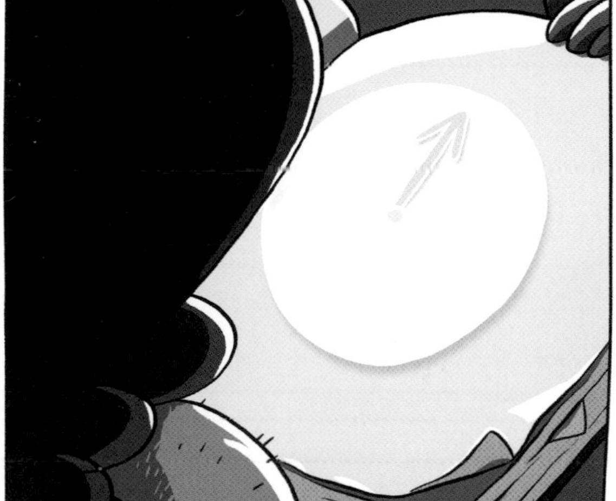

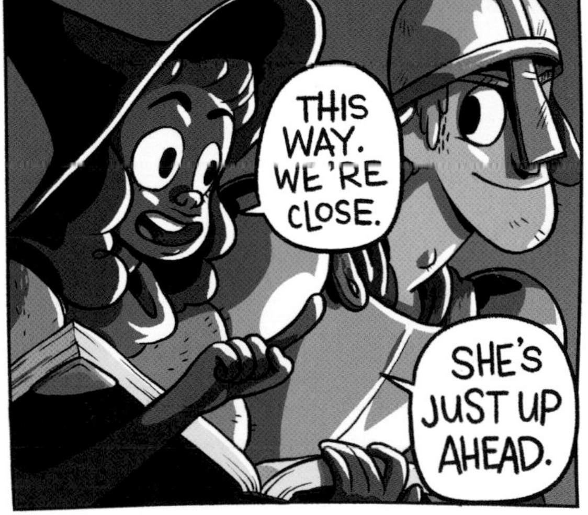
THIS WAY. WE'RE CLOSE.
SHE'S JUST UP AHEAD.

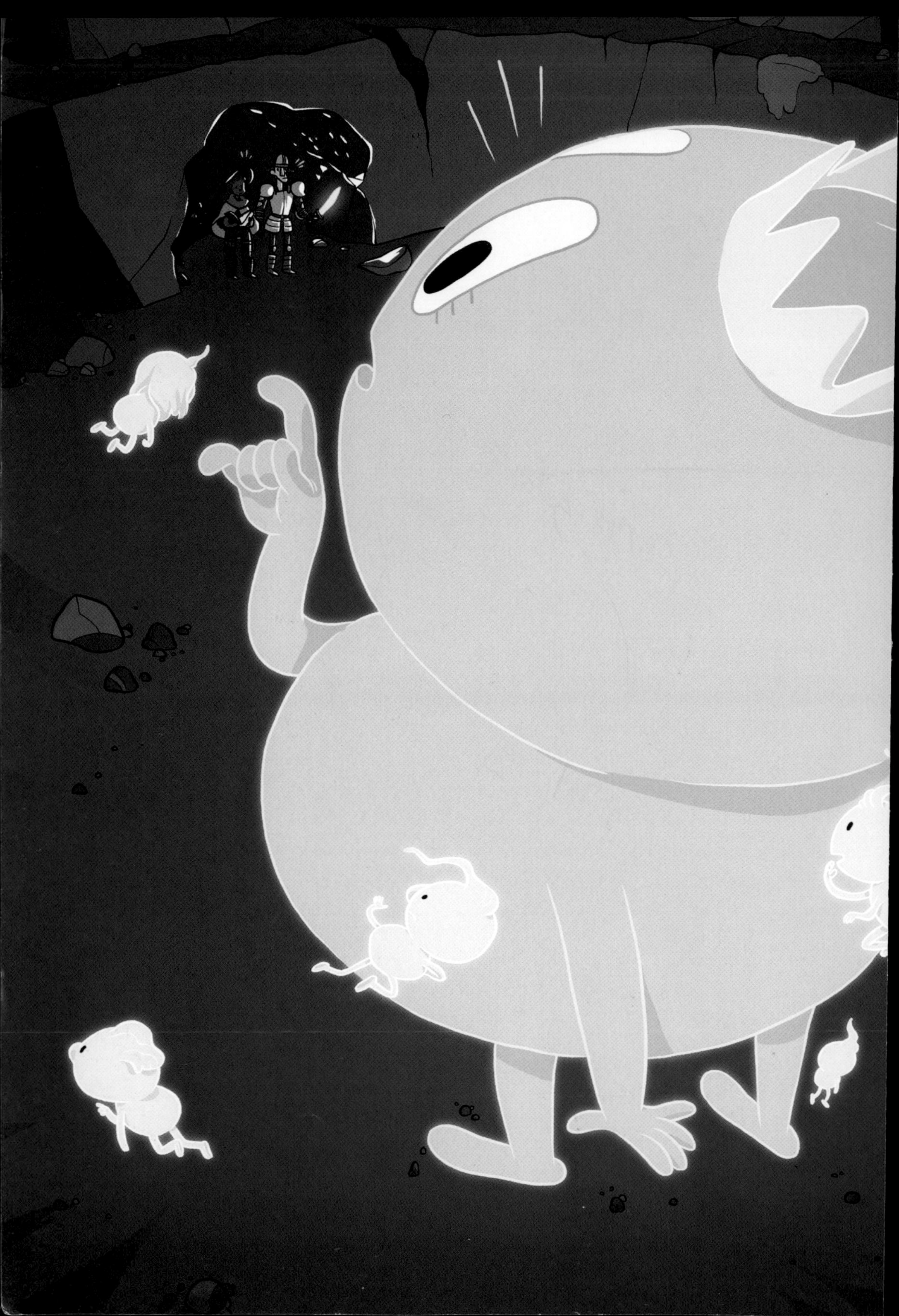

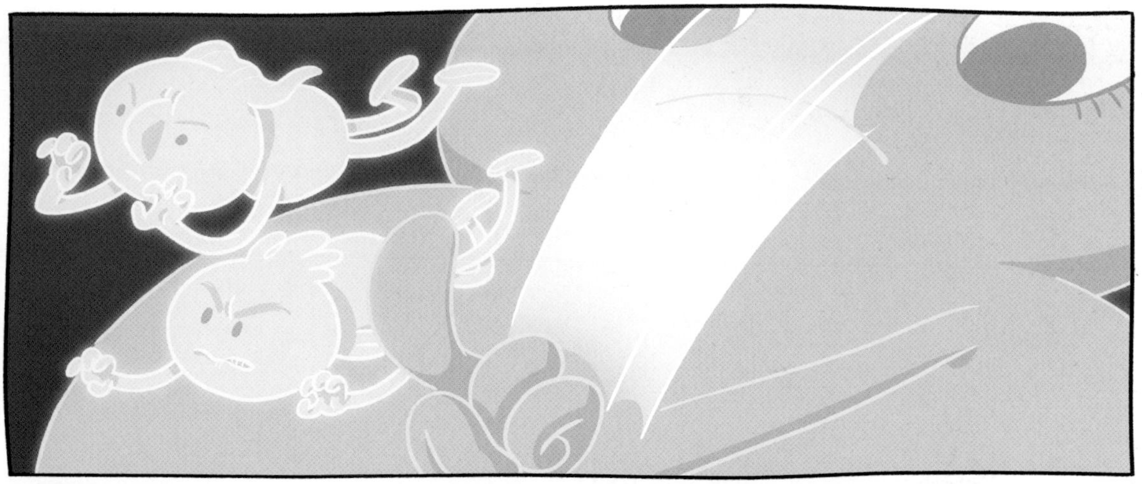

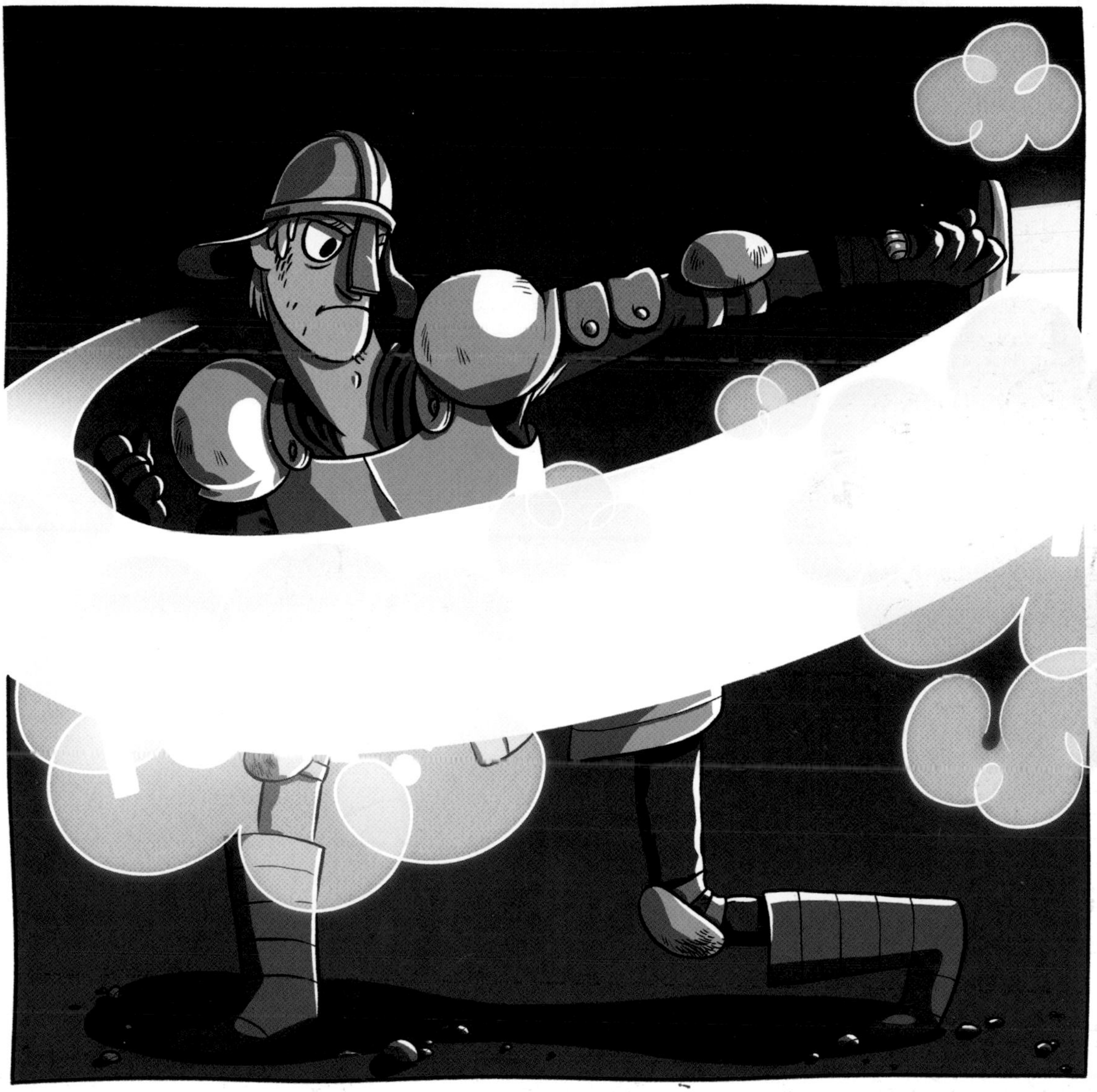

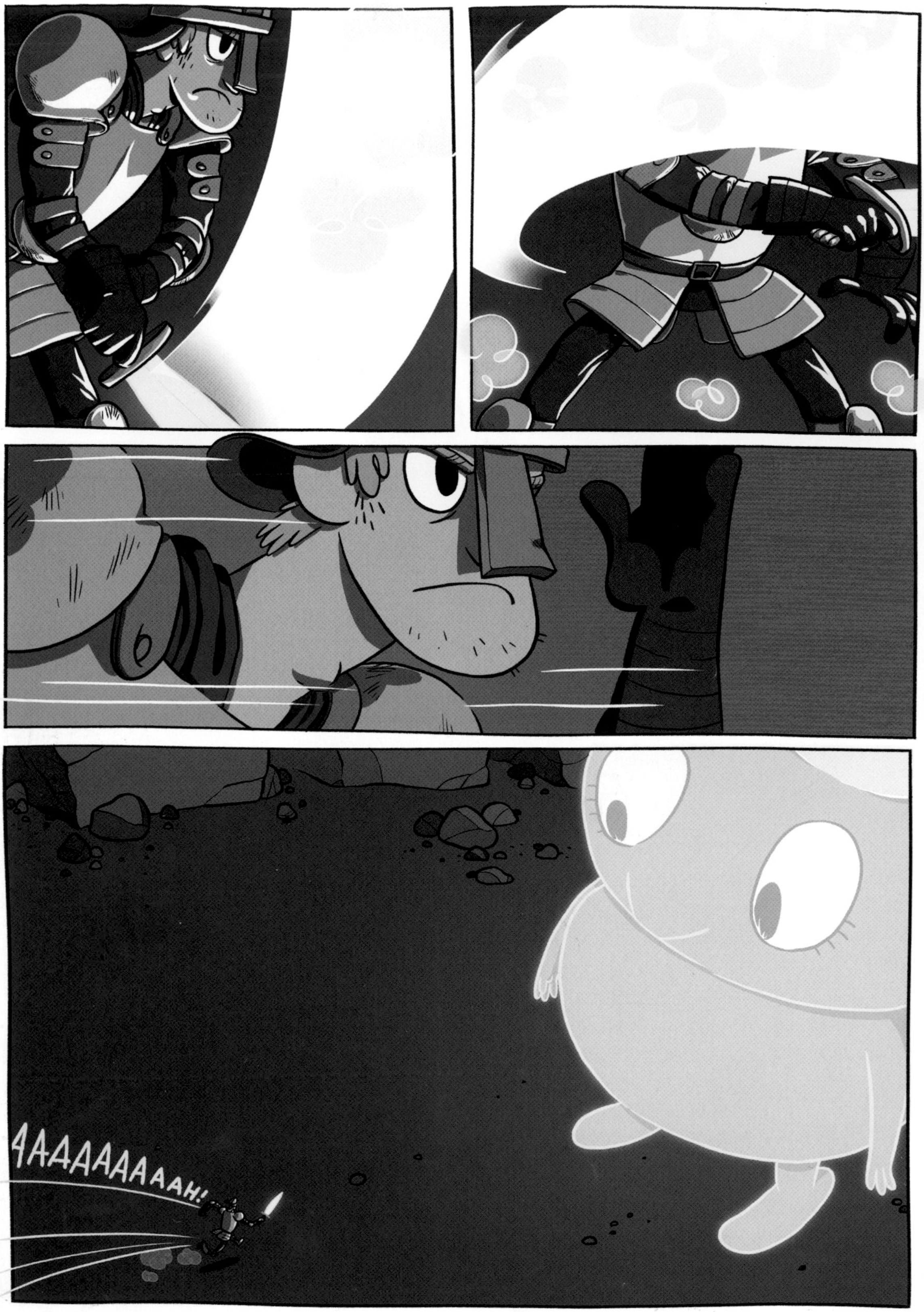
AAAAAAAAAAH!

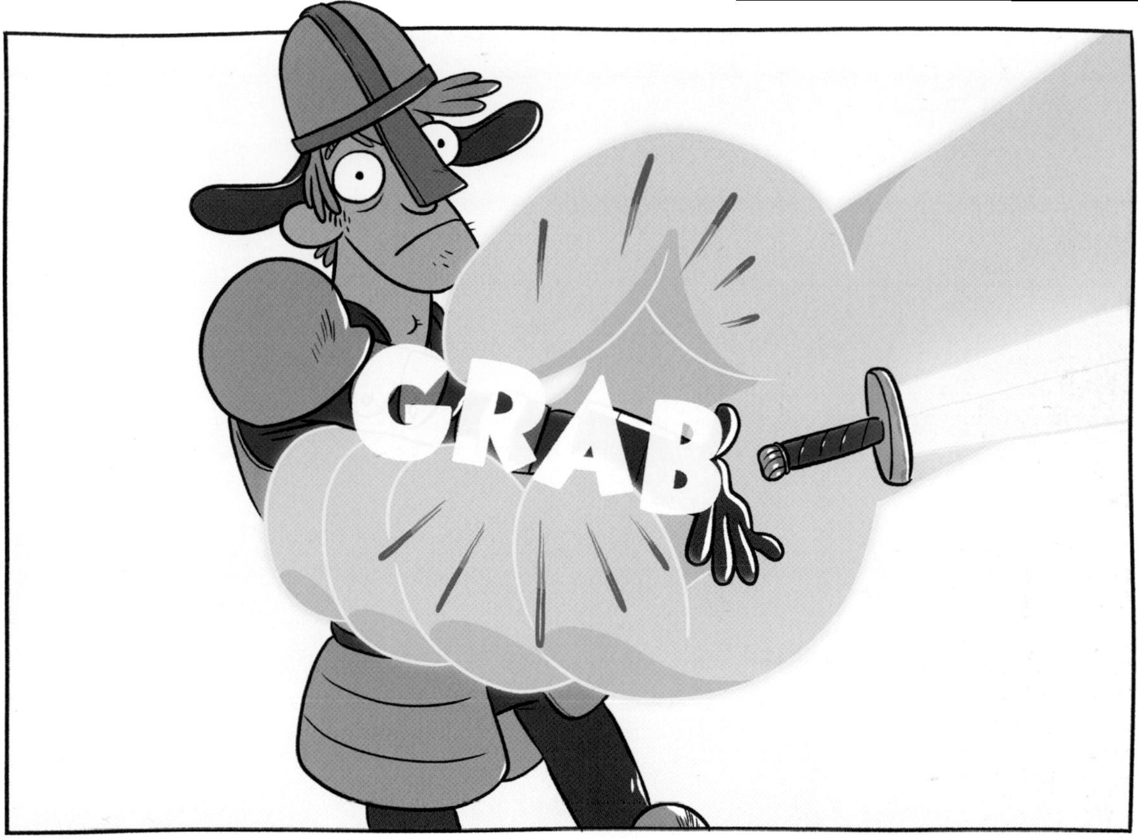
GRAB

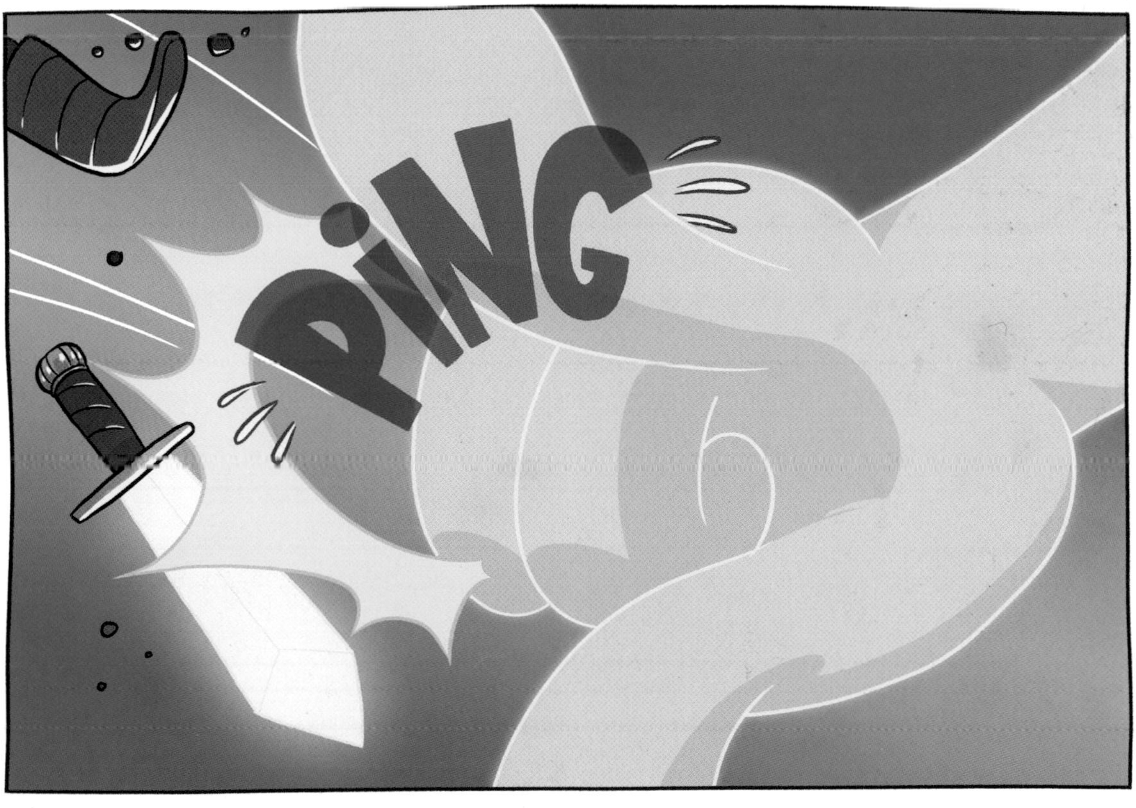
PING

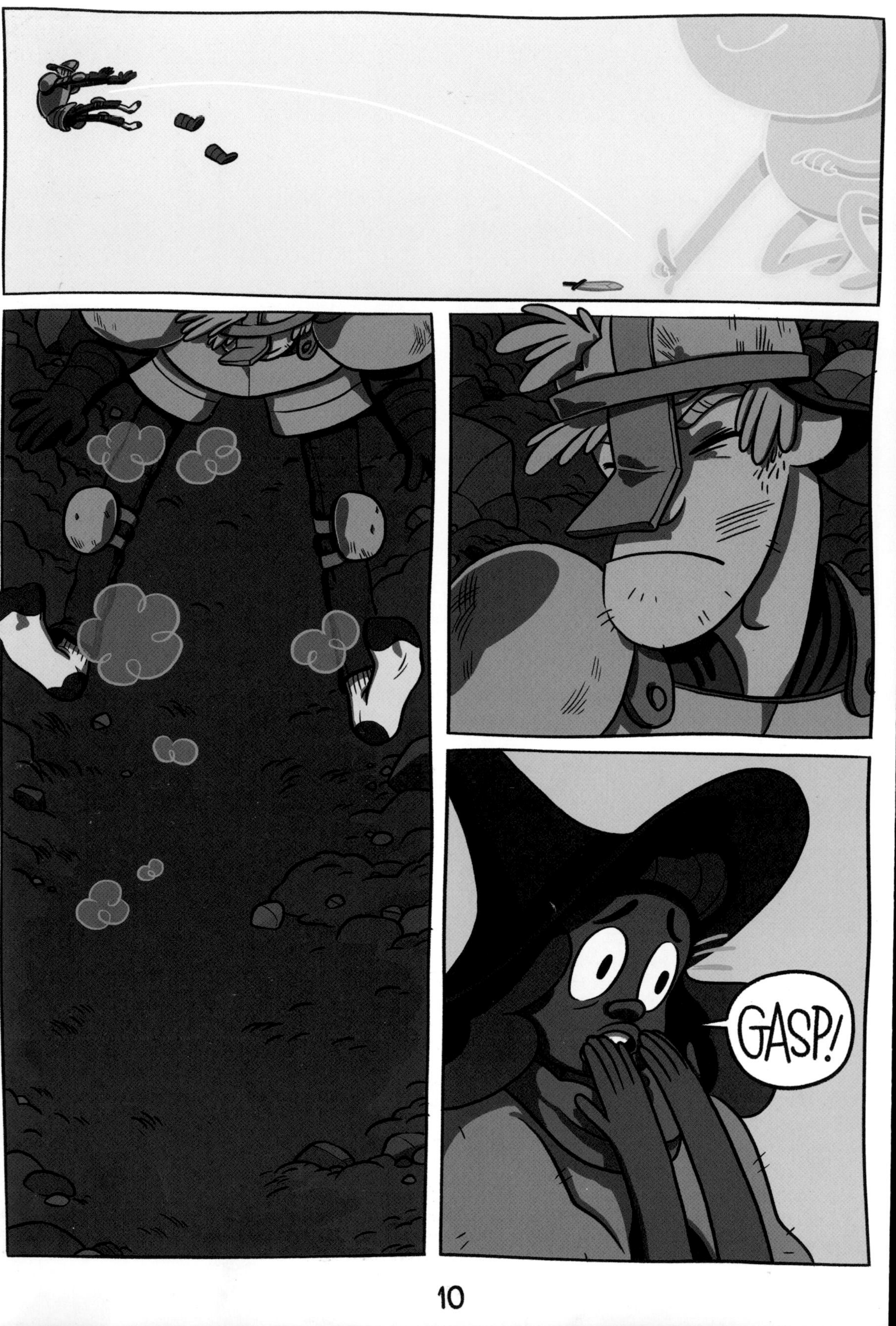
GASP!

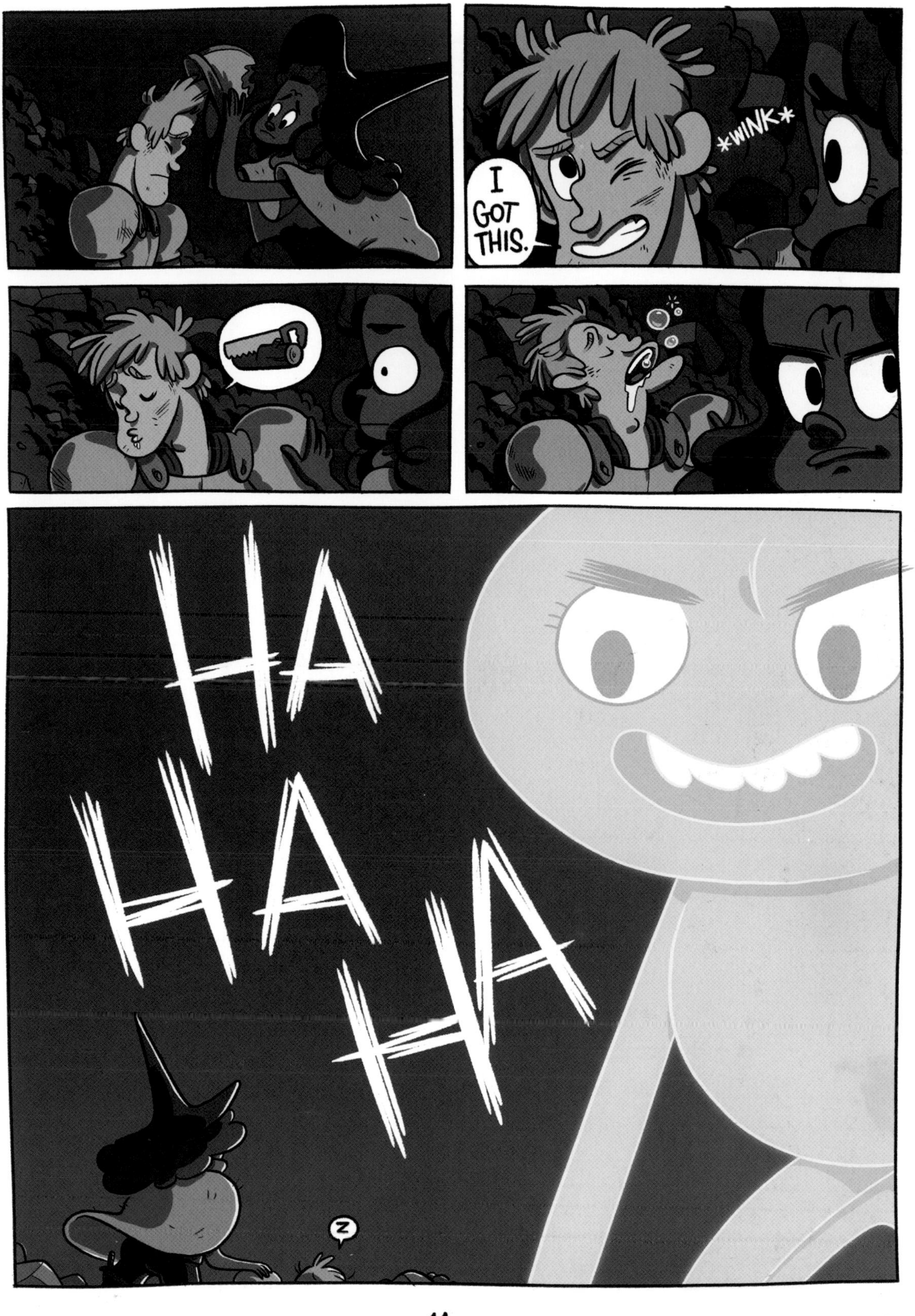
I GOT THIS.
WINK
HA HA HA HA
Z

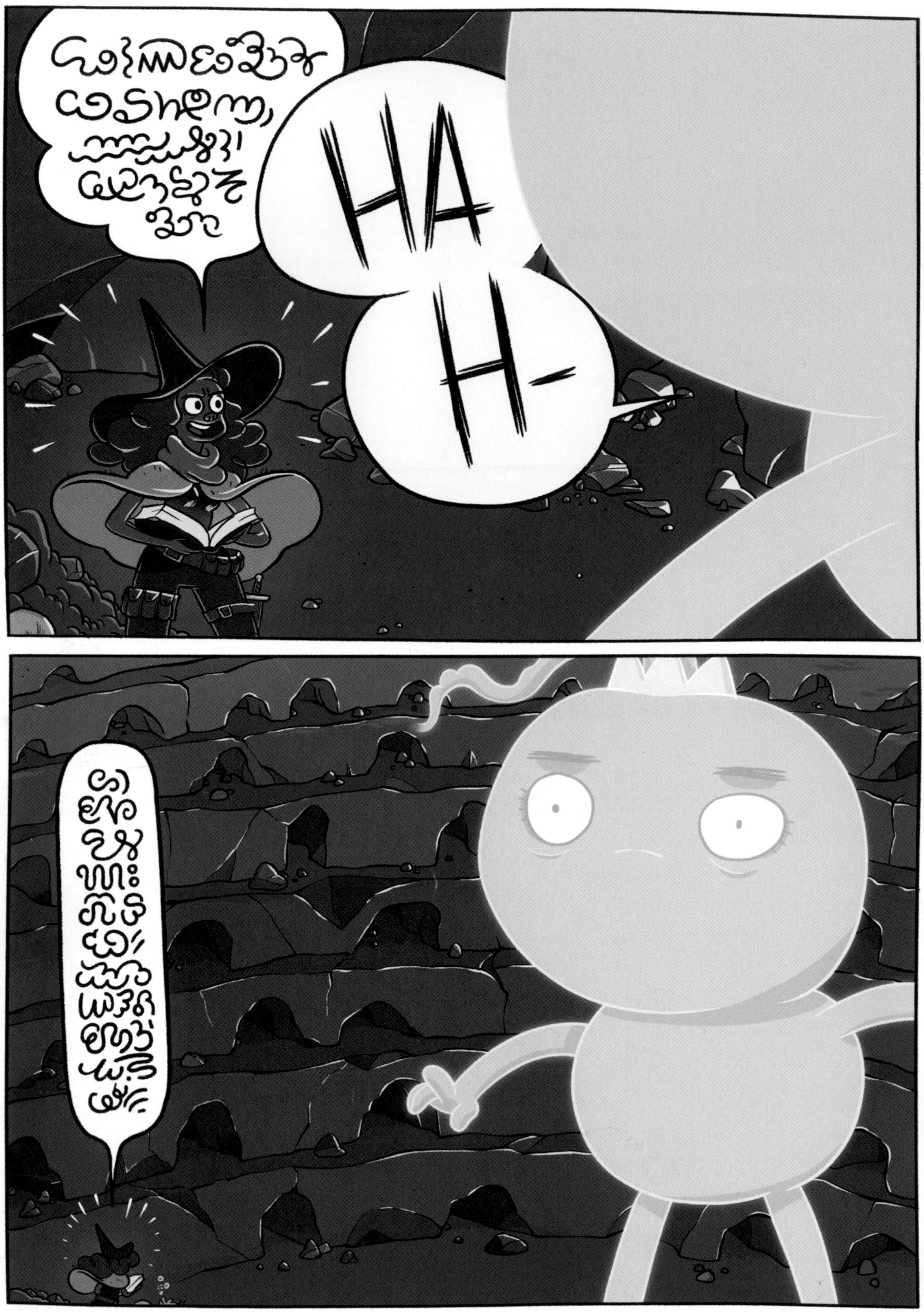
HA
H-

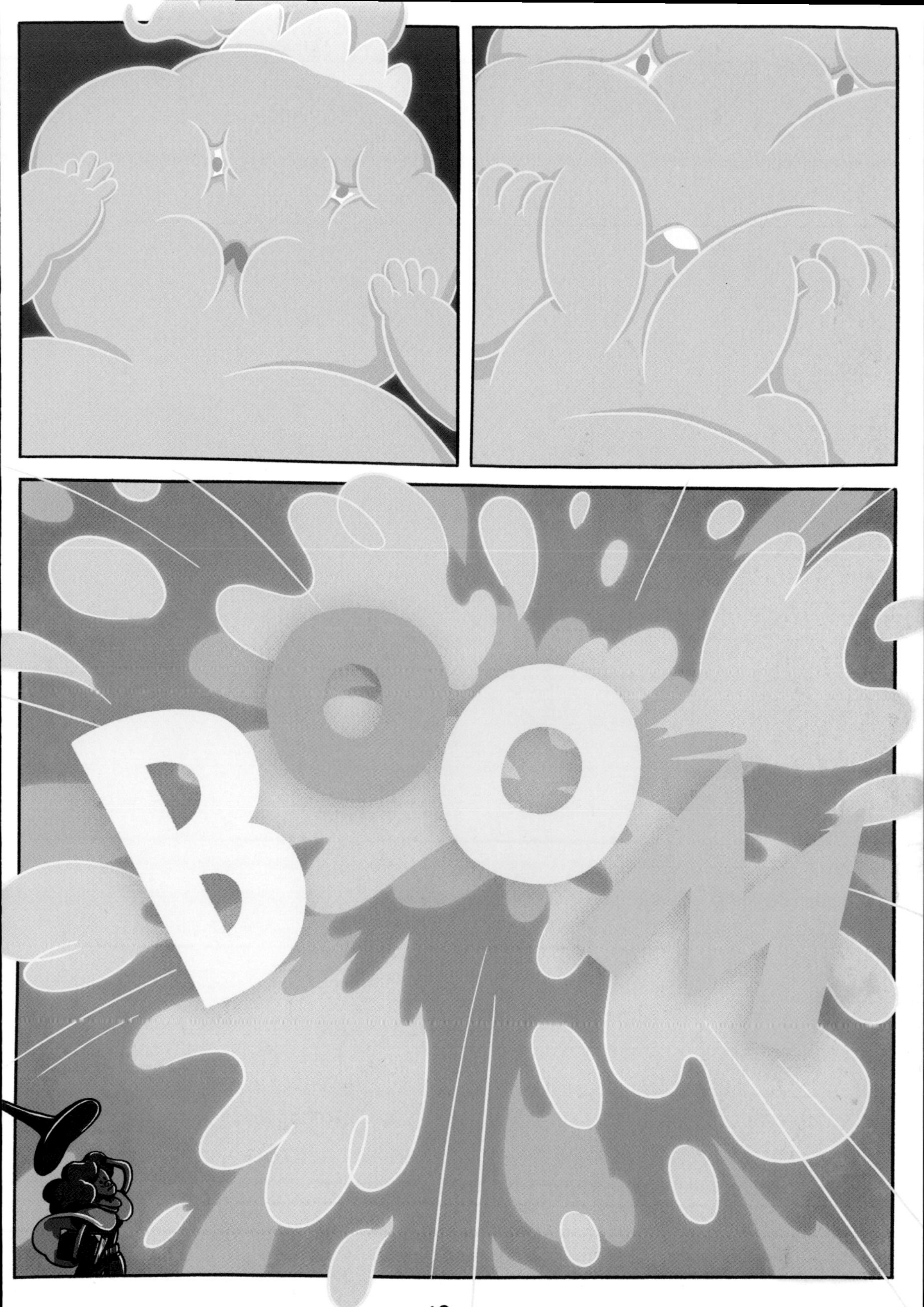
BOOM

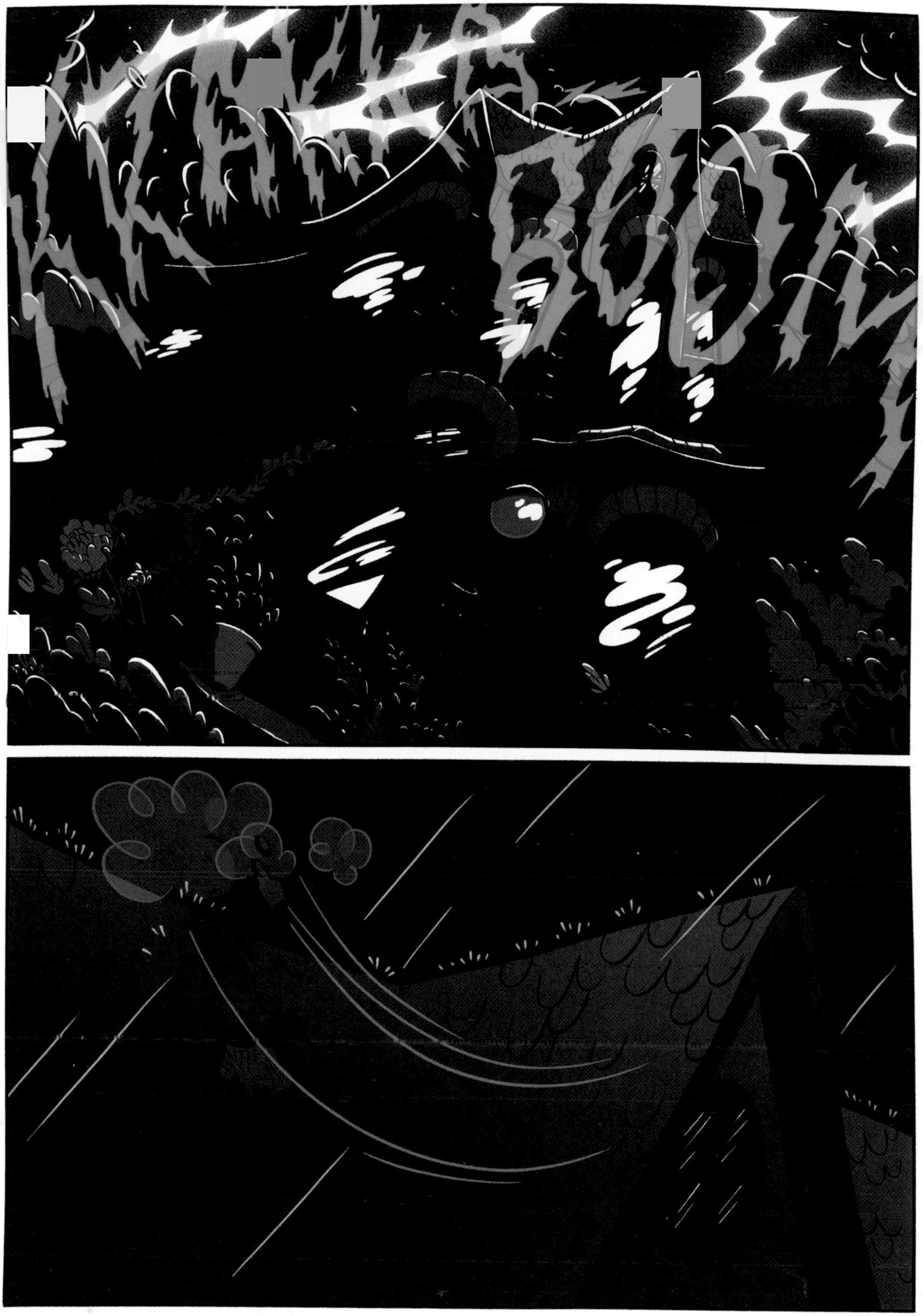
BOOM

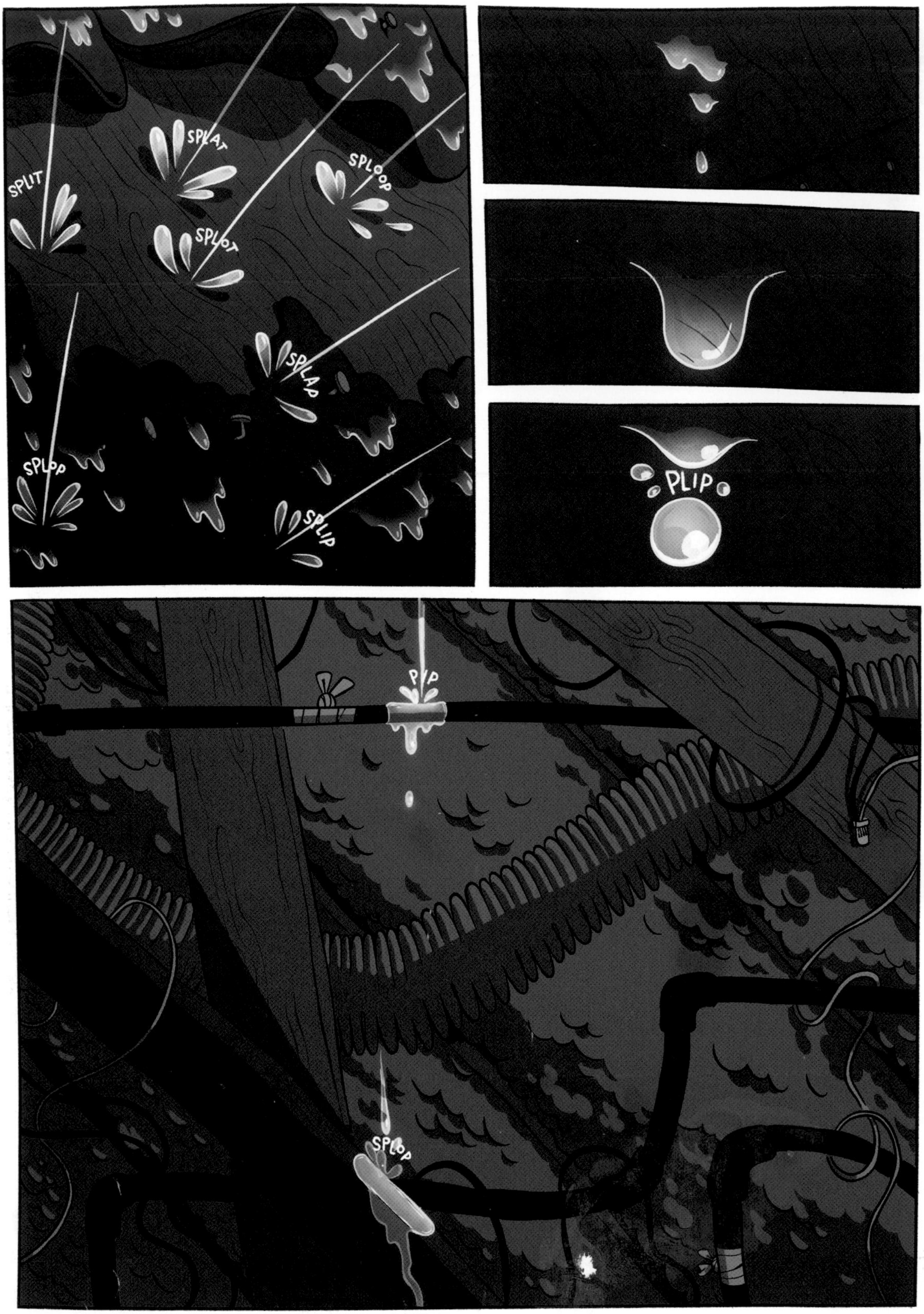
SPLIT
SPLAT
SPLOOP
SPLOT
SPLAP
SPLOP
SPLIP
PLIP
PLIP
SPLOP

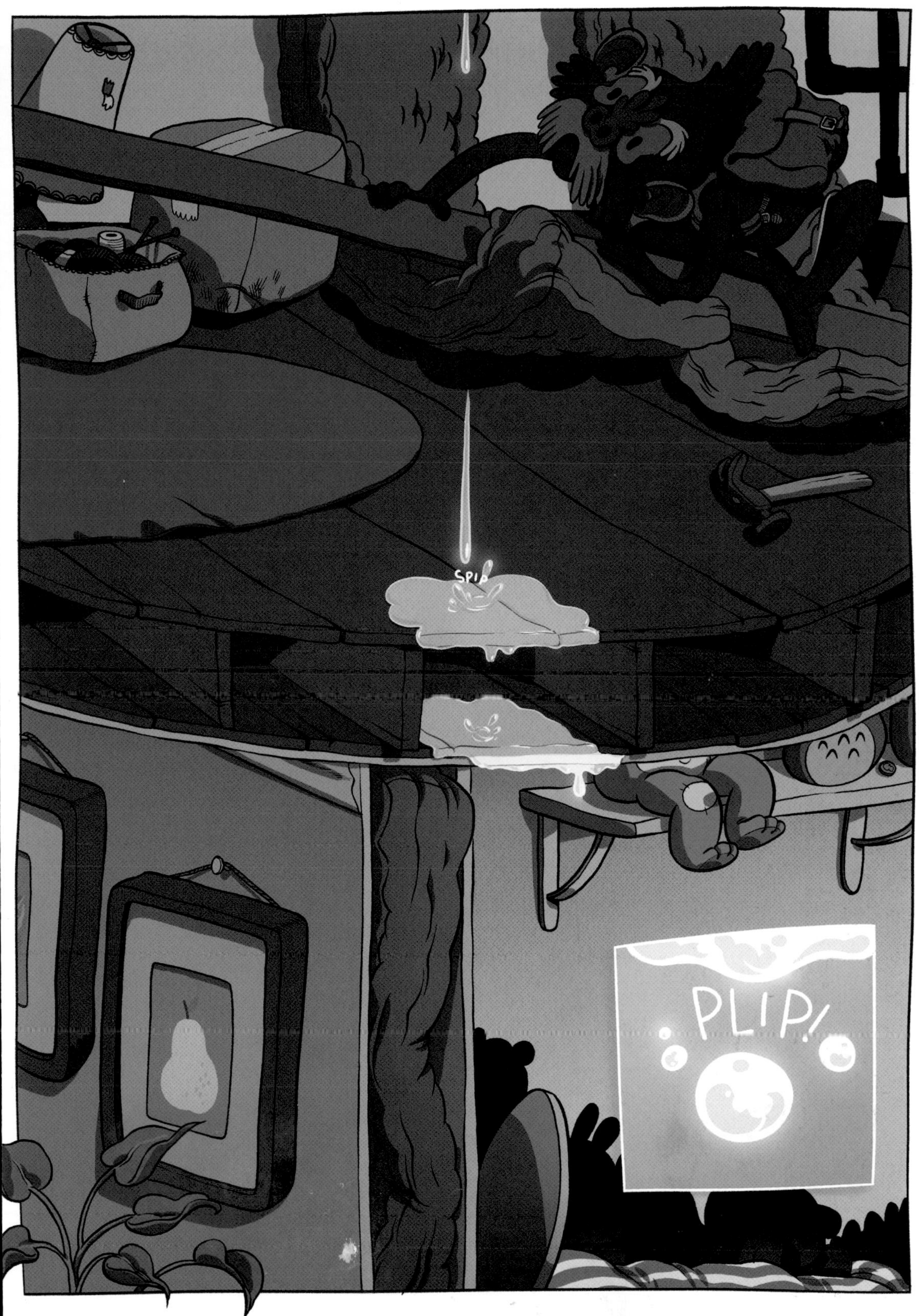
SPIP
PLIP!

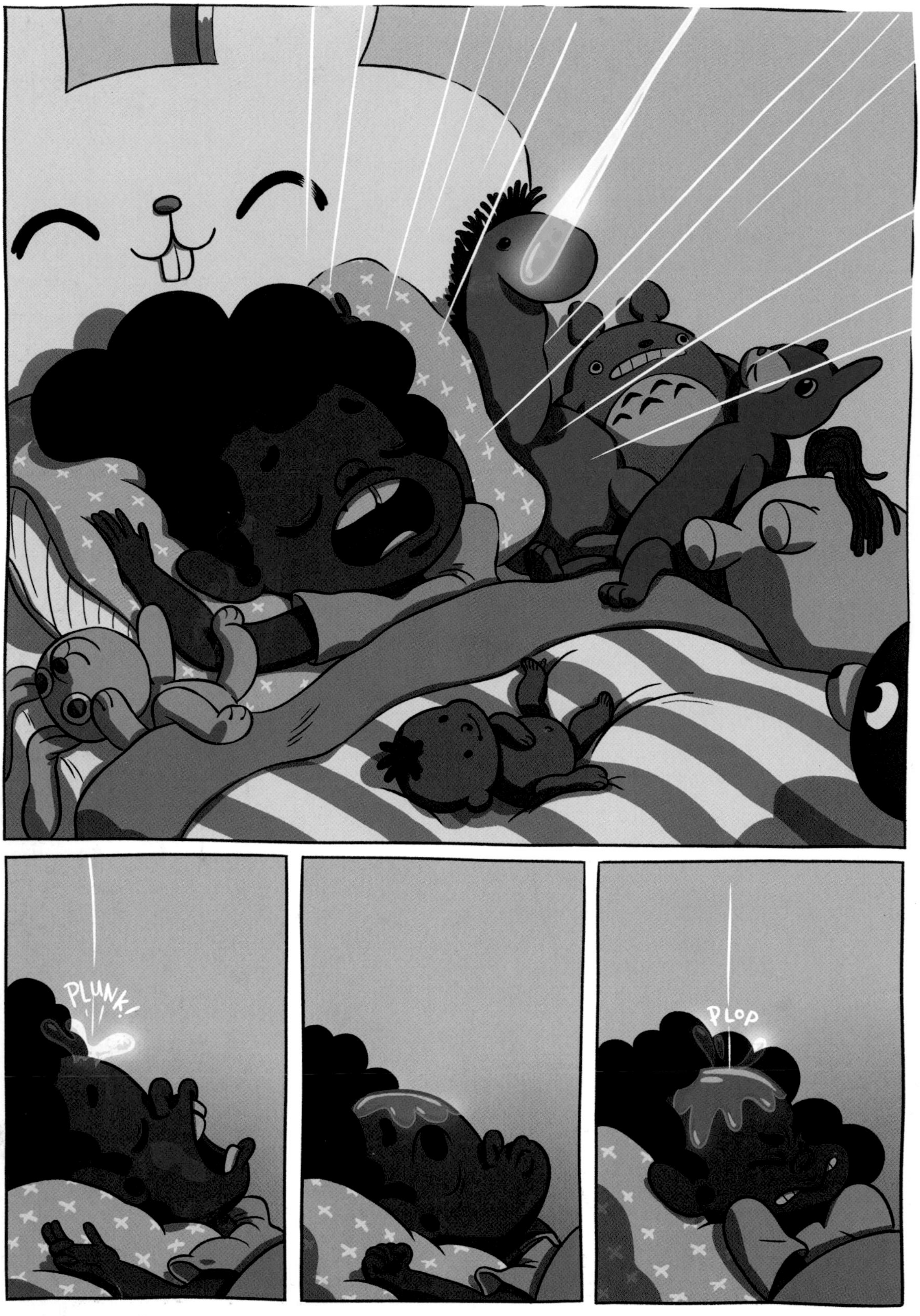
PLUNK!
PLOP

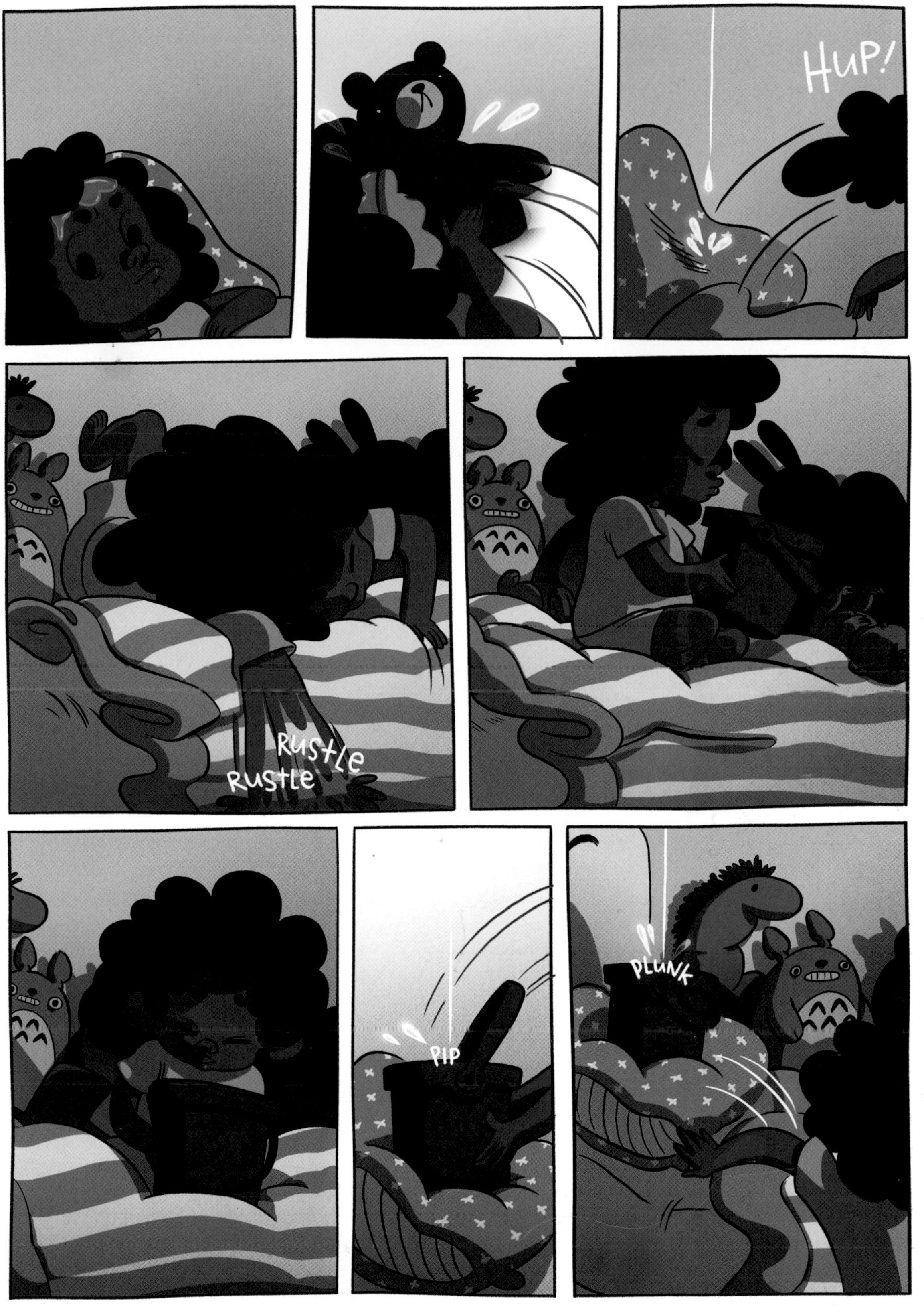
HUP!
RUSTLE
RUSTLE
PIP
PLUNK

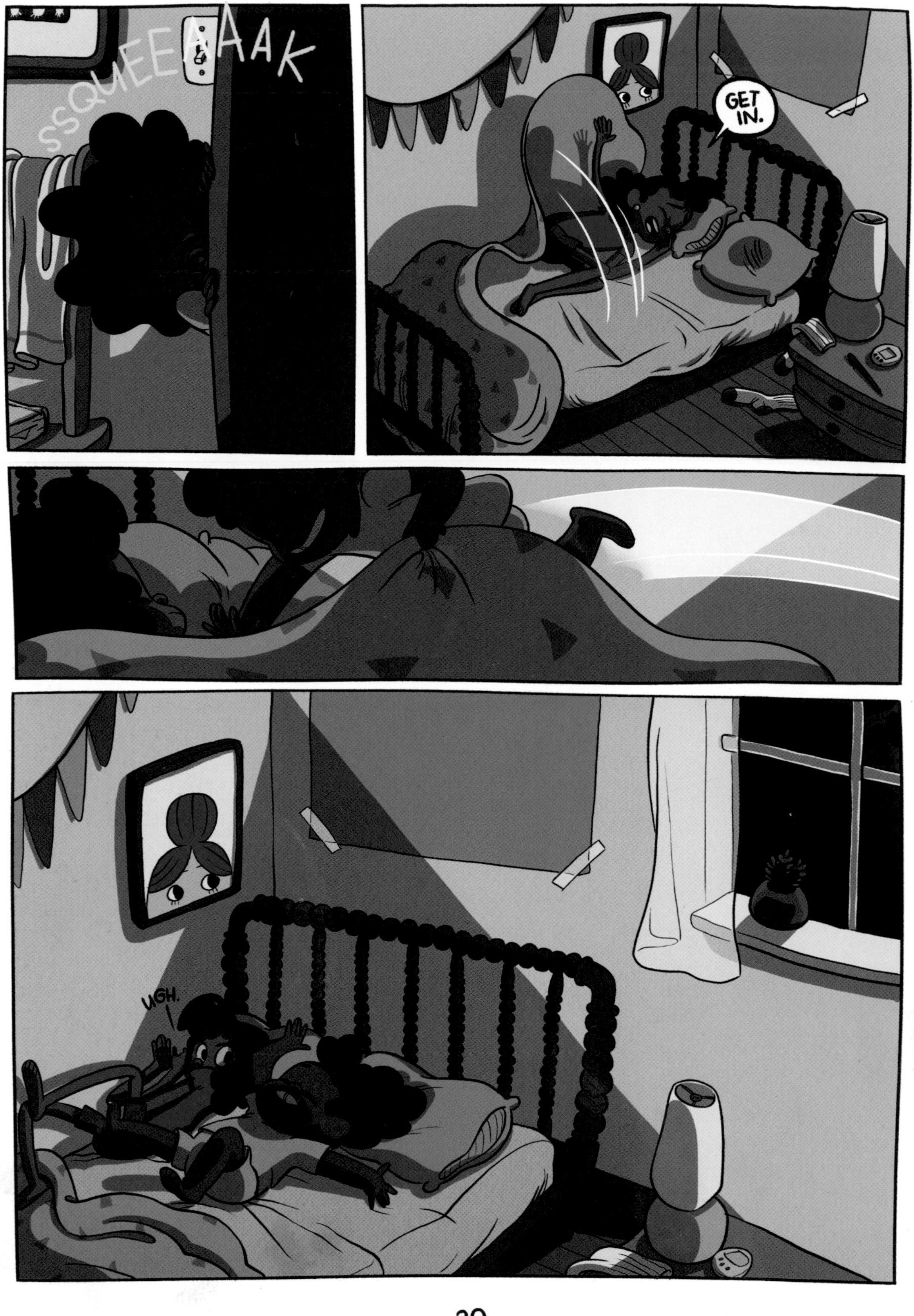
SSQUEEAAAK
GET IN.
UGH.

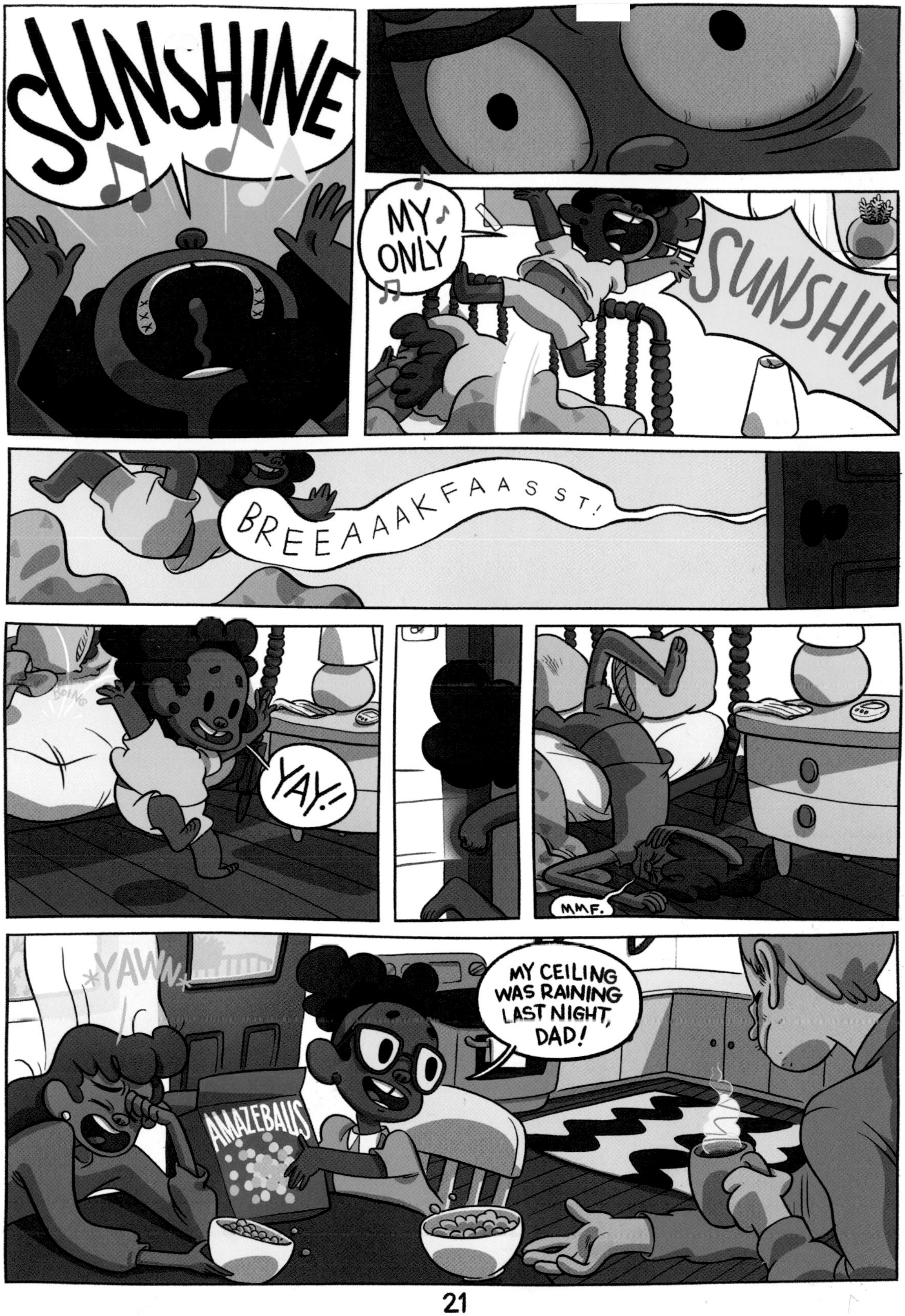
SUNSHINE
MY ONLY
SUNSHIN
BREEAAAKFAAS ST!
BOING
YAY!
MMF.
YAWN
MY CEILING WAS RAINING LAST NIGHT, DAD!
AMAZEBALLS

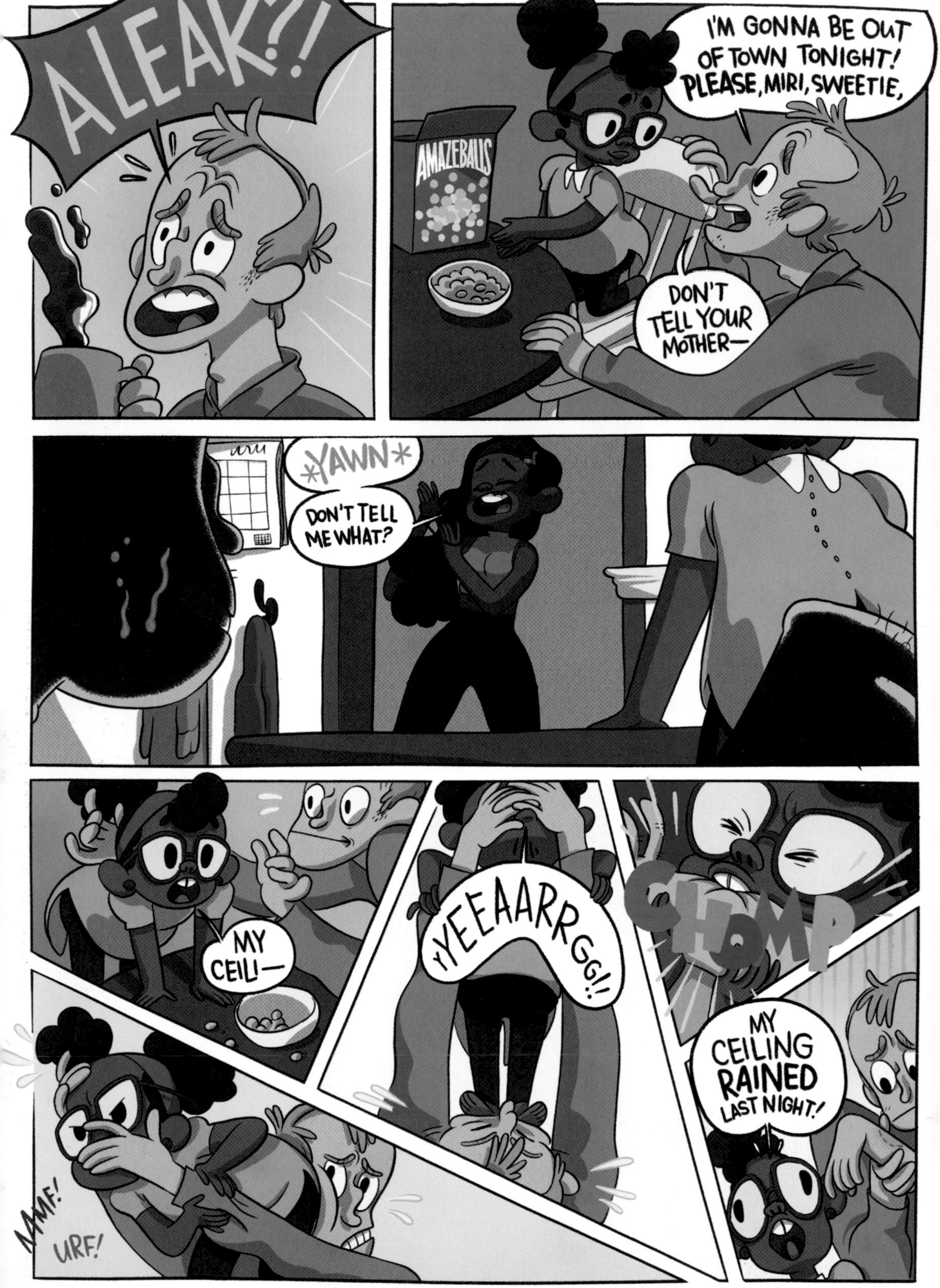
ALEAK?!
I'M GONNA BE OUT OF TOWN TONIGHT! PLEASE, MIRI, SWEETIE,
AMAZEBALLS
DON'T TELL YOUR MOTHER—
YAWN
DON'T TELL ME WHAT?
MY CEILI—
¡YEEAARRGG!!
CHOMP
MY CEILING RAINED LAST NIGHT!
MMF!
URF!

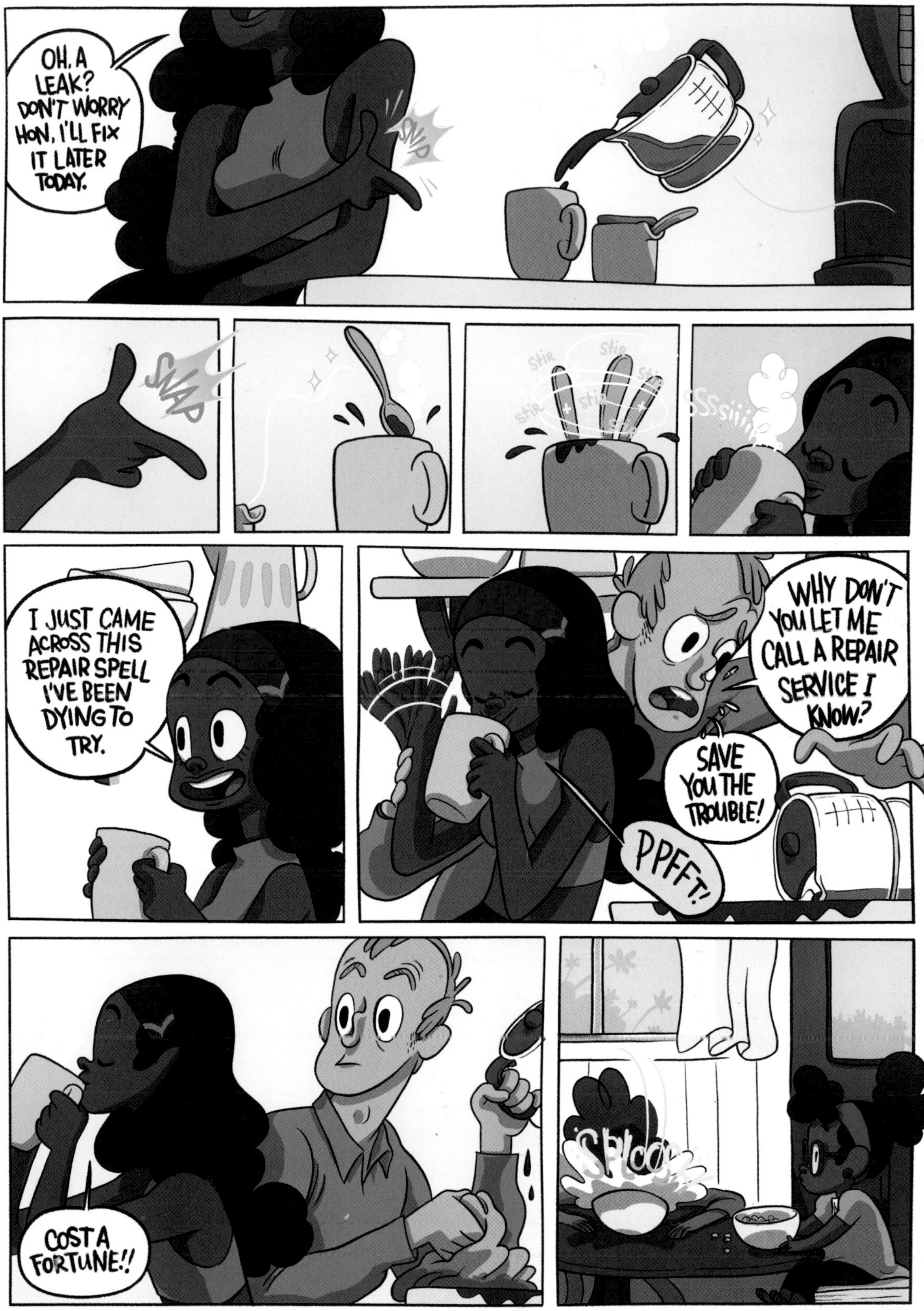
OH, A LEAK? DON'T WORRY HON, I'LL FIX IT LATER TODAY.
SNAP
SNAP
stir
stir
stir
stir
I JUST CAME ACROSS THIS REPAIR SPELL I'VE BEEN DYING TO TRY.
WHY DON'T YOU LET ME CALL A REPAIR SERVICE I KNOW?
SAVE YOU THE TROUBLE!
PPFFT!
COST A FORTUNE!!

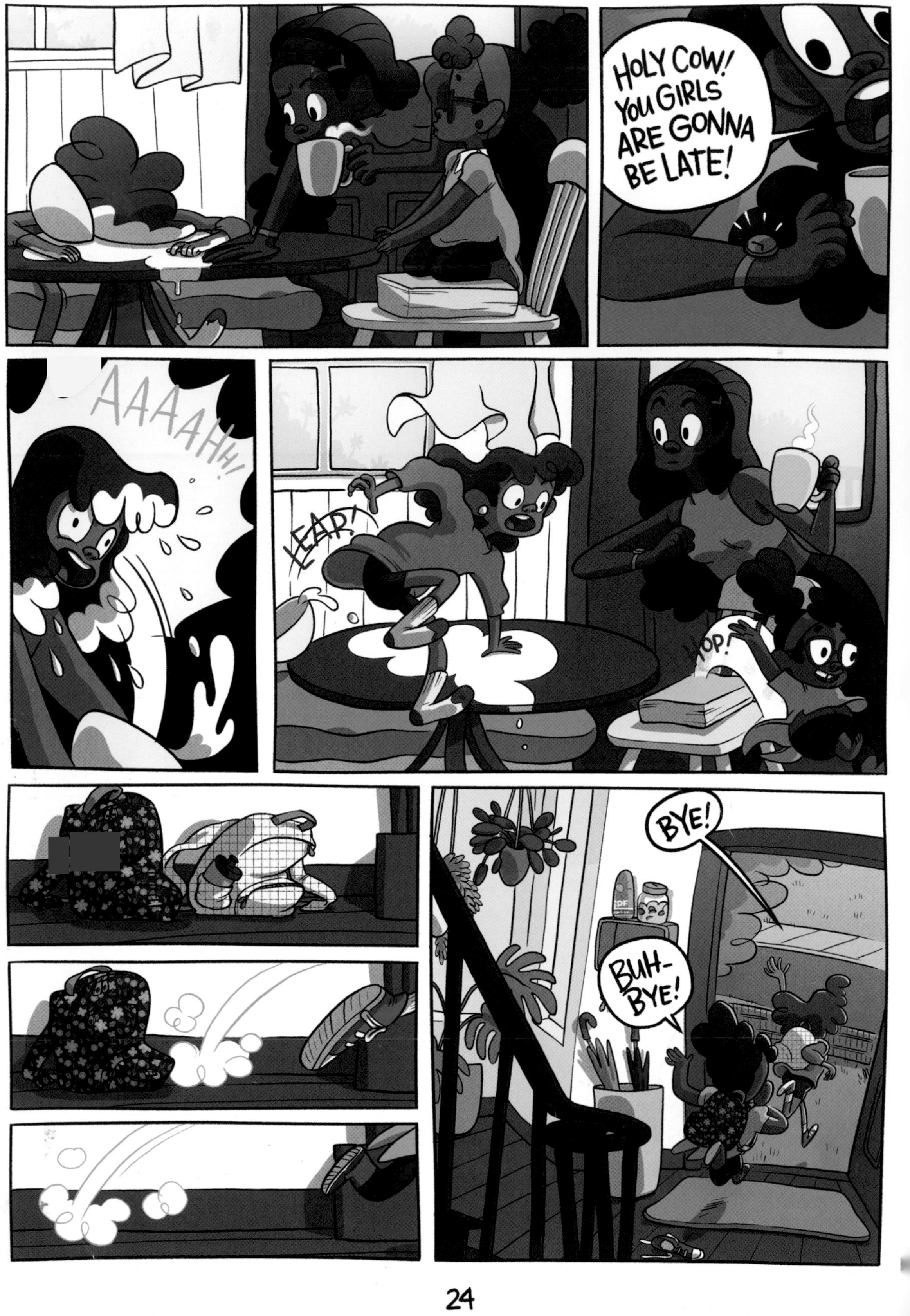
HOLY COW! YOU GIRLS ARE GONNA BE LATE!
AAAAHH!!
LEAP!
HOP!
BYE!
SPF
BUH-BYE!

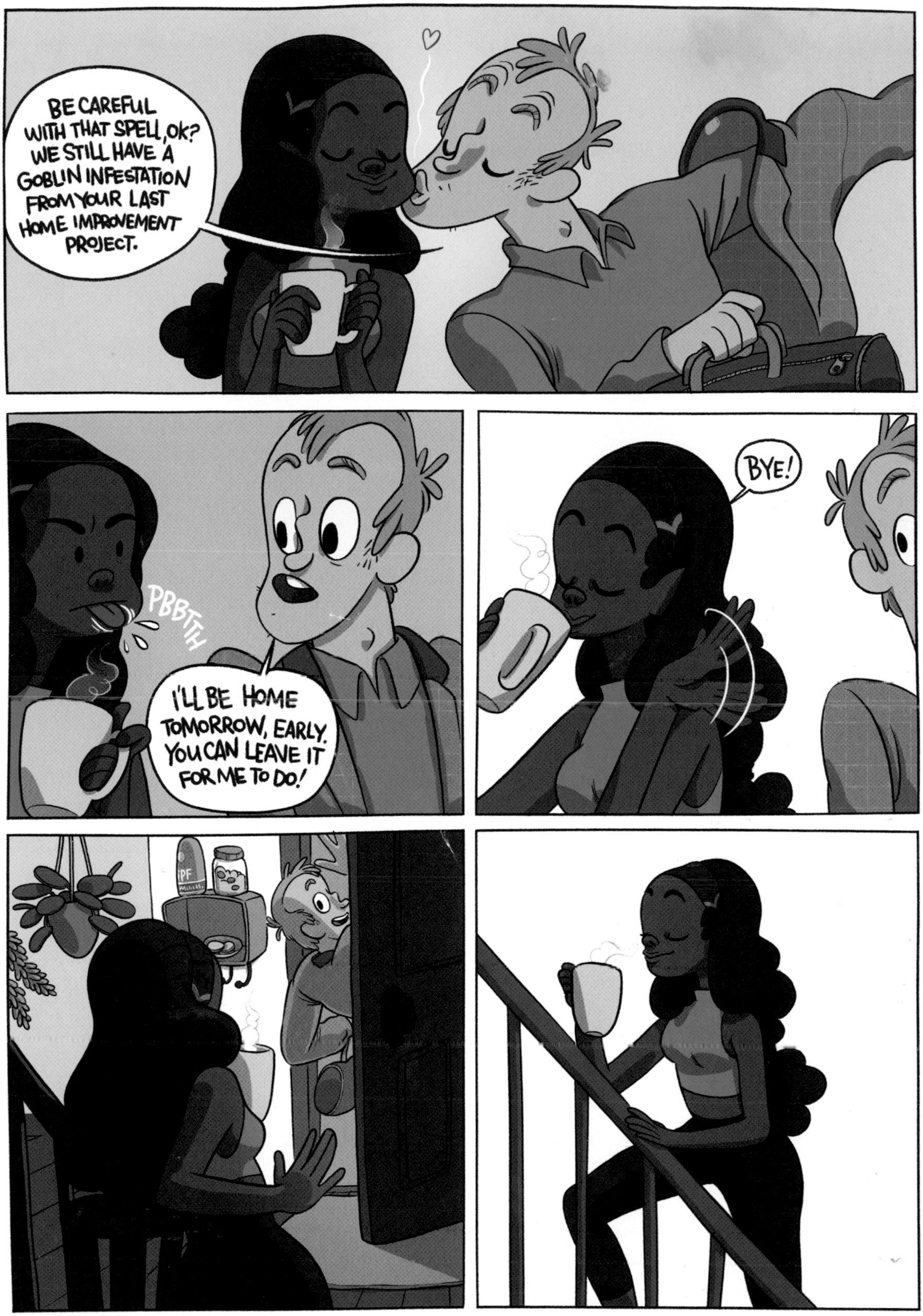
BE CAREFUL WITH THAT SPELL, OK? WE STILL HAVE A GOBLIN INFESTATION FROM YOUR LAST HOME IMPROVEMENT PROJECT.
PBBTTH
I'LL BE HOME TOMORROW, EARLY. YOU CAN LEAVE IT FOR ME TO DO!
BYE!

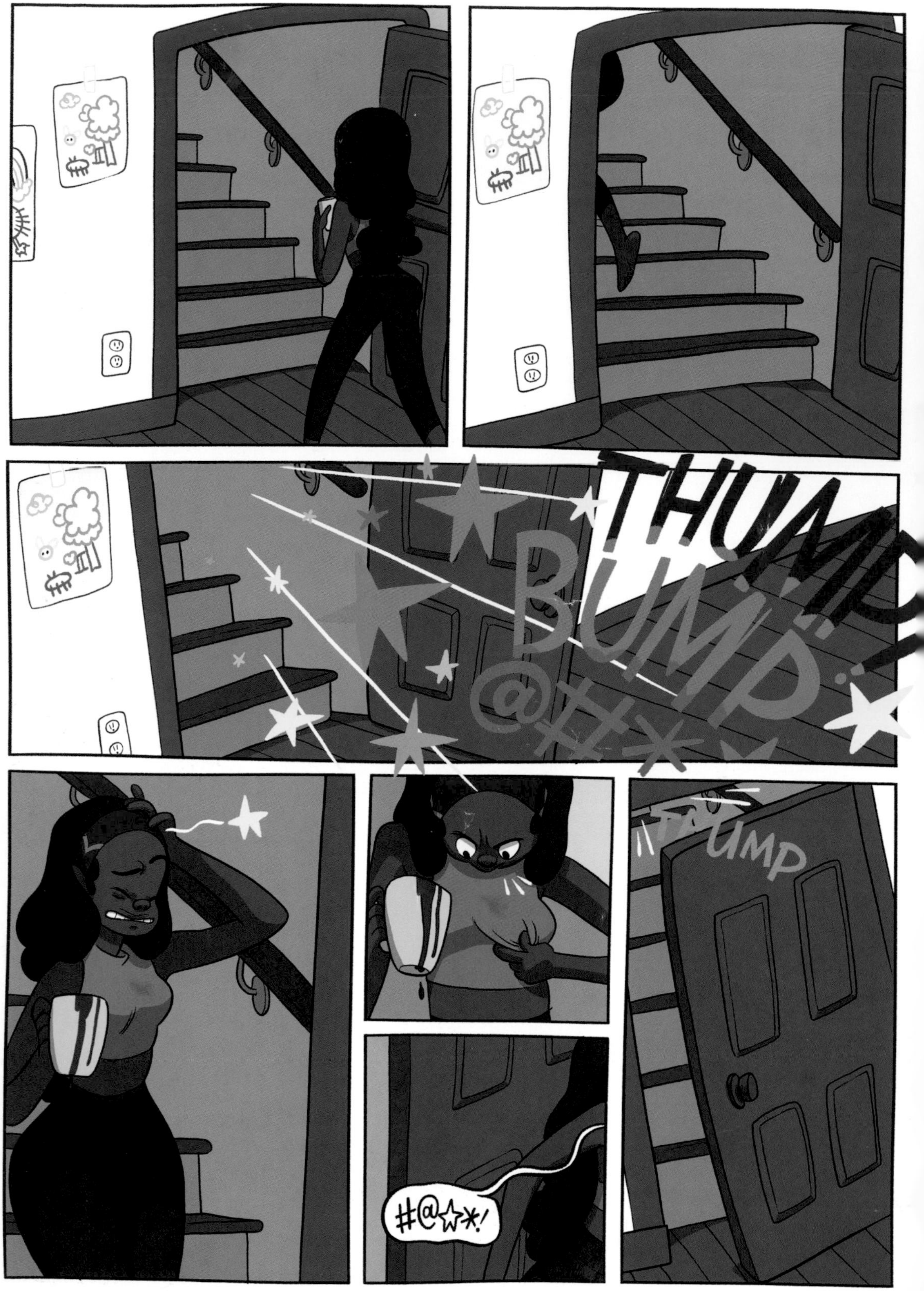
THUMP!
BUMP!
@#*
THUMP
#@☆*!

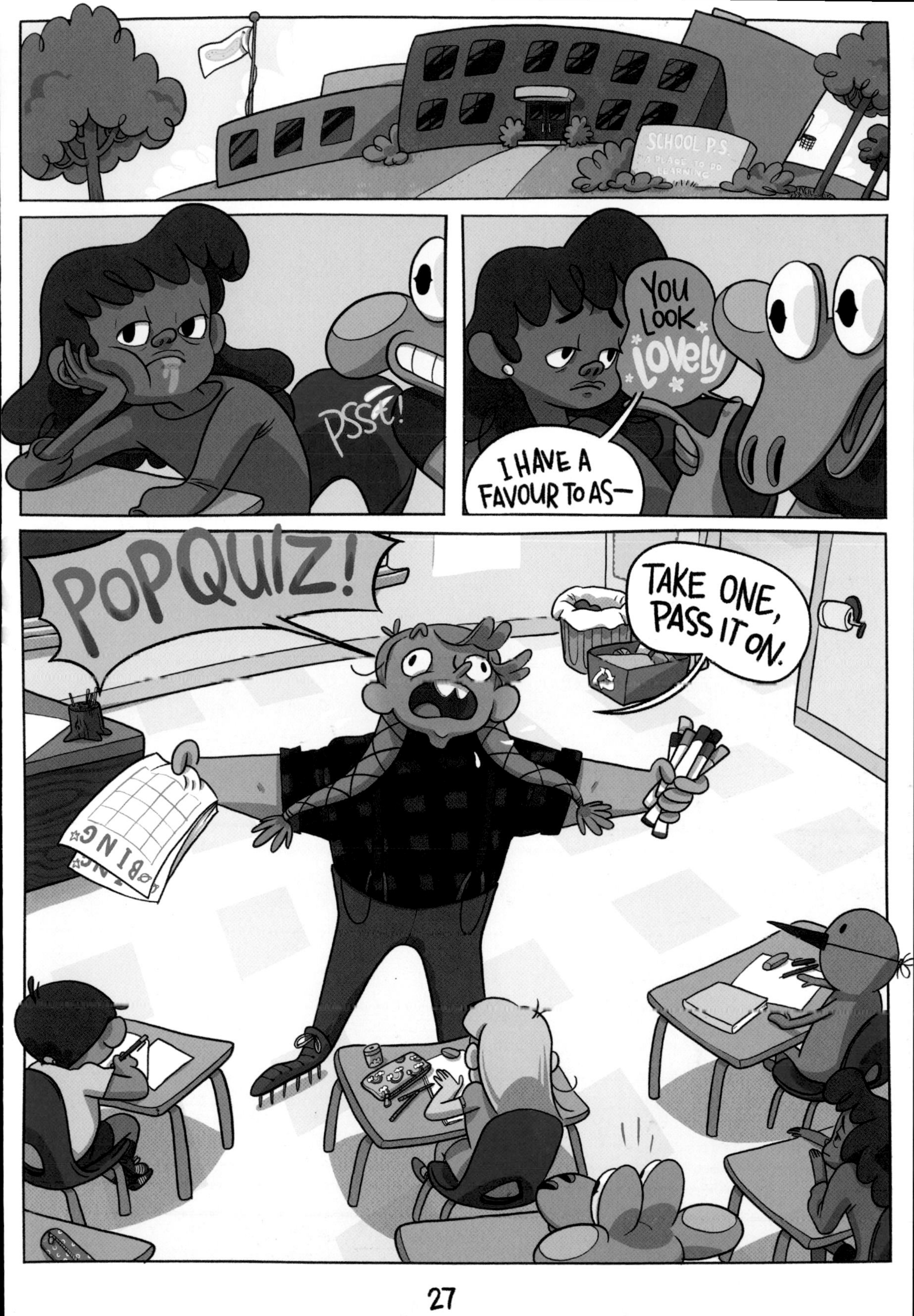
SCHOOL P.S.
A PLACE TO DO LEARNING
PSST!
YOU LOOK Lovely
I HAVE A FAVOUR TO AS—
POP QUIZ!
TAKE ONE, PASS IT ON.
BING

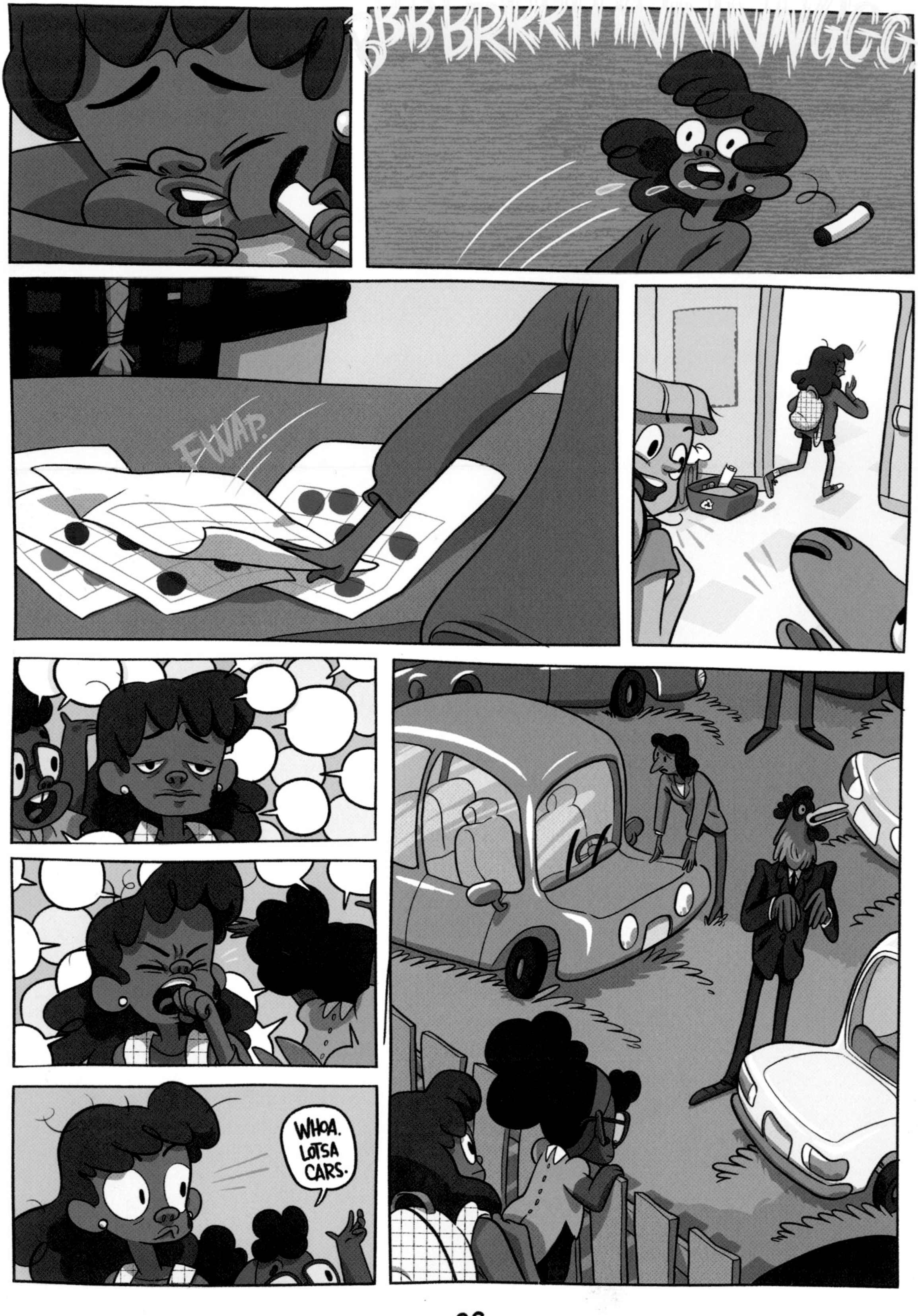
BBBRRRIIINNNNNGGG!
FWAP.
WHOA. LOTSA CARS.

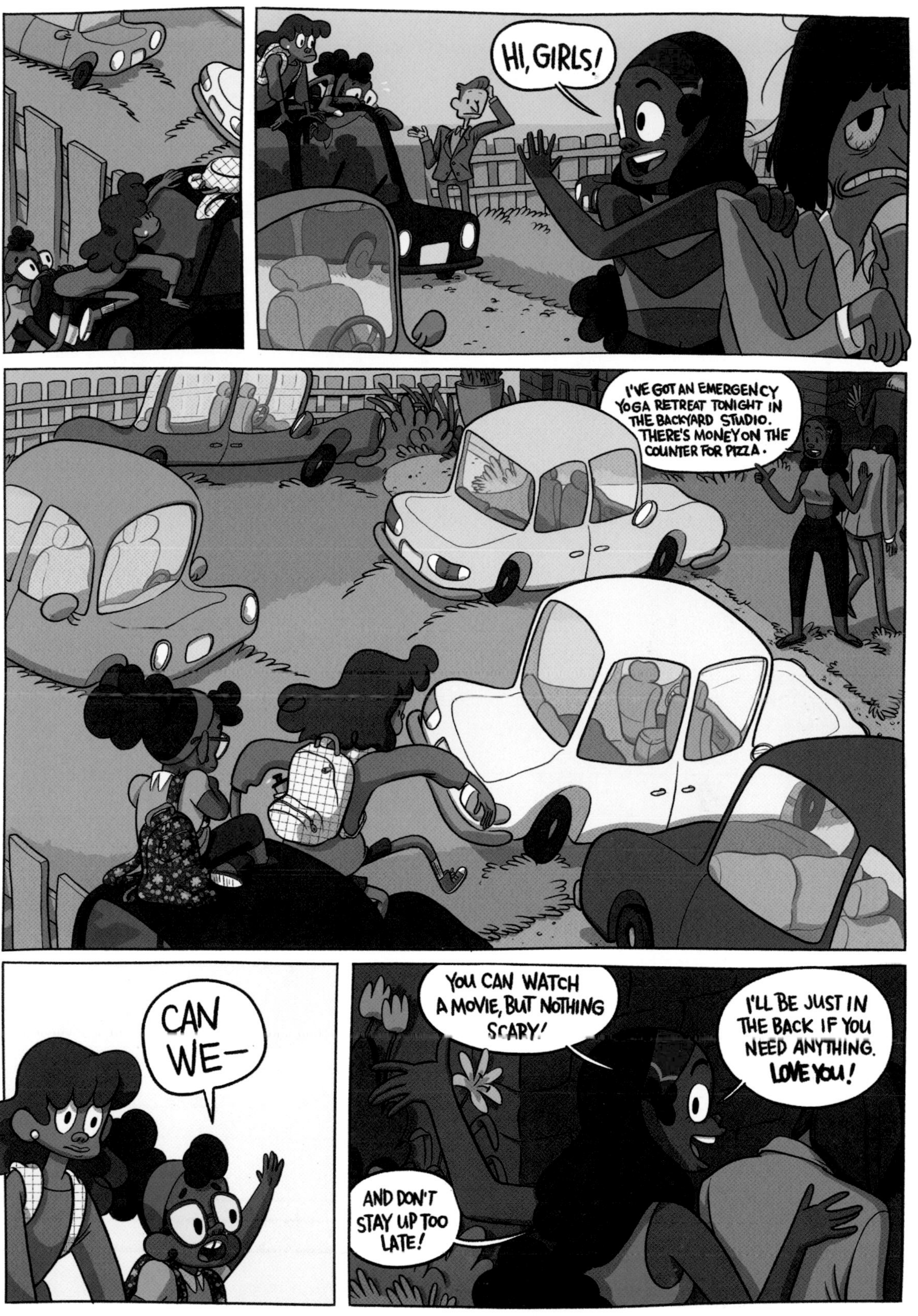
HI, GIRLS!
I'VE GOT AN EMERGENCY YOGA RETREAT TONIGHT IN THE BACKYARD STUDIO. THERE'S MONEY ON THE COUNTER FOR PIZZA.
CAN WE—
YOU CAN WATCH A MOVIE, BUT NOTHING SCARY!
I'LL BE JUST IN THE BACK IF YOU NEED ANYTHING. LOVE YOU!
AND DON'T STAY UP TOO LATE!

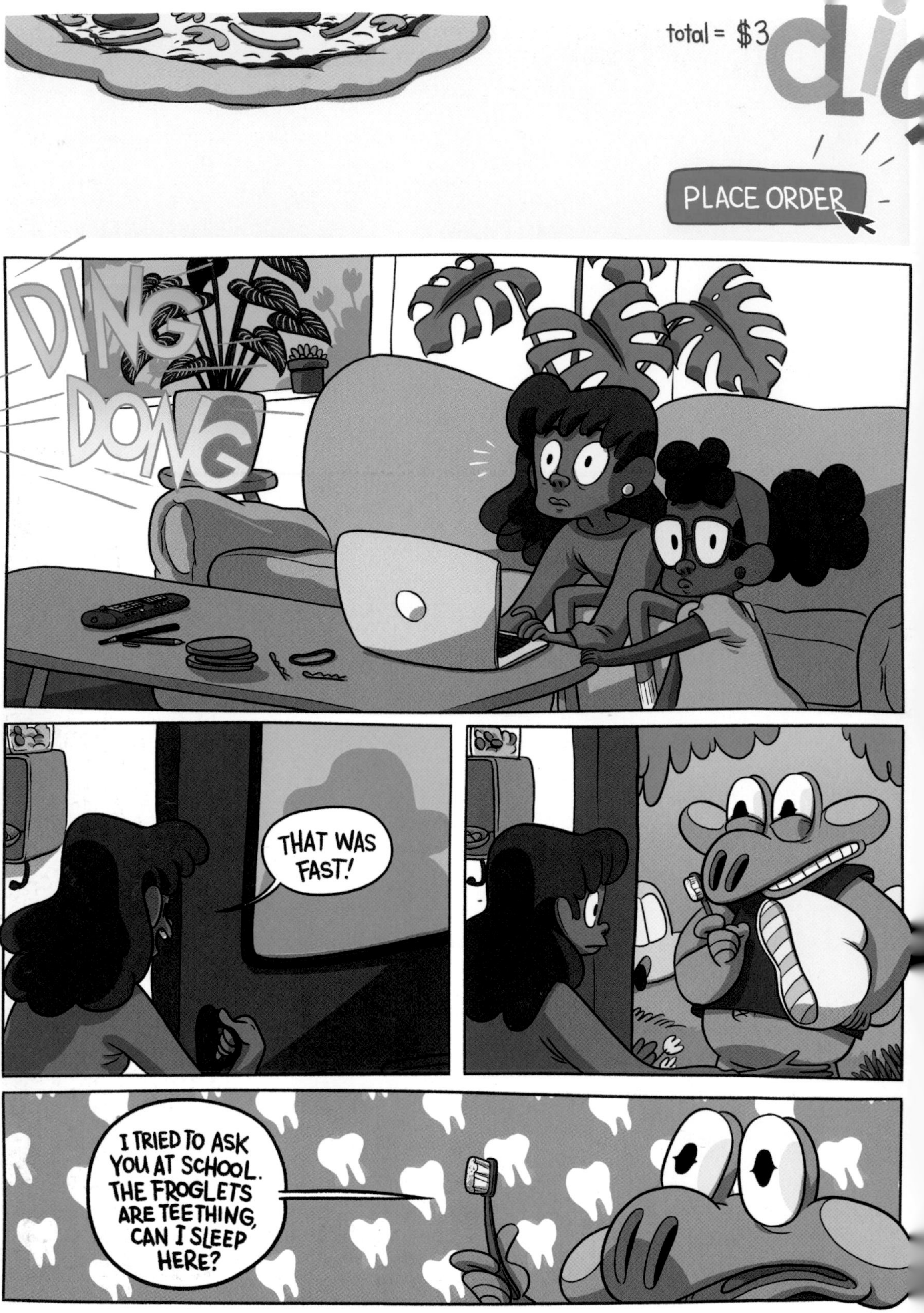
total = $3
CLIC
PLACE ORDER
DING DONG
THAT WAS FAST!
I TRIED TO ASK YOU AT SCHOOL. THE FROGLETS ARE TEETHING, CAN I SLEEP HERE?

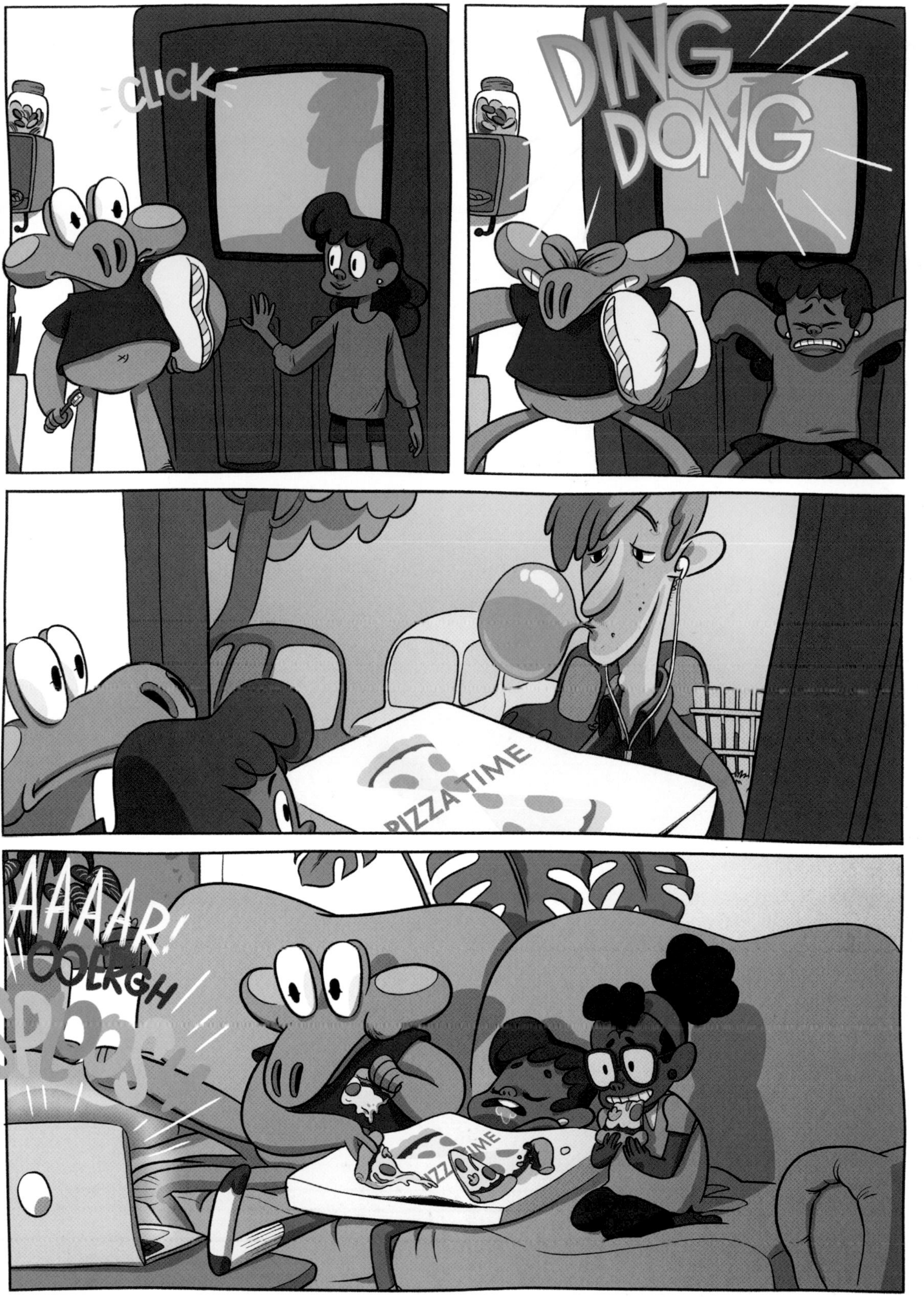
CLICK
DING DONG
PIZZA TIME
AAAAR!
OOERGH
SPLOSH
PIZZA TIME

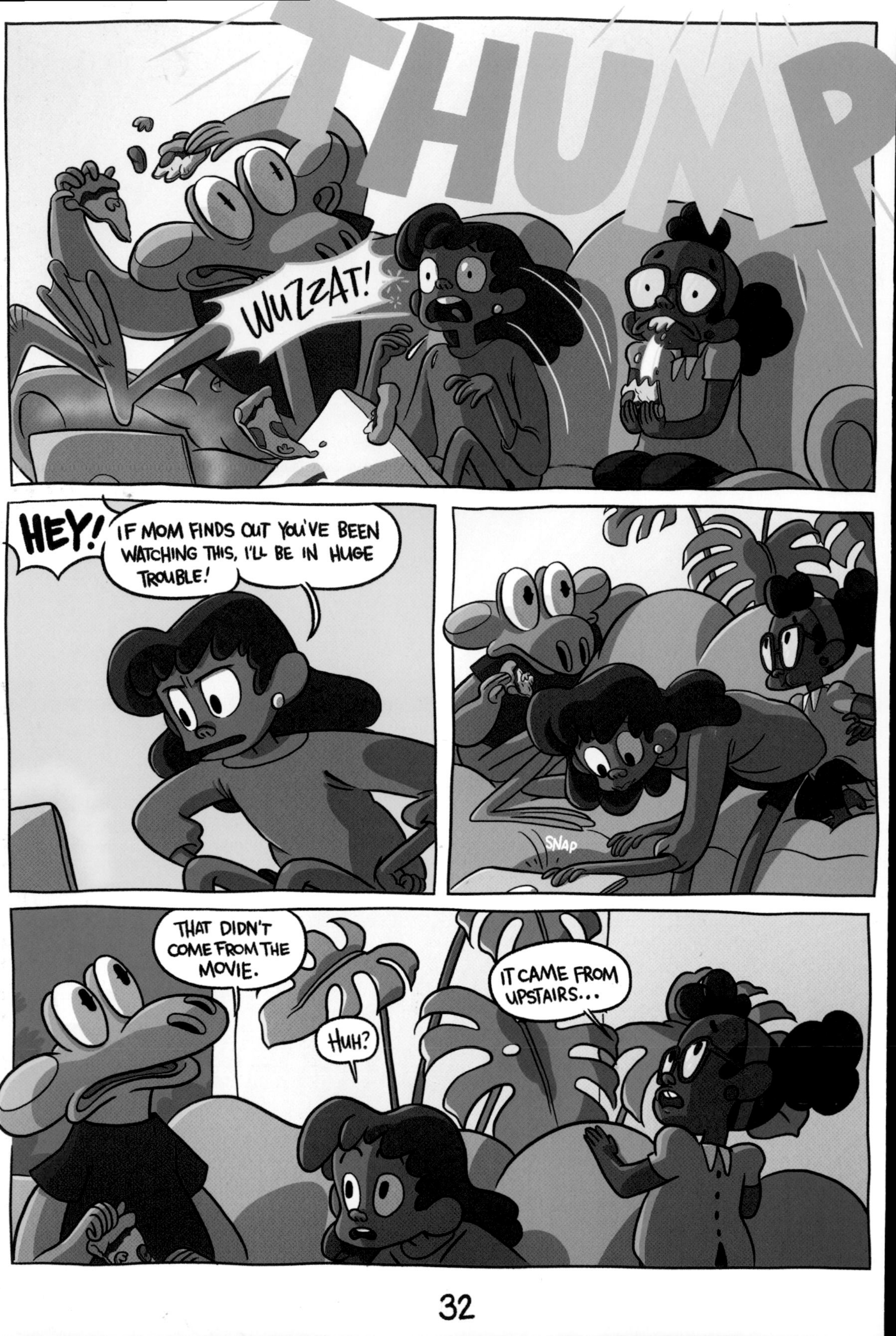
THUMP
WUZZAT!
HEY!
IF MOM FINDS OUT YOU'VE BEEN WATCHING THIS, I'LL BE IN HUGE TROUBLE!
SNAP
THAT DIDN'T COME FROM THE MOVIE.
HUH?
IT CAME FROM UPSTAIRS...

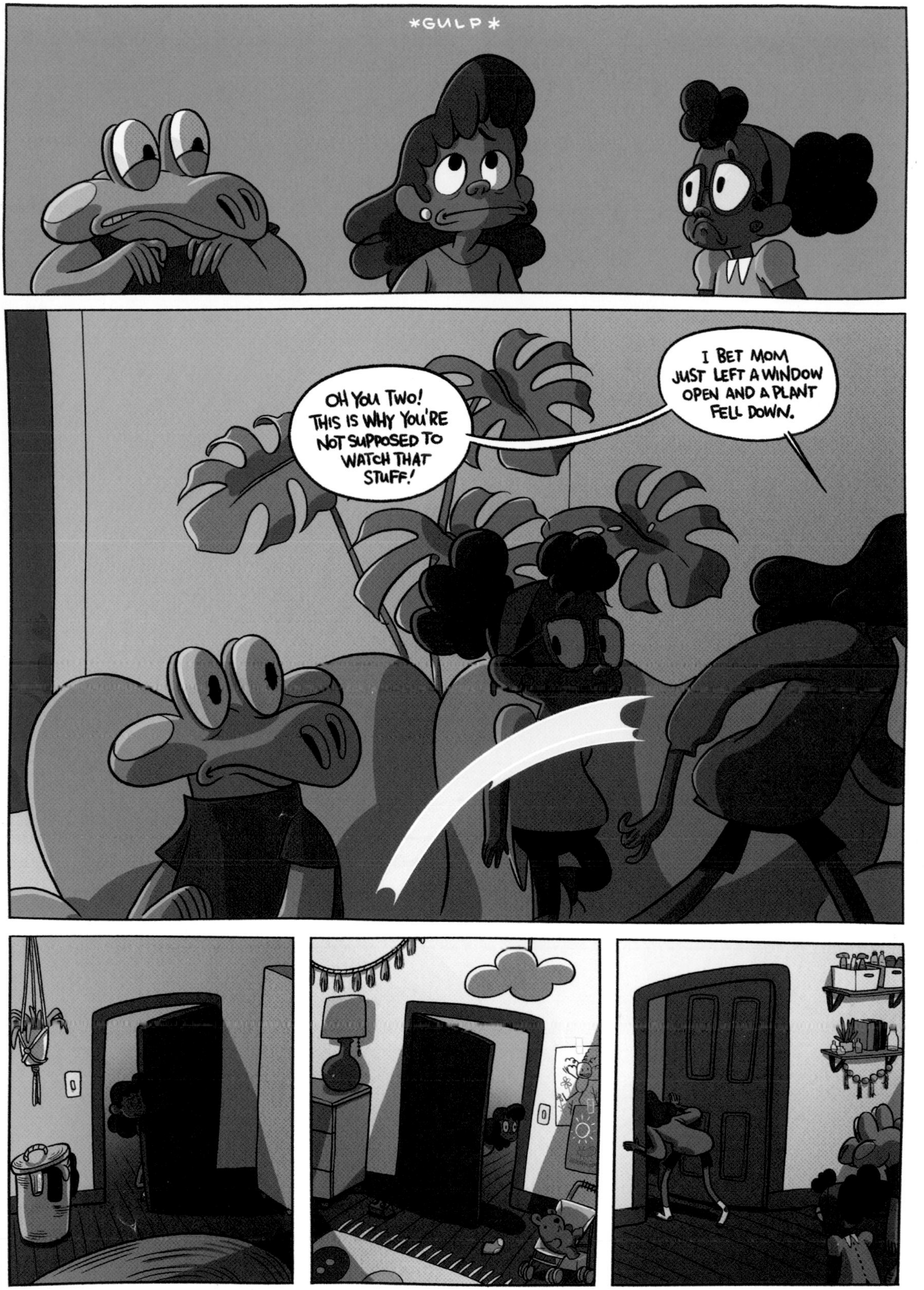
GULP
OH YOU TWO! THIS IS WHY YOU'RE NOT SUPPOSED TO WATCH THAT STUFF!
I BET MOM JUST LEFT A WINDOW OPEN AND A PLANT FELL DOWN.

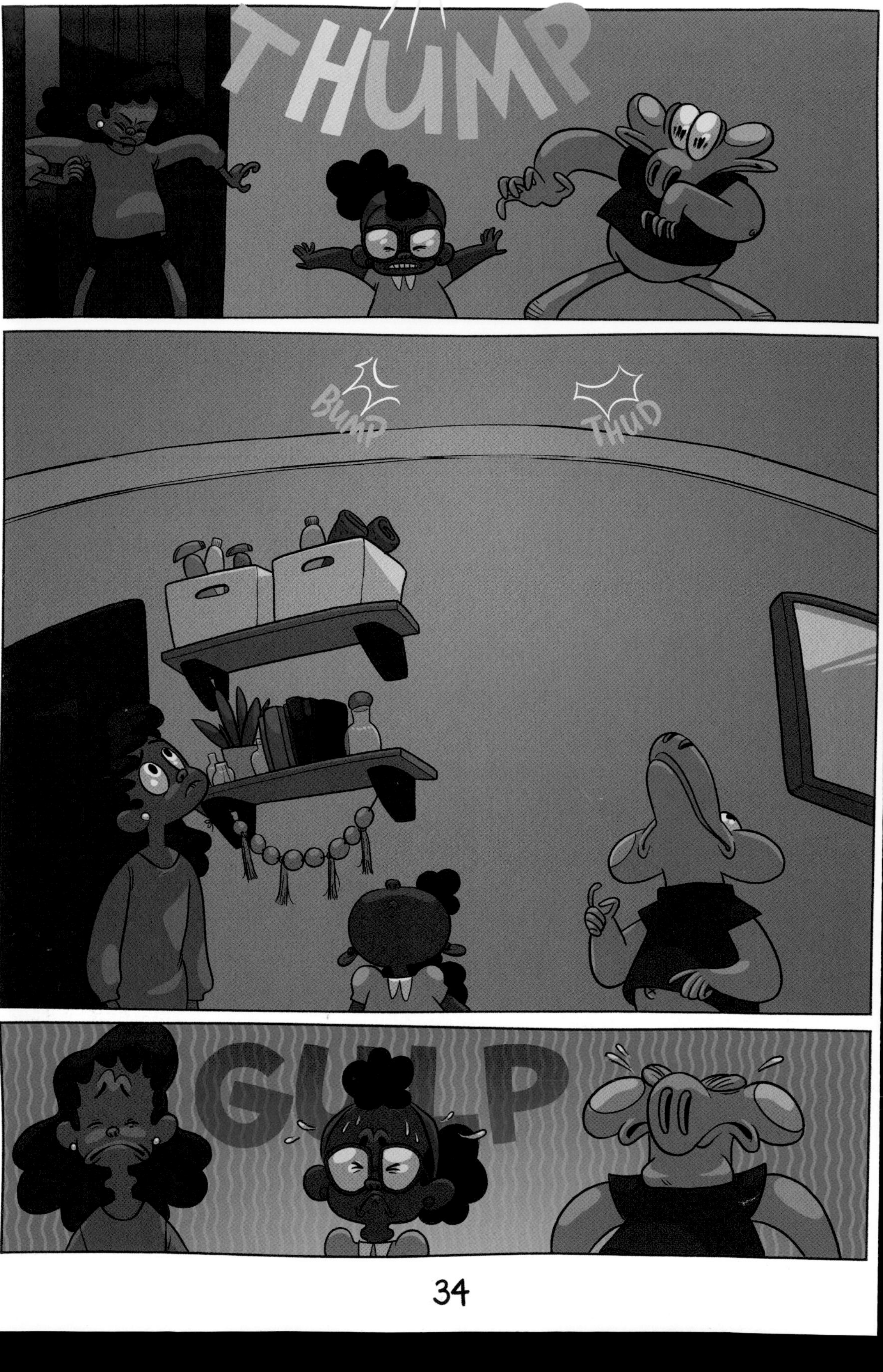

THUMP
BUMP
THUD
GULP

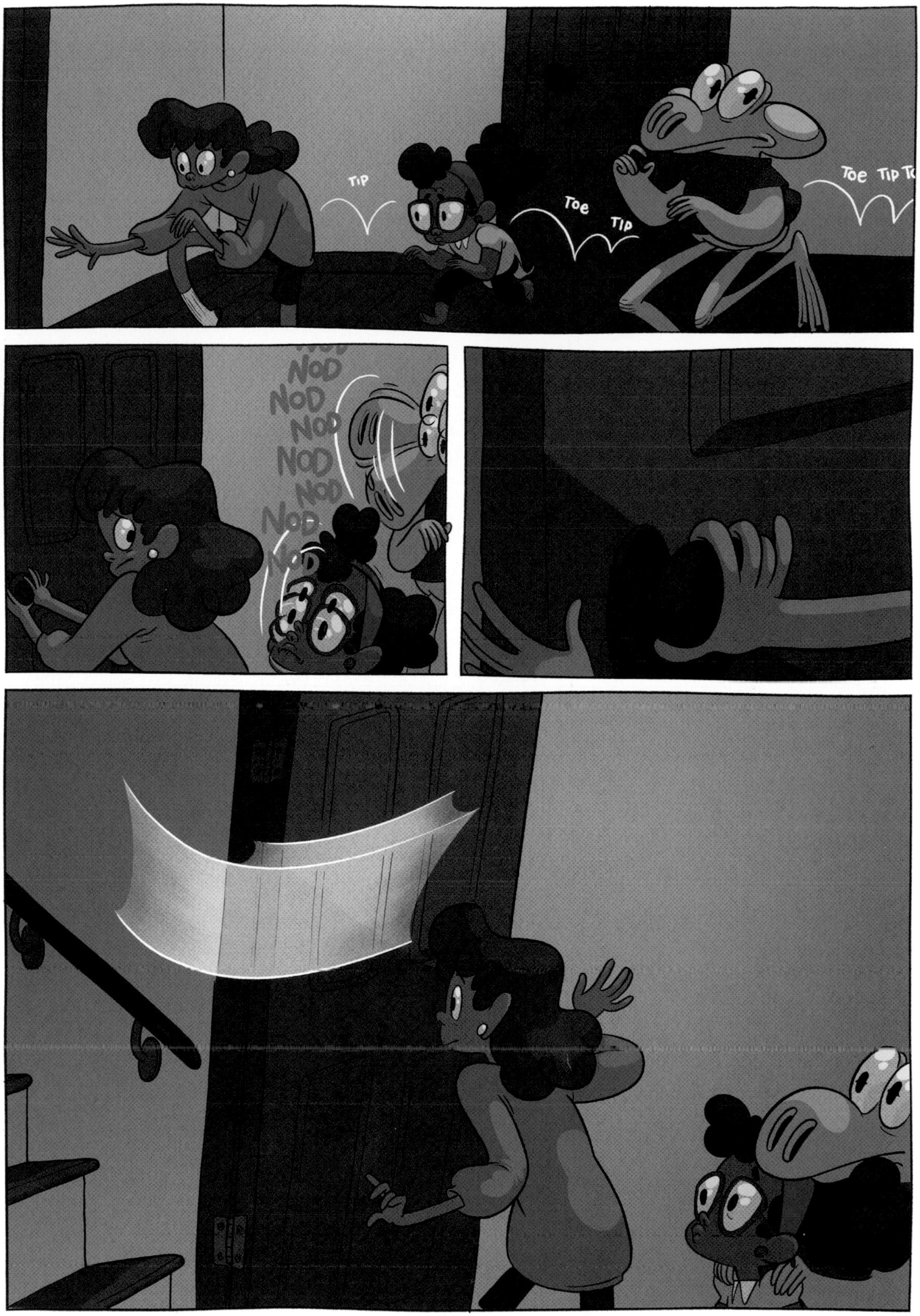

TIP
TOE
TIP
TOE TIP
NOD
NOD
NOD
NOD
NOD
NOD

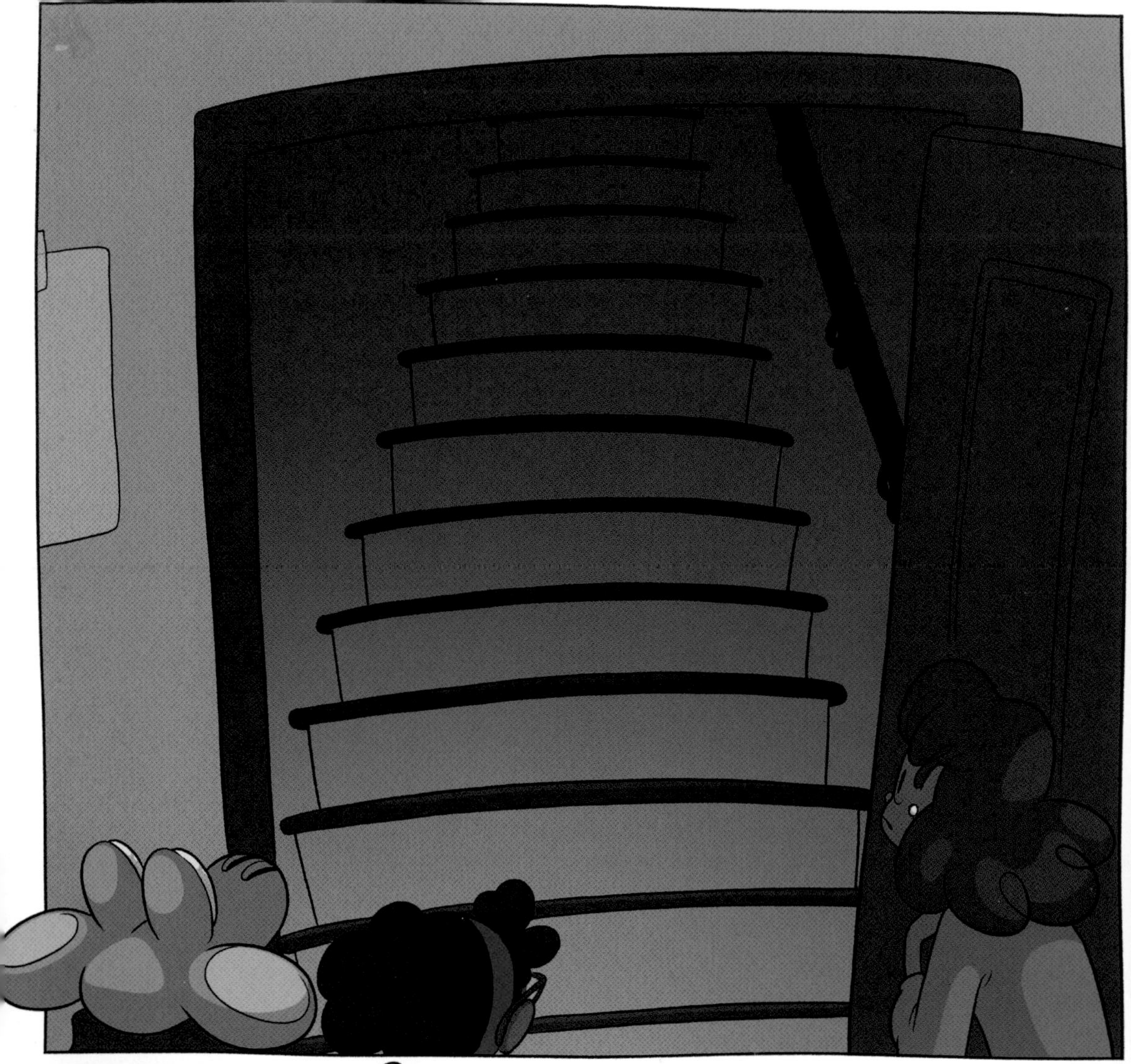

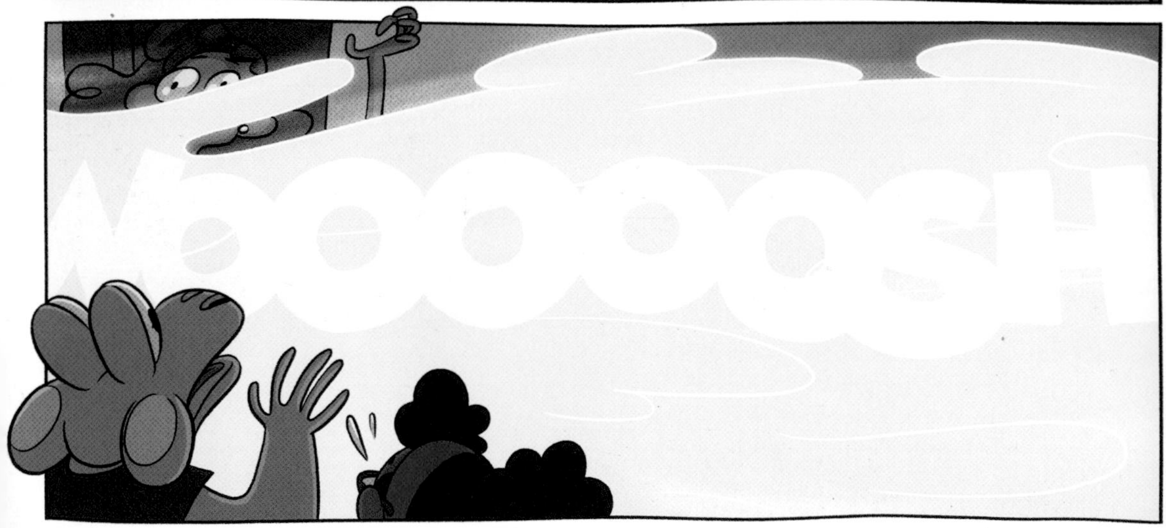
WOOOOOSH

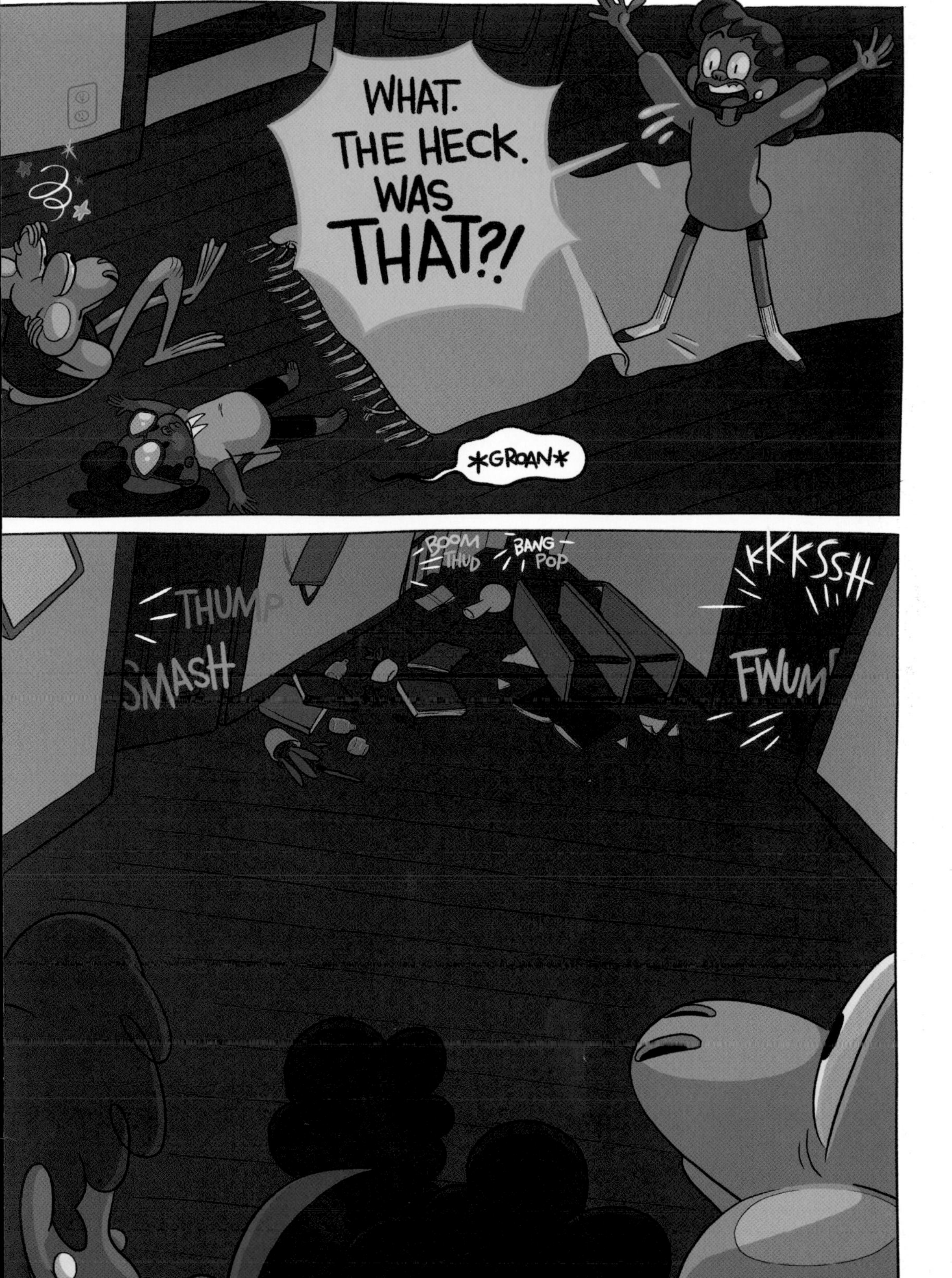
WHAT. THE HECK. WAS THAT?!
GROAN
BOOM
THUD
BANG
POP
THUMP
SMASH
KKKSSH
FWUM

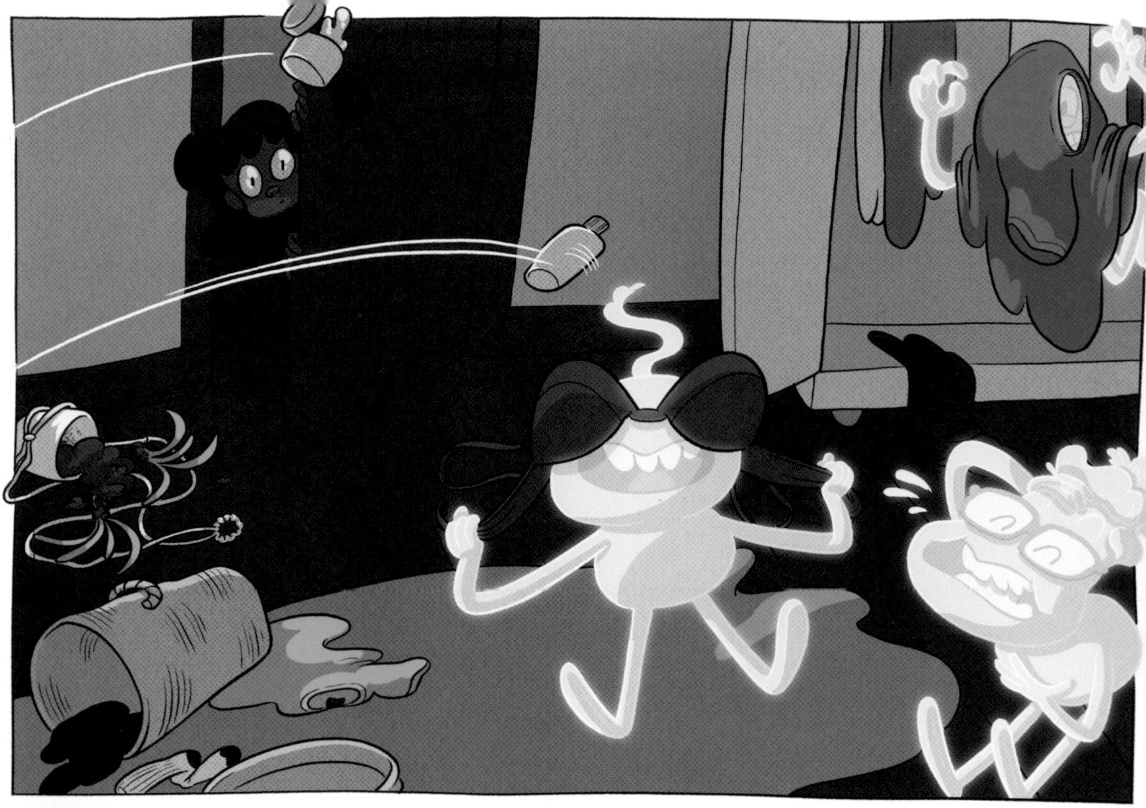

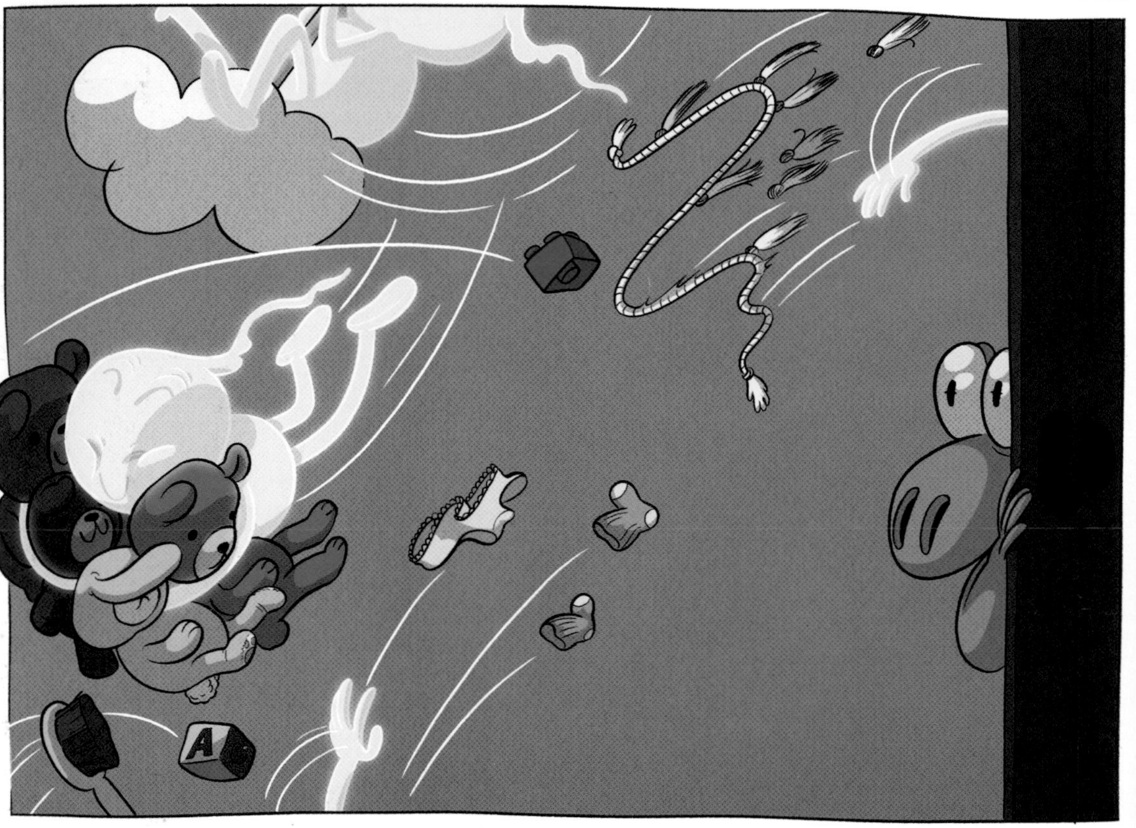

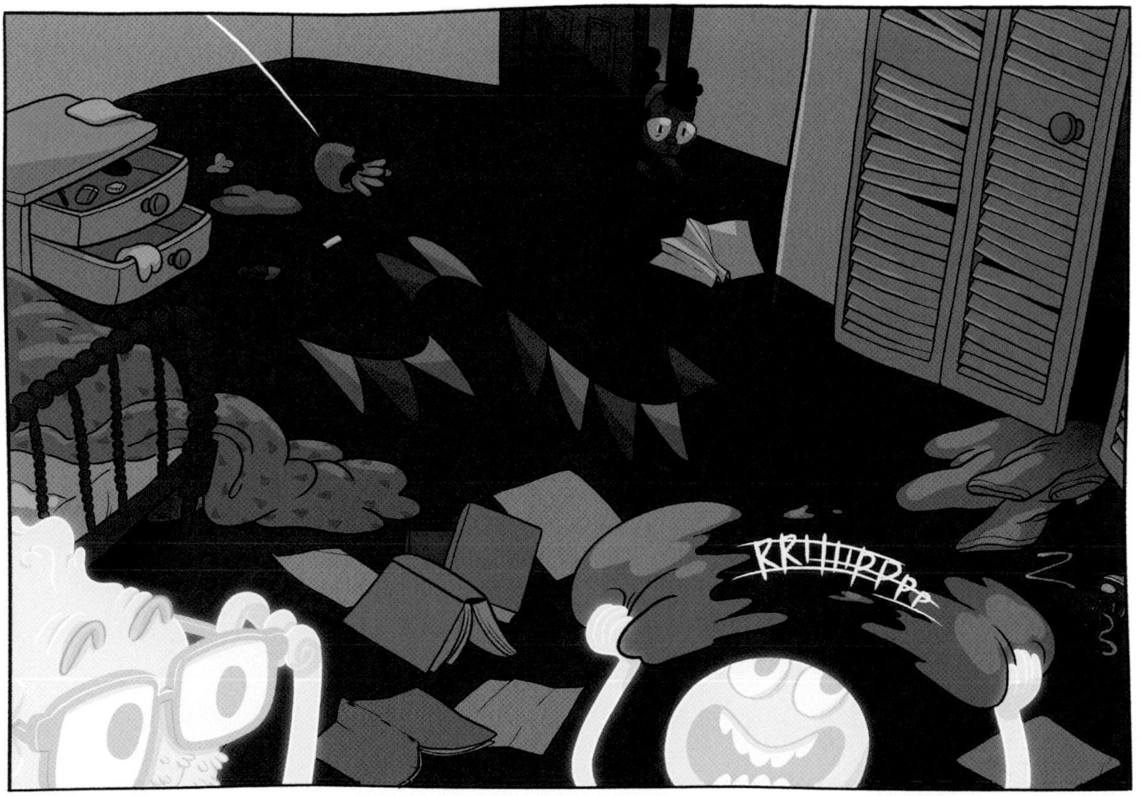
KRIIIIIPPPP

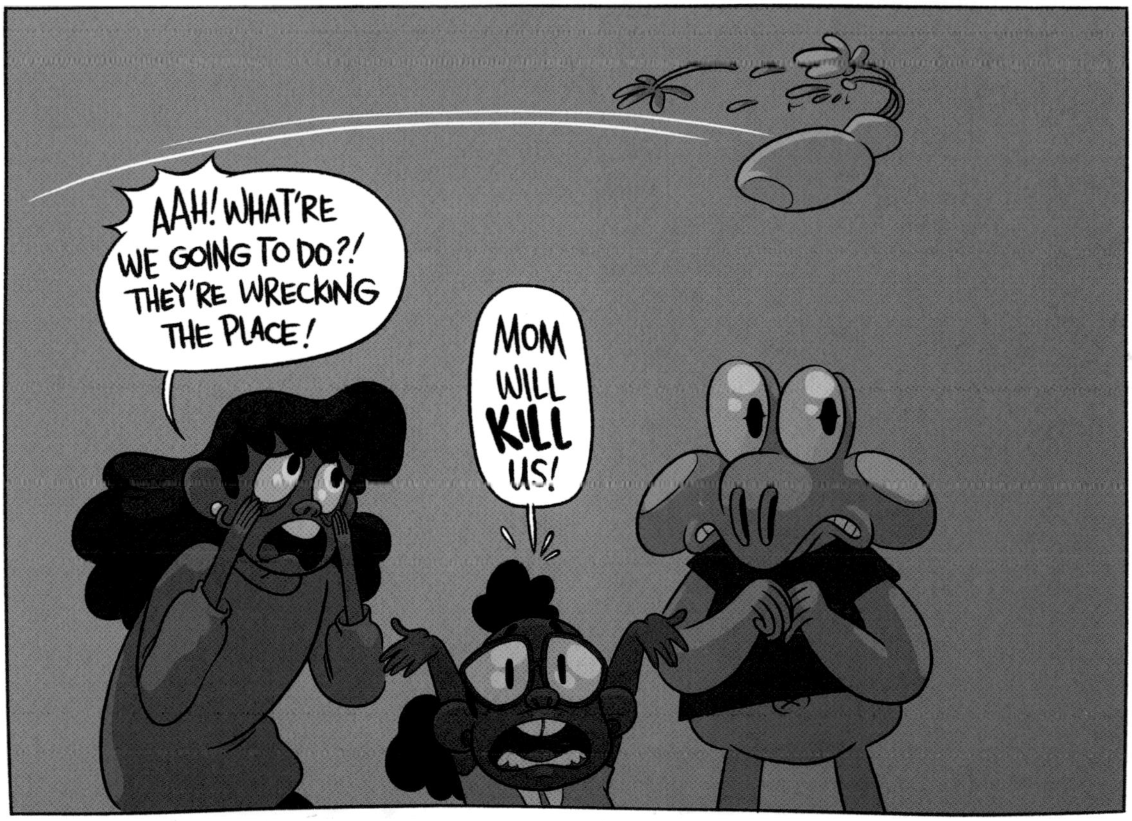
AAH! WHAT'RE WE GOING TO DO?! THEY'RE WRECKING THE PLACE!
MOM WILL **KILL** US!

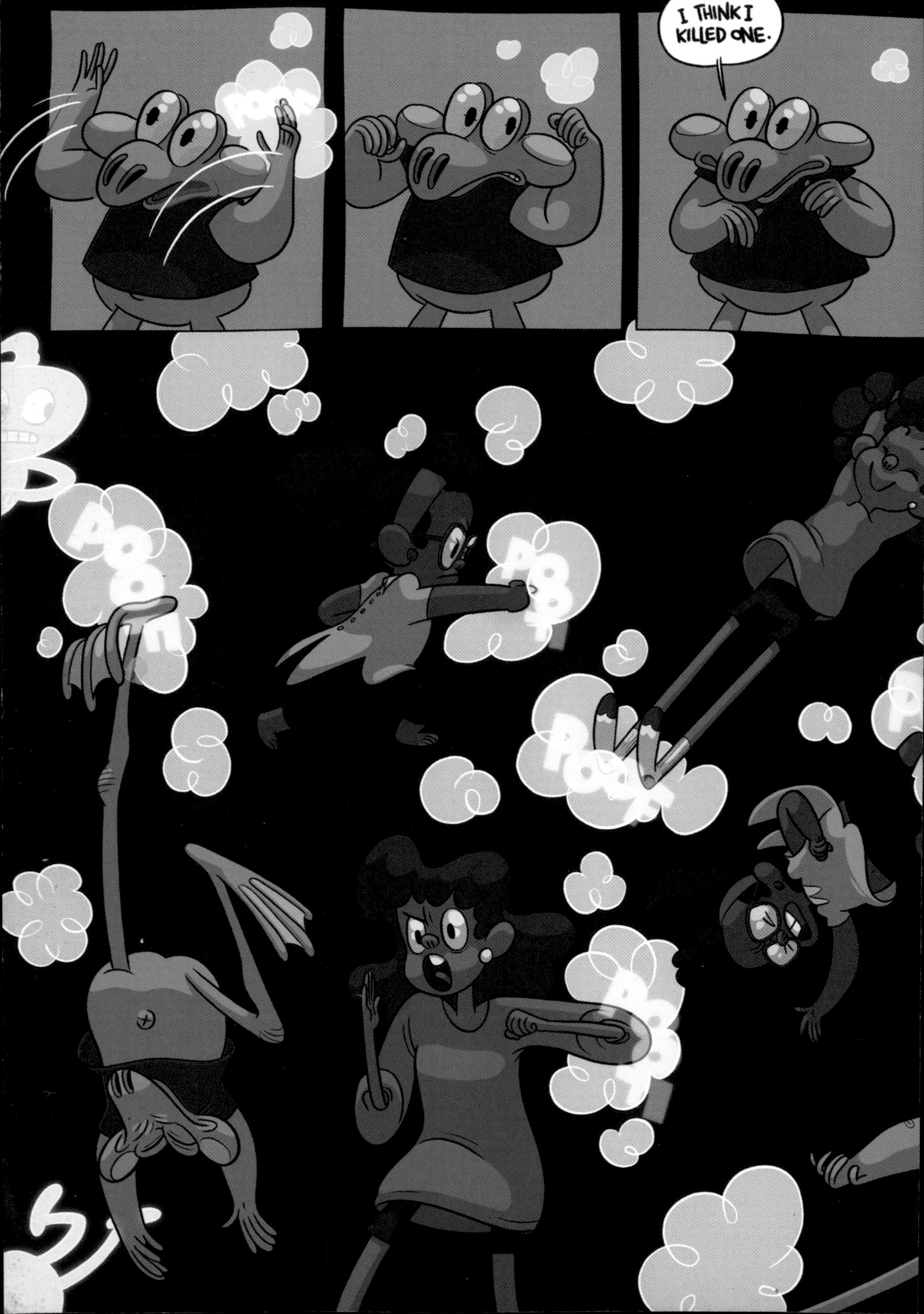
POOF
I THINK I KILLED ONE.
POOF
POOF

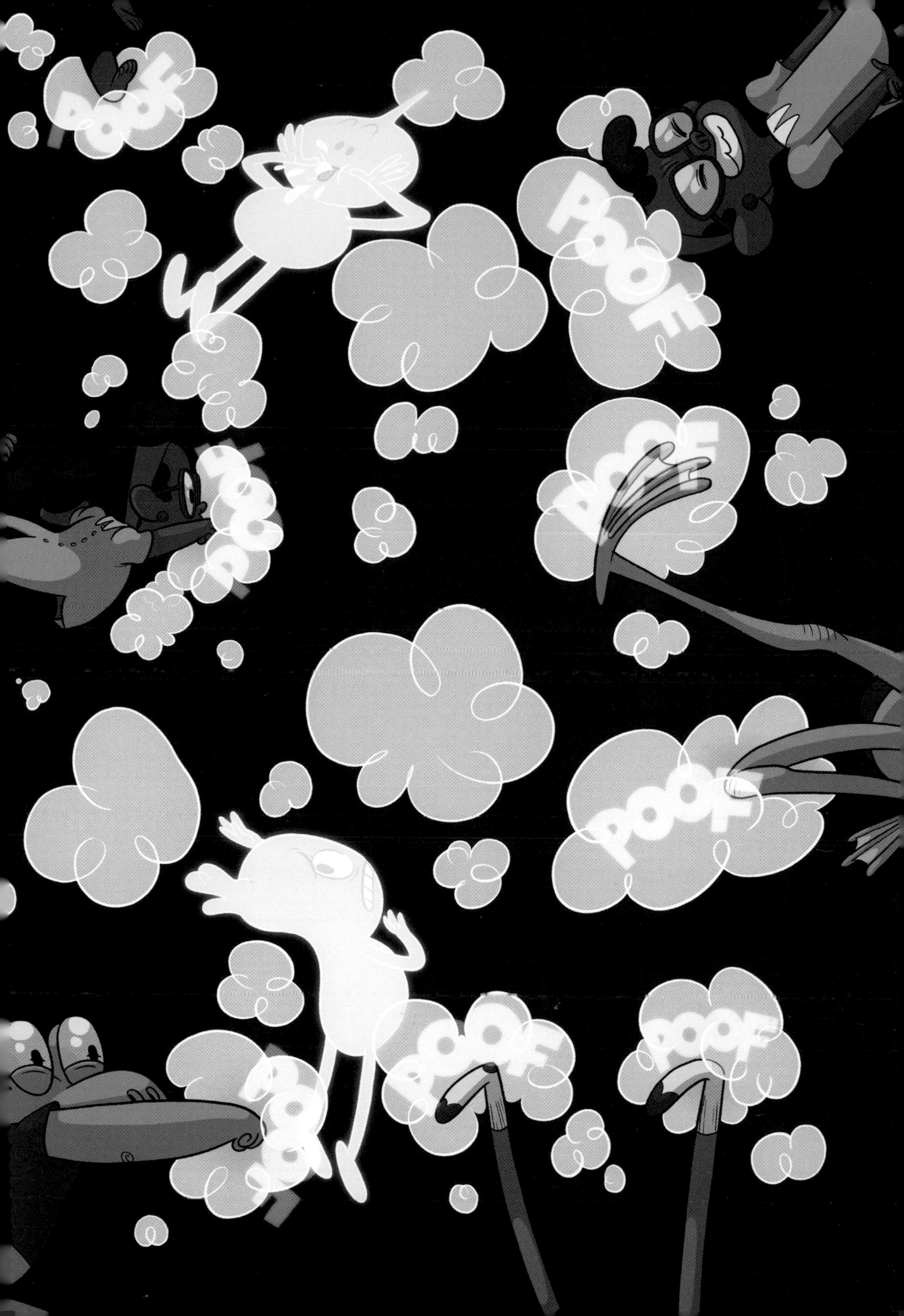
POOF
POOF
POOF
POOF
POOF
POOF
POOF
POOF

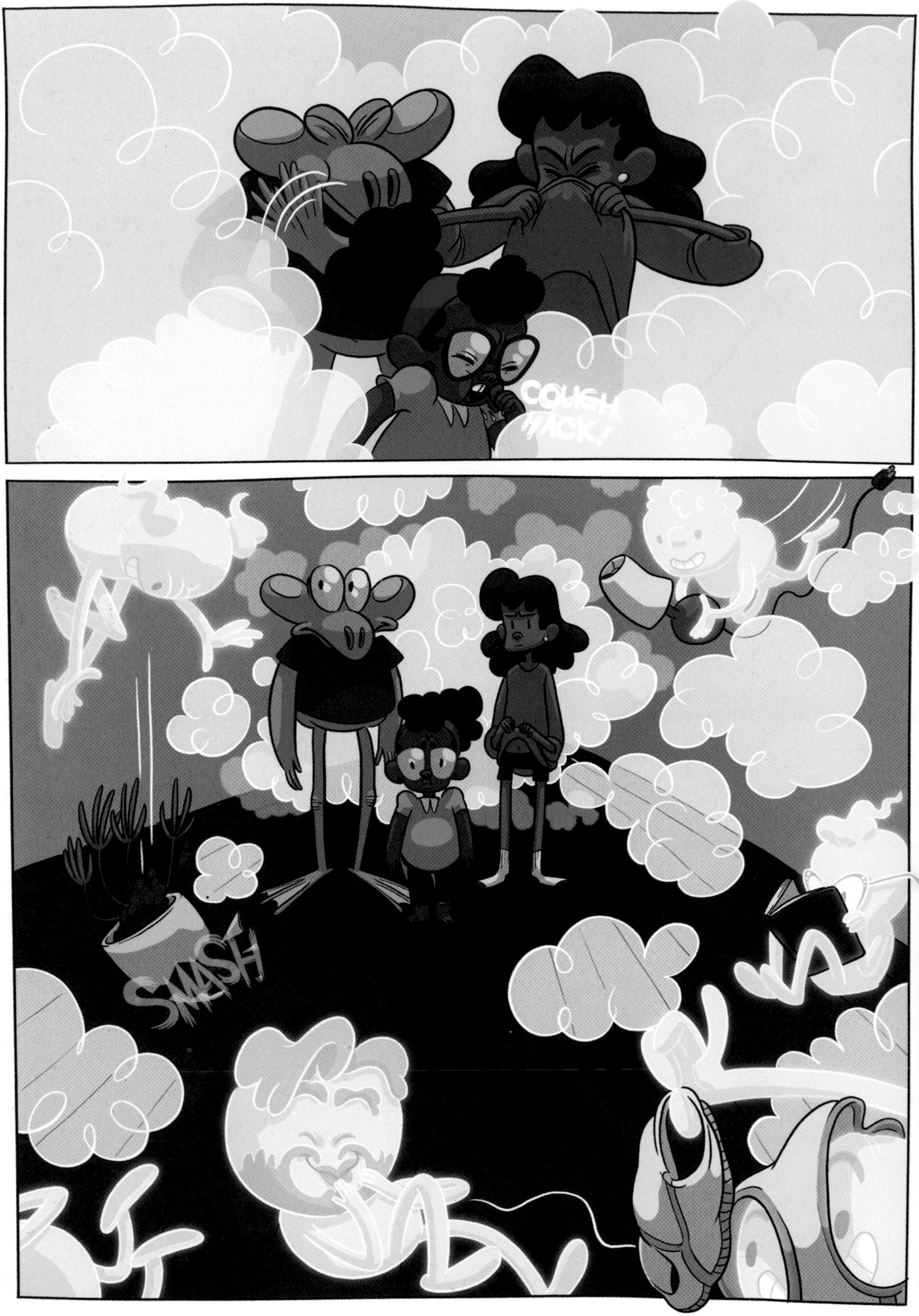
COUGH
HACK!
SMASH

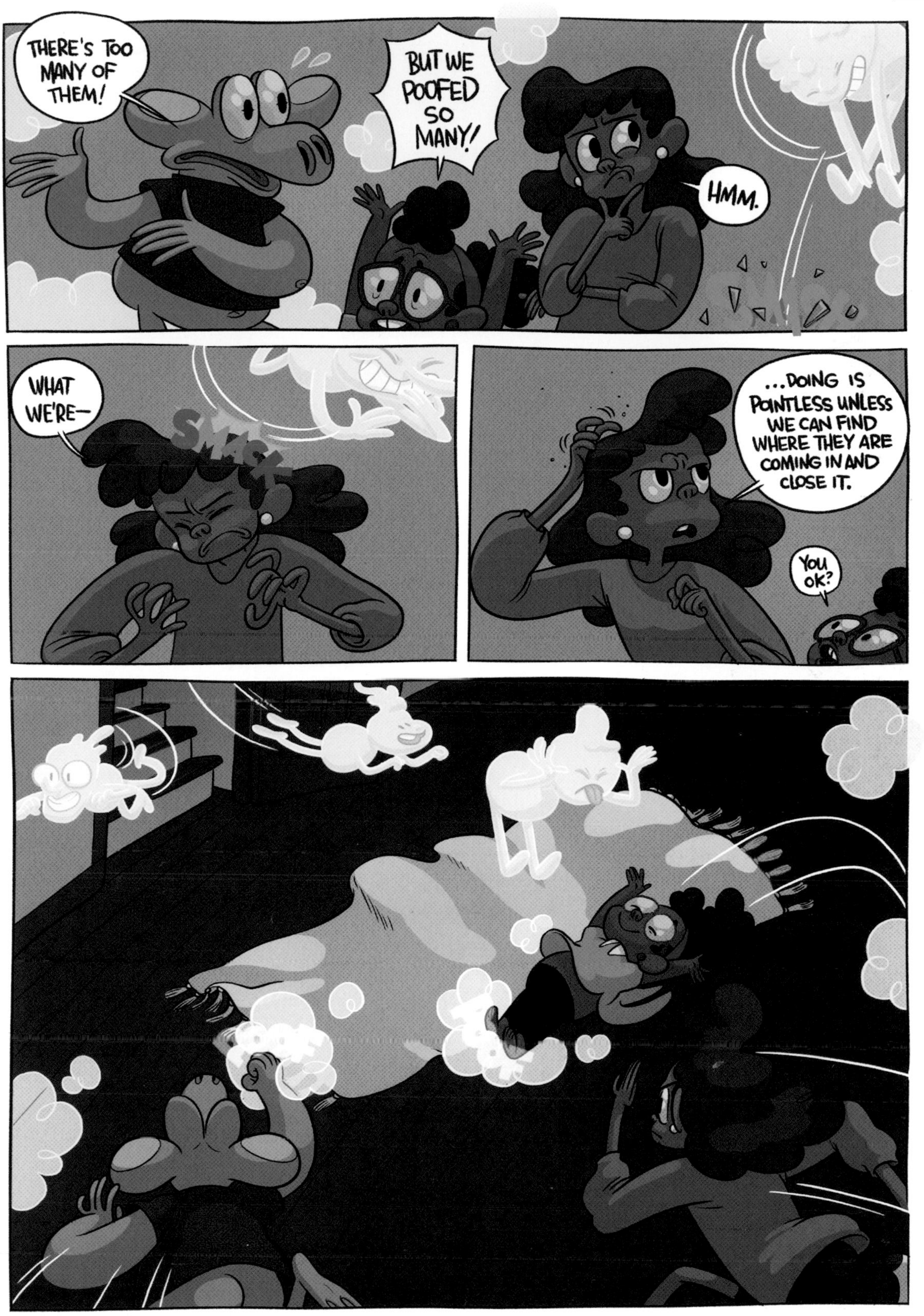
THERE'S TOO MANY OF THEM!
BUT WE POOFED SO MANY!
HMM.
WHAT WE'RE—
SMACK
...DOING IS POINTLESS UNLESS WE CAN FIND WHERE THEY ARE COMING IN AND CLOSE IT.
YOU OK?

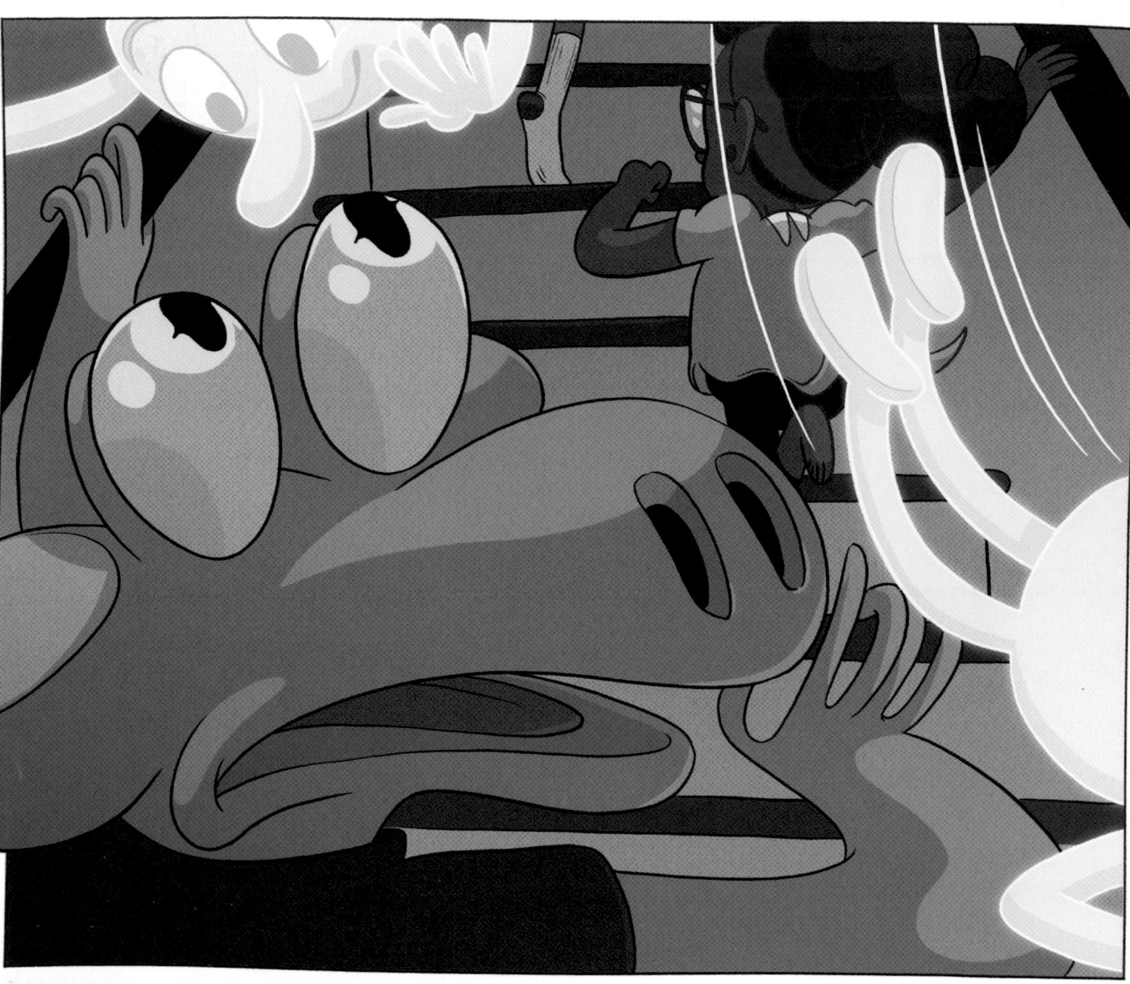

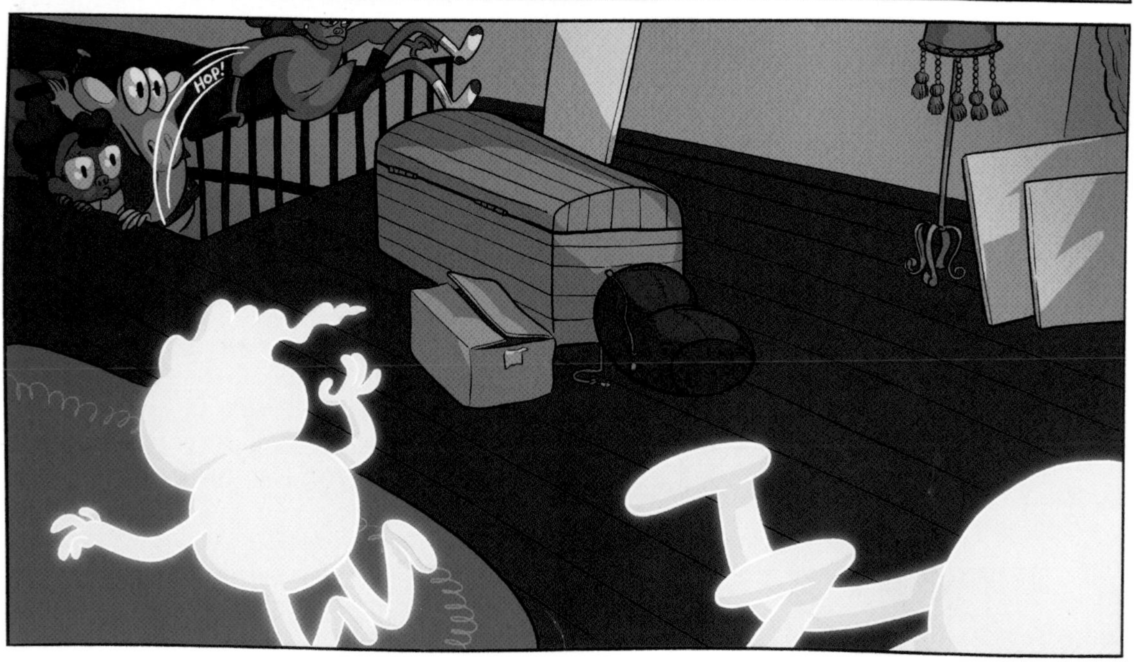
HOP!

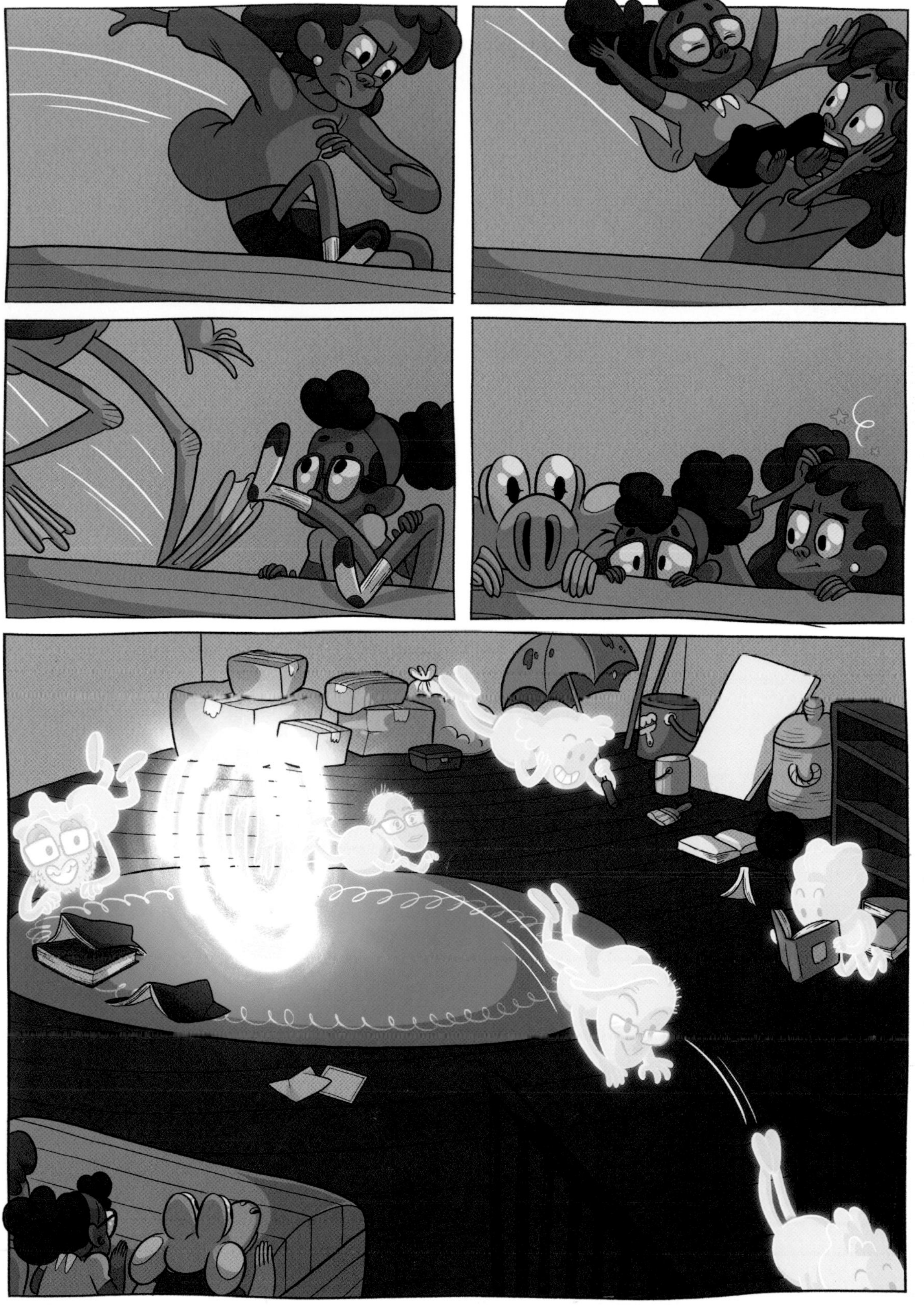

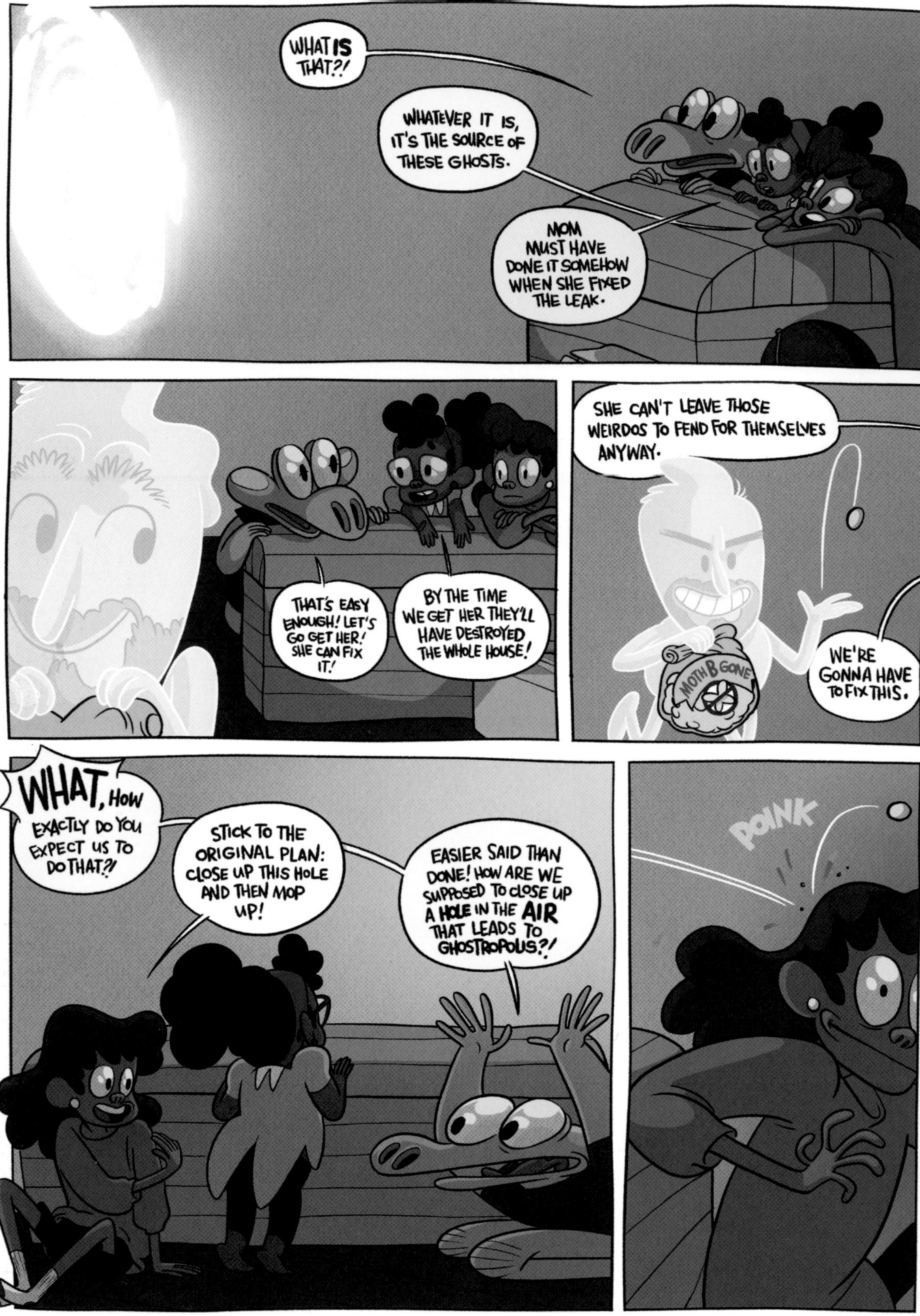
WHAT IS THAT?!
WHATEVER IT IS, IT'S THE SOURCE OF THESE GHOSTS.
MOM MUST HAVE DONE IT SOMEHOW WHEN SHE FIXED THE LEAK.
THAT'S EASY ENOUGH! LET'S GO GET HER! SHE CAN FIX IT!
BY THE TIME WE GET HER THEY'LL HAVE DESTROYED THE WHOLE HOUSE!
SHE CAN'T LEAVE THOSE WEIRDOS TO FEND FOR THEMSELVES ANYWAY.
MOTH B GONE
WE'RE GONNA HAVE TO FIX THIS.
WHAT, HOW EXACTLY DO YOU EXPECT US TO DO THAT?!
STICK TO THE ORIGINAL PLAN: CLOSE UP THIS HOLE AND THEN MOP UP!
EASIER SAID THAN DONE! HOW ARE WE SUPPOSED TO CLOSE UP A HOLE IN THE AIR THAT LEADS TO GHOSTROPOLIS?!
POINK

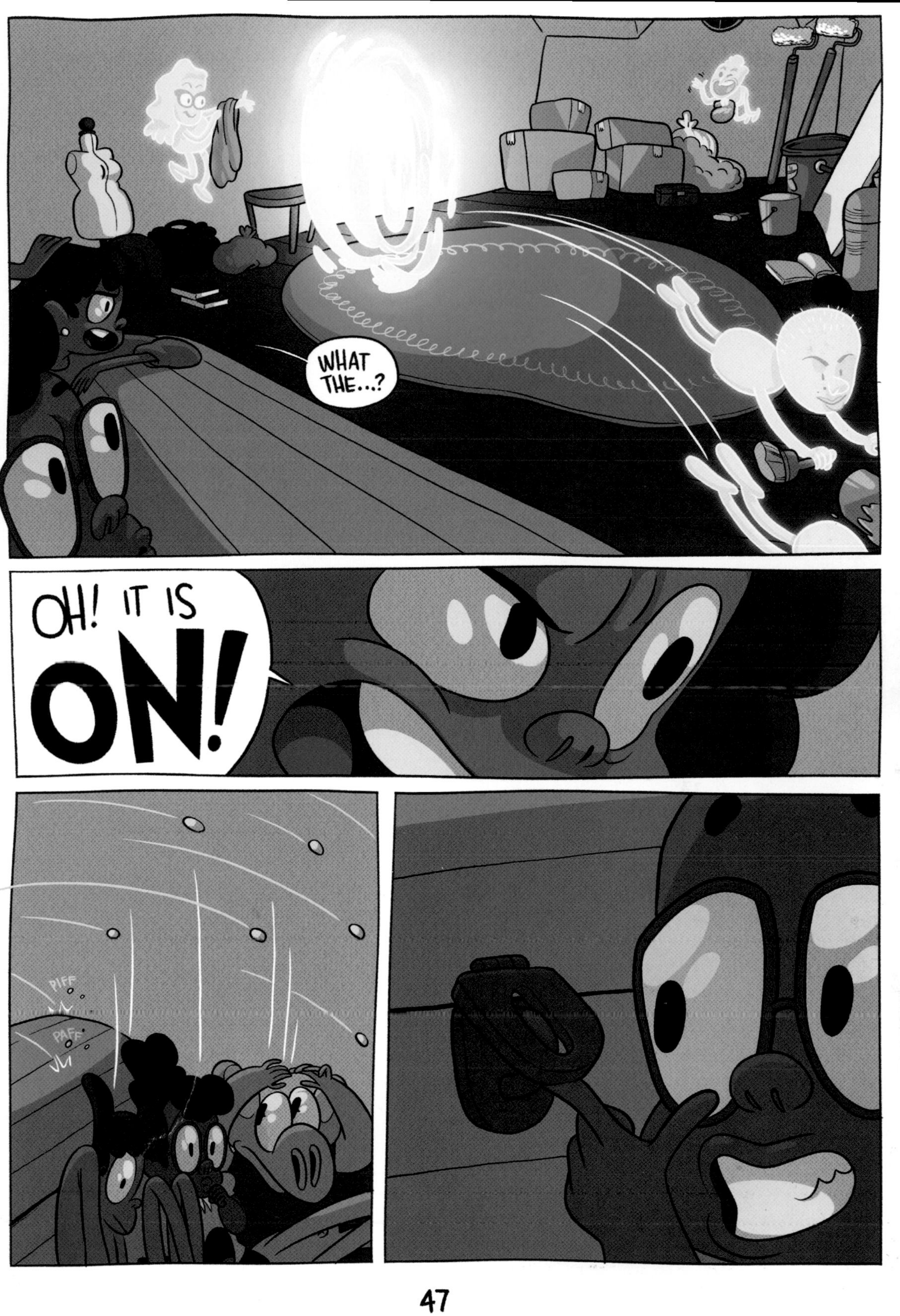
WHAT THE...?
OH! IT IS ON!
PIFF
PAFF

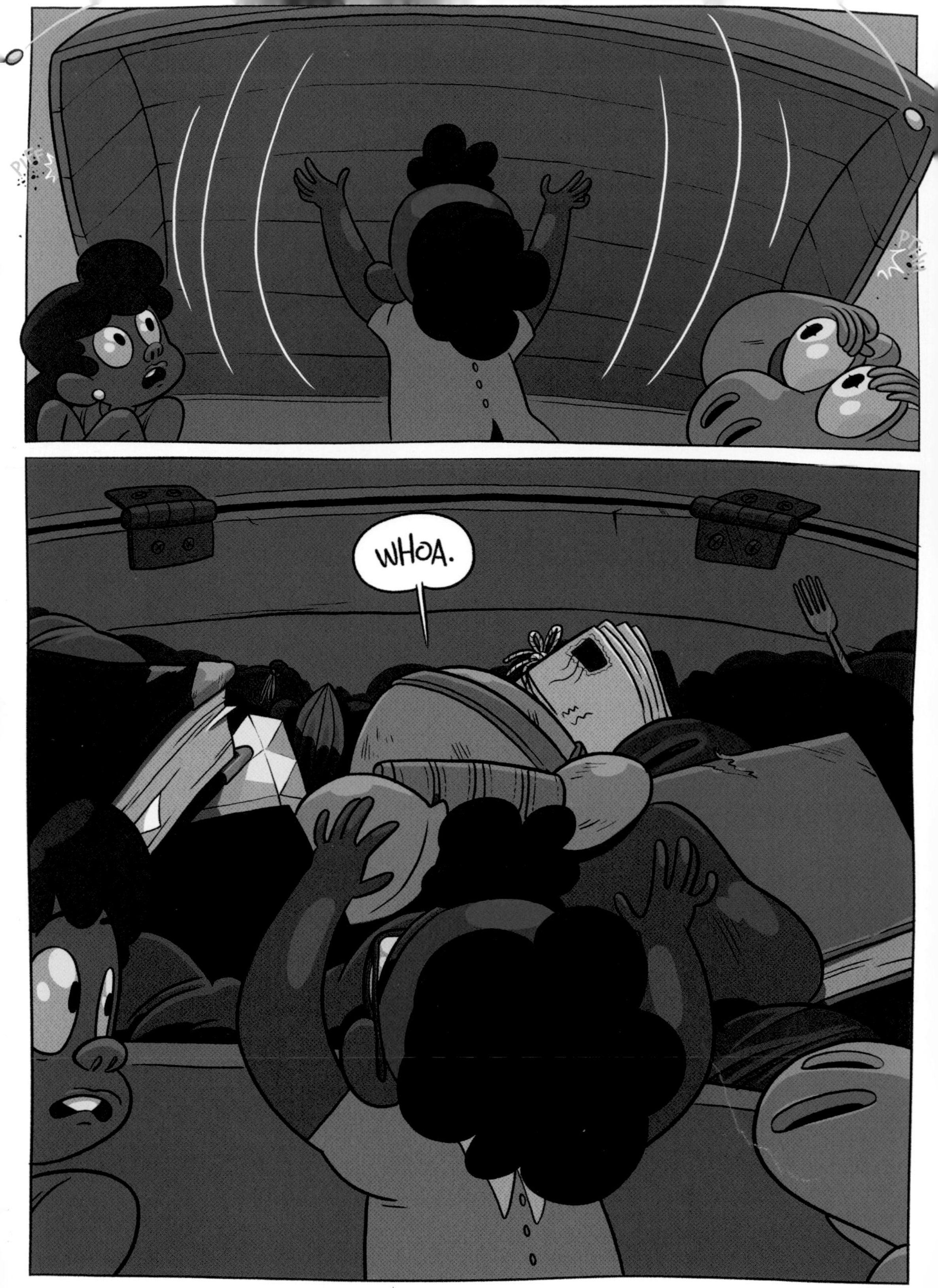
WHOA.

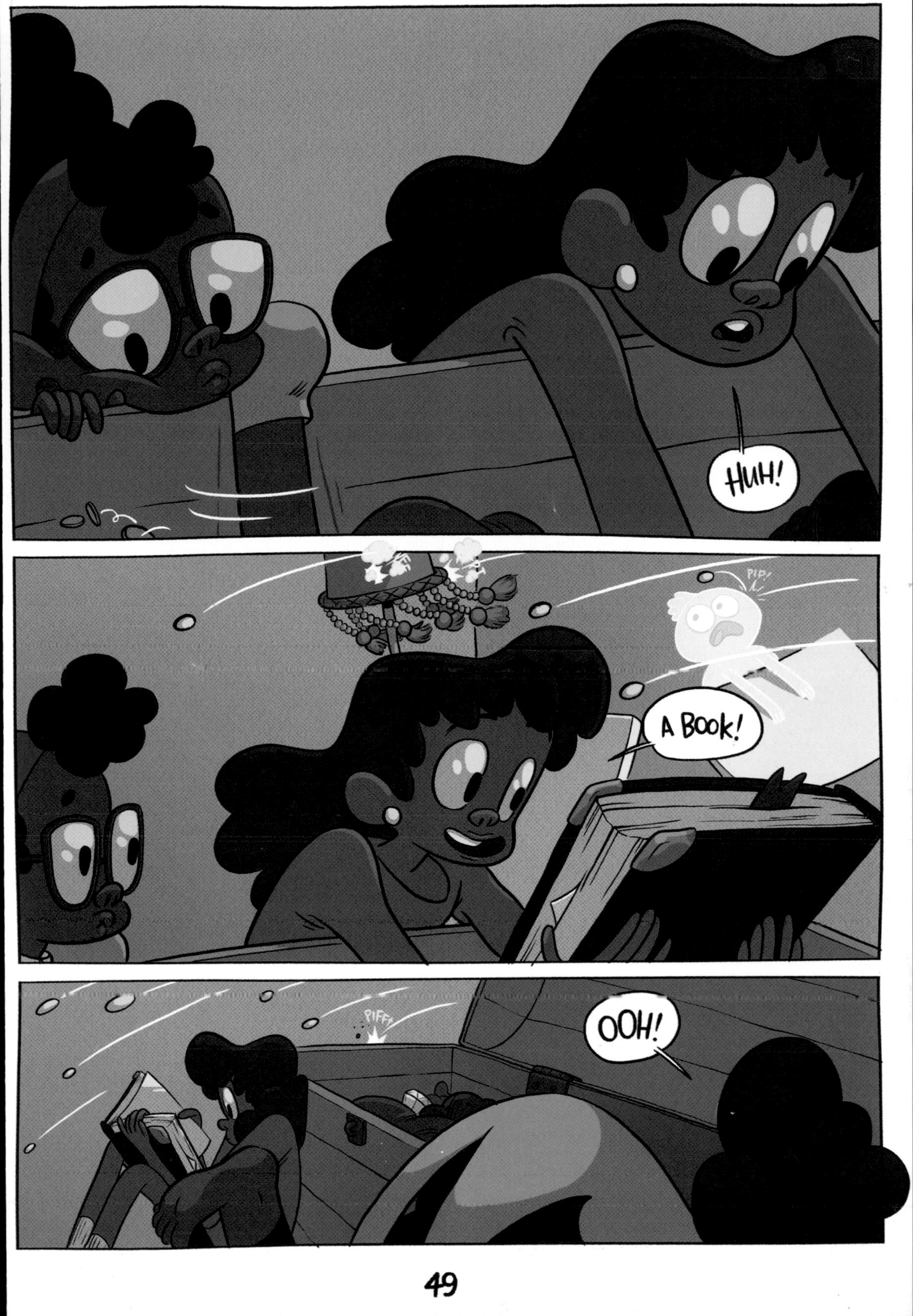
HUH!
PIP!
A BOOK!
PIFF
OOH!

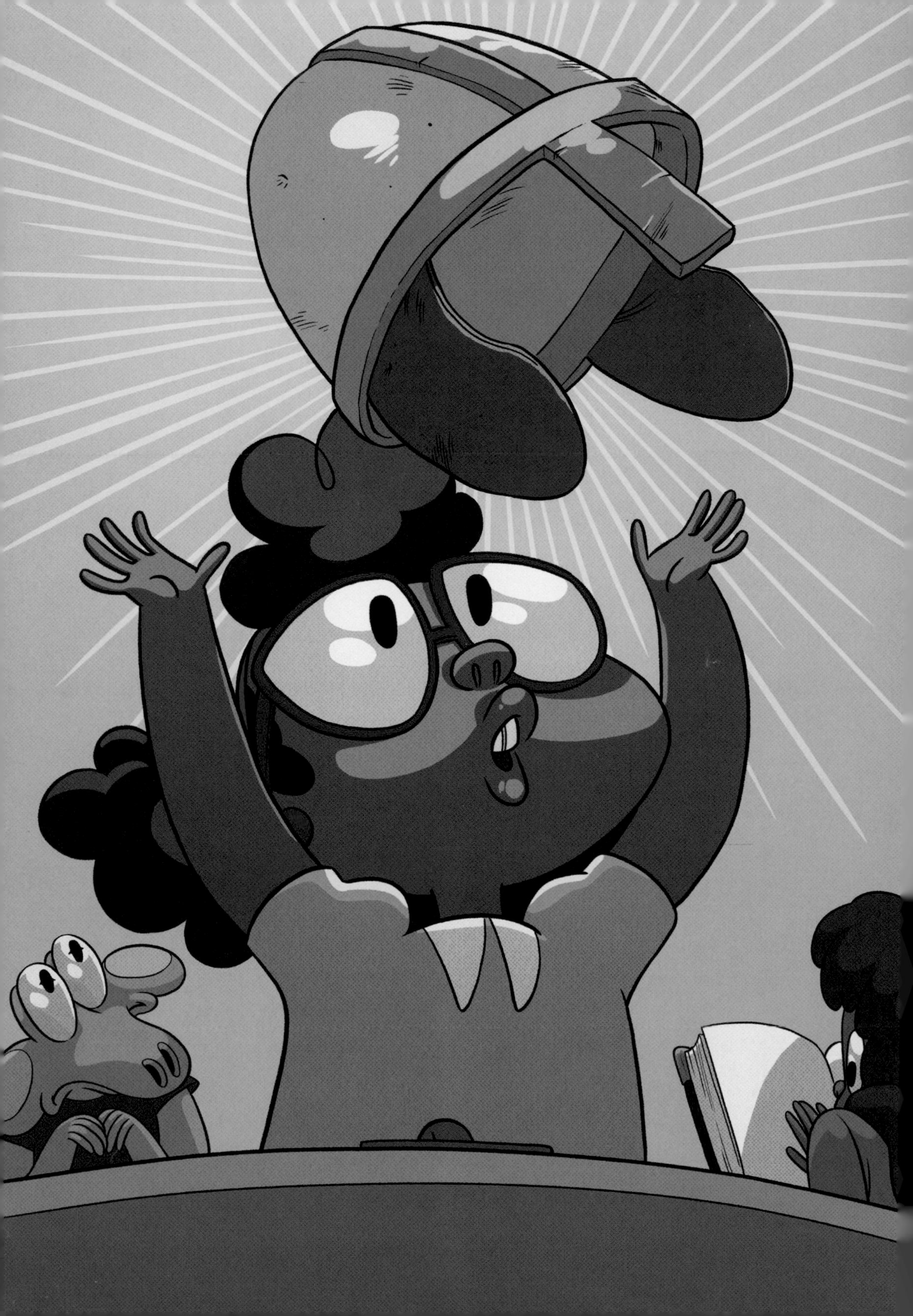

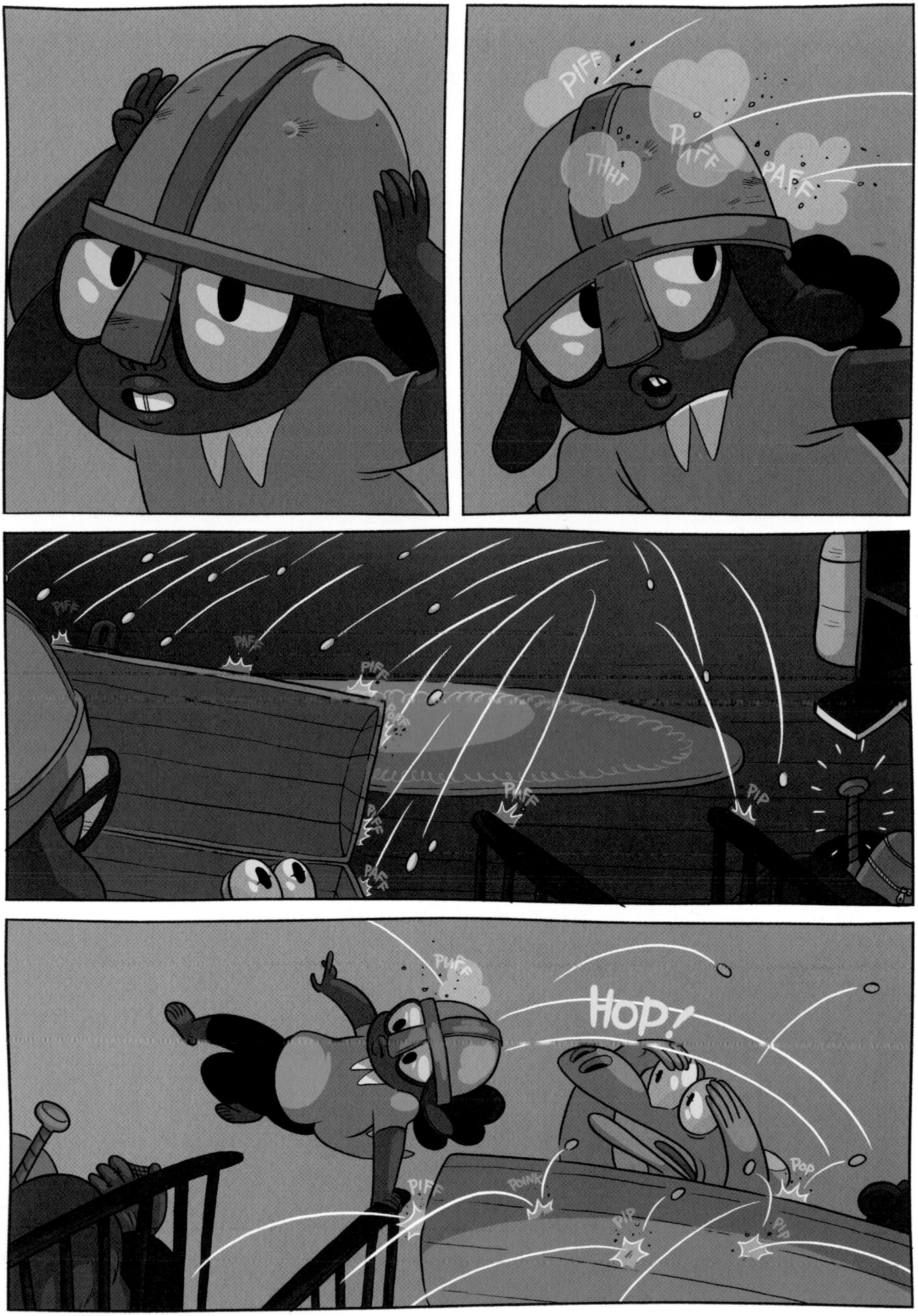
PIFF
THHT
PAFF
PAFF
PAFF
PIFF
PAFF
PIP
PUFF
HOP!
PIFF
POINK
PIP
POP
PIP

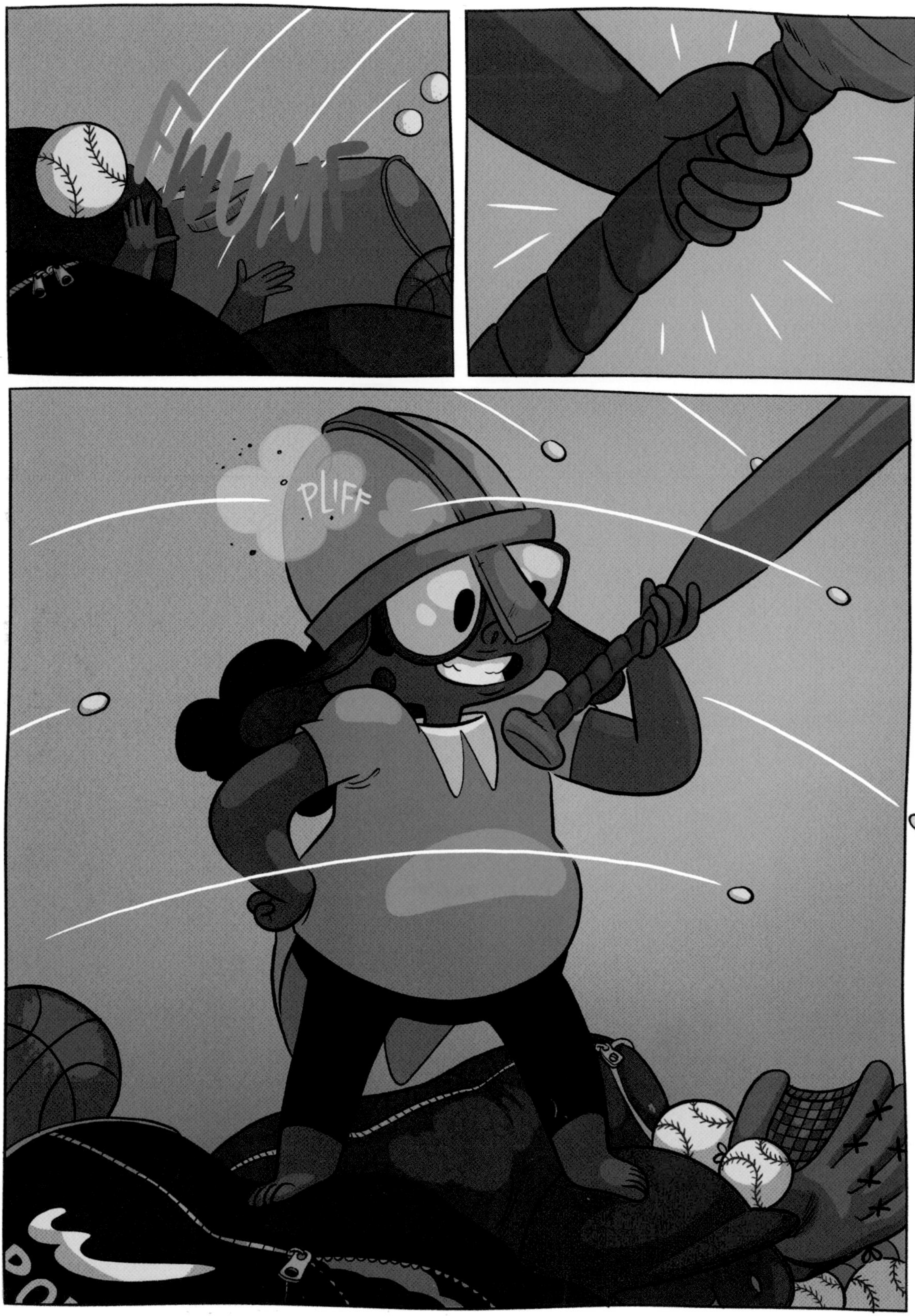
FWUMF
PLIFF

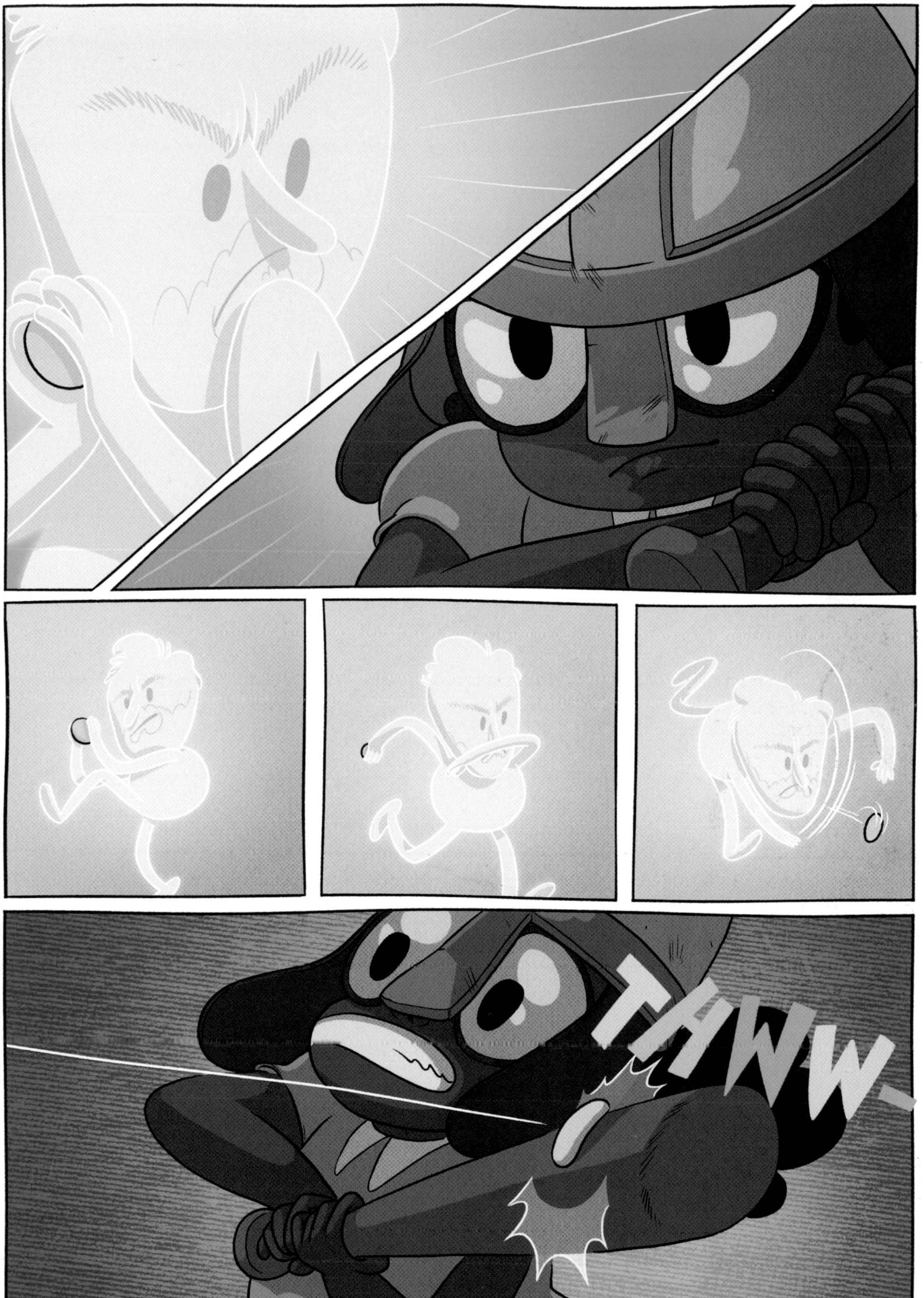
THWW-

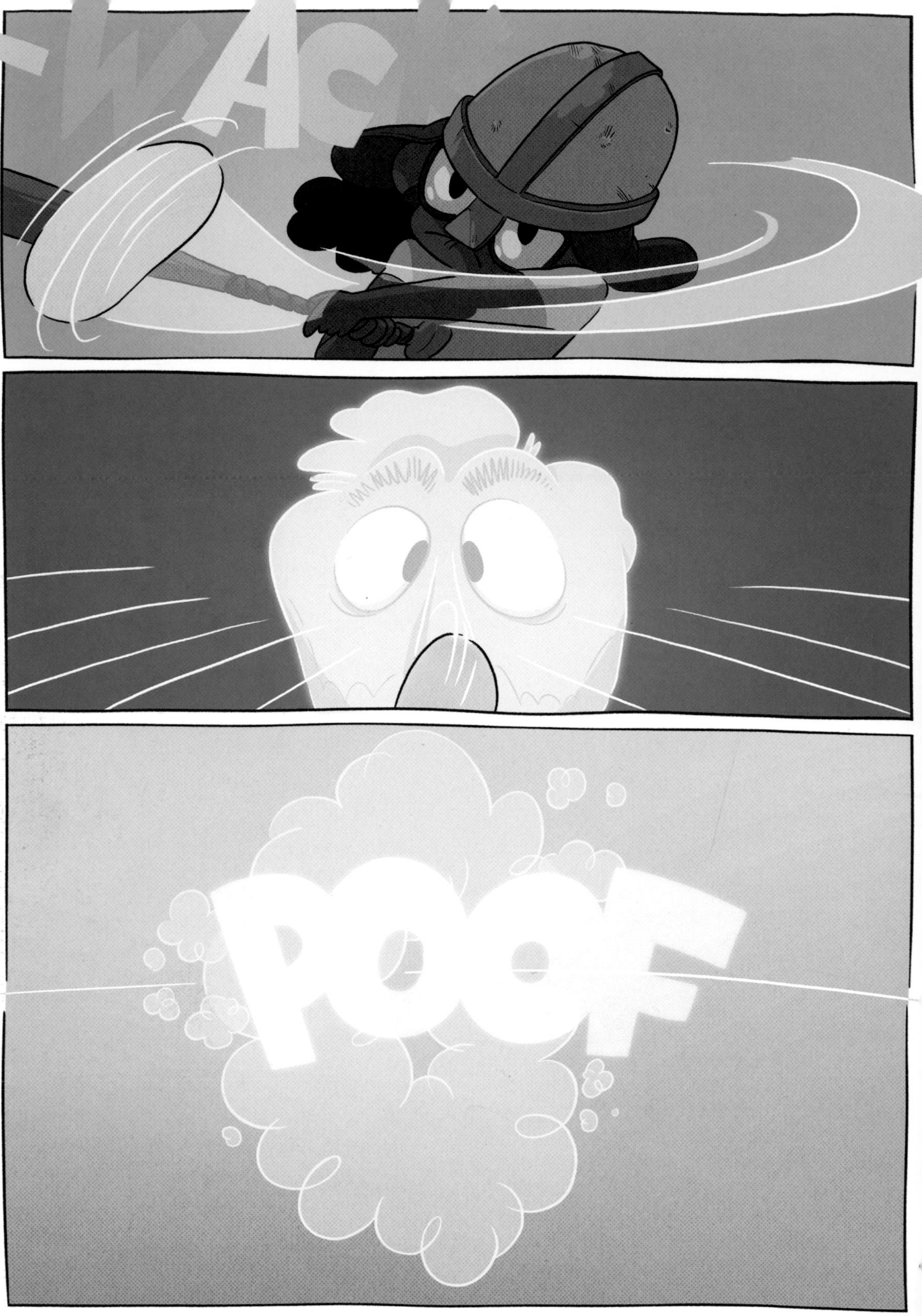
POOF

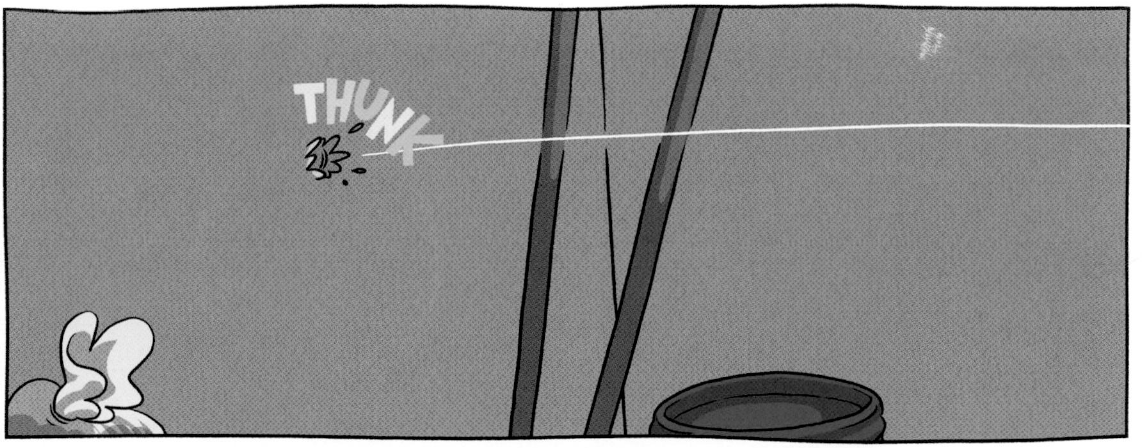
THUNK

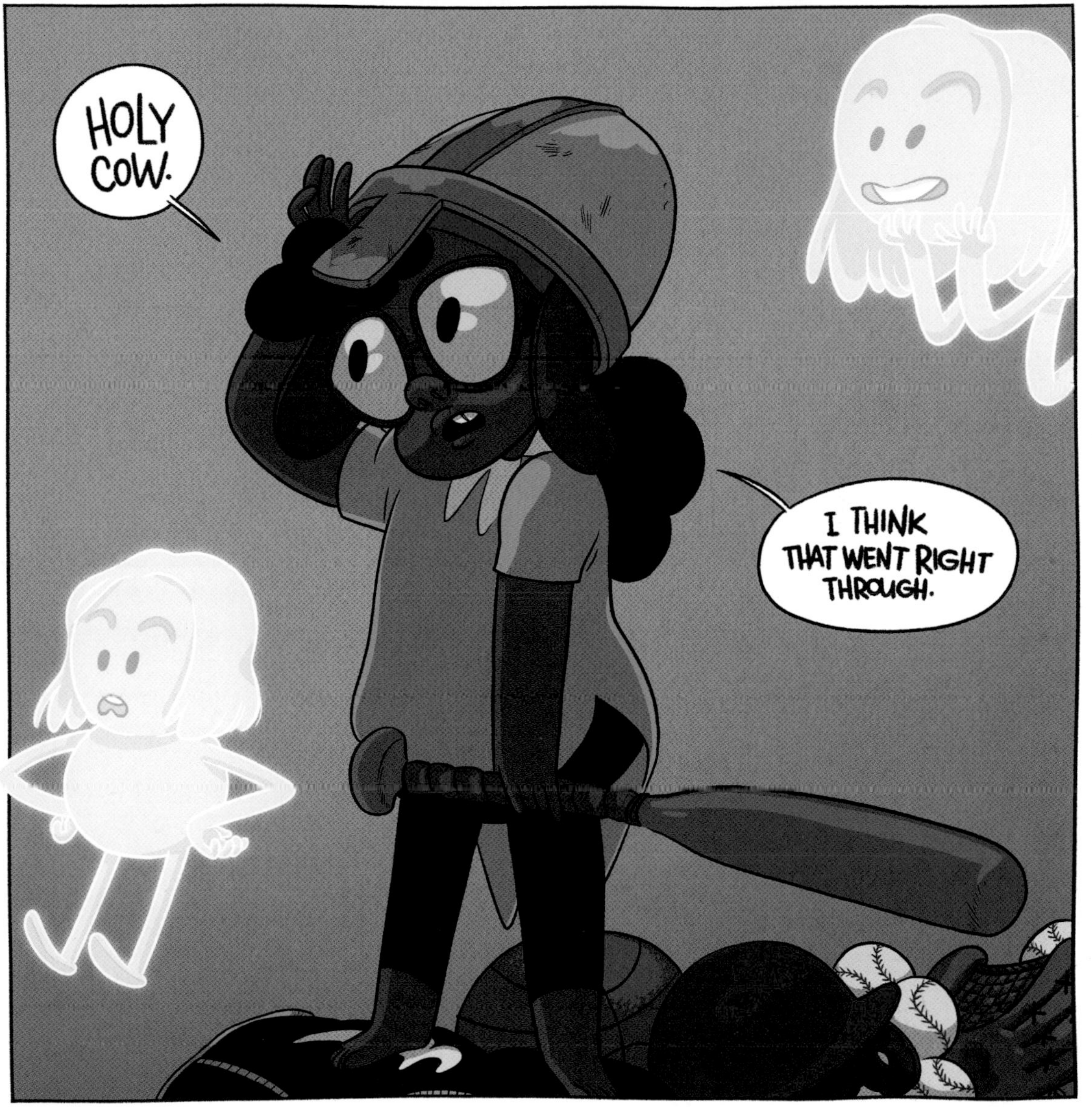
HOLY COW.
I THINK THAT WENT RIGHT THROUGH.

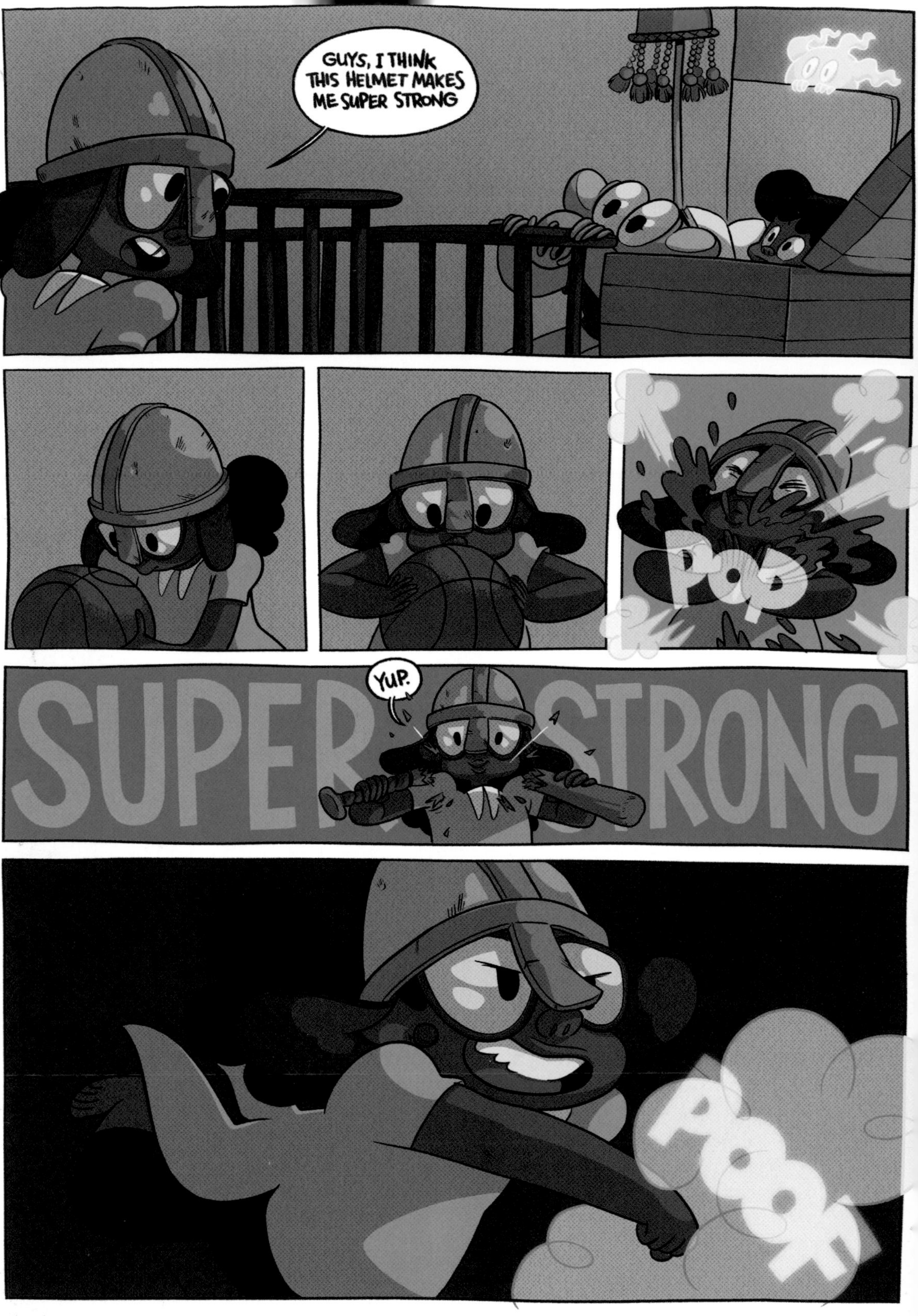
GUYS, I THINK THIS HELMET MAKES ME SUPER STRONG
POP
YUP.
SUPER STRONG
POOF

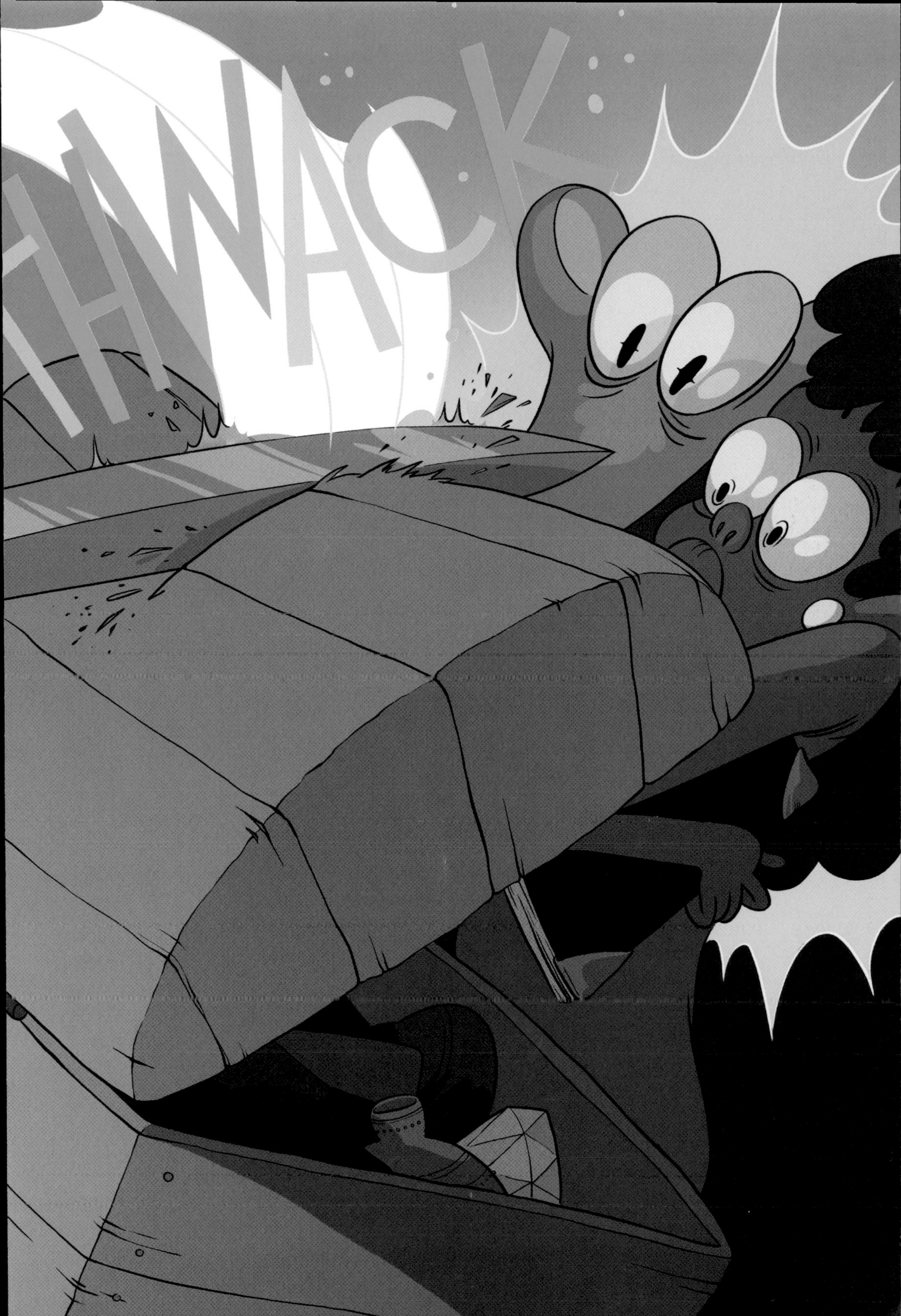
THWACK

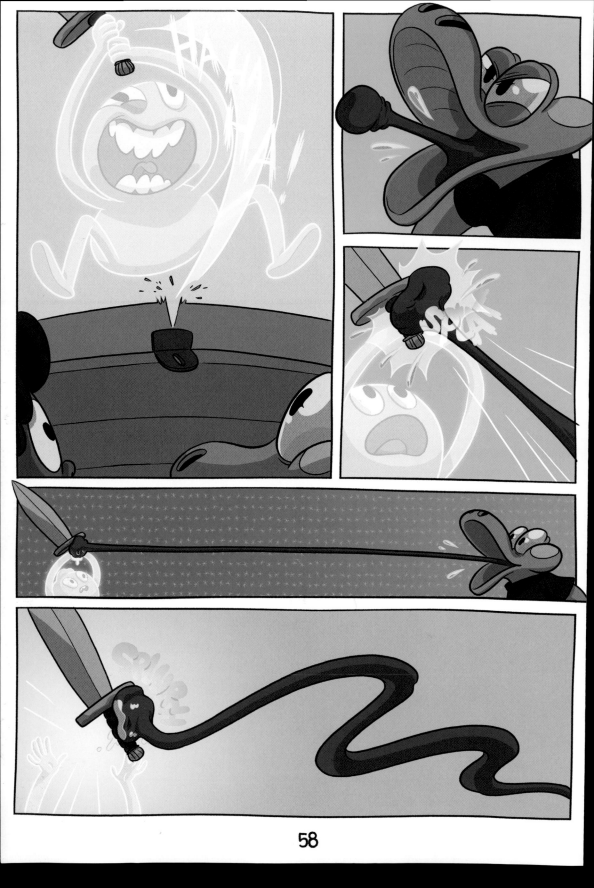

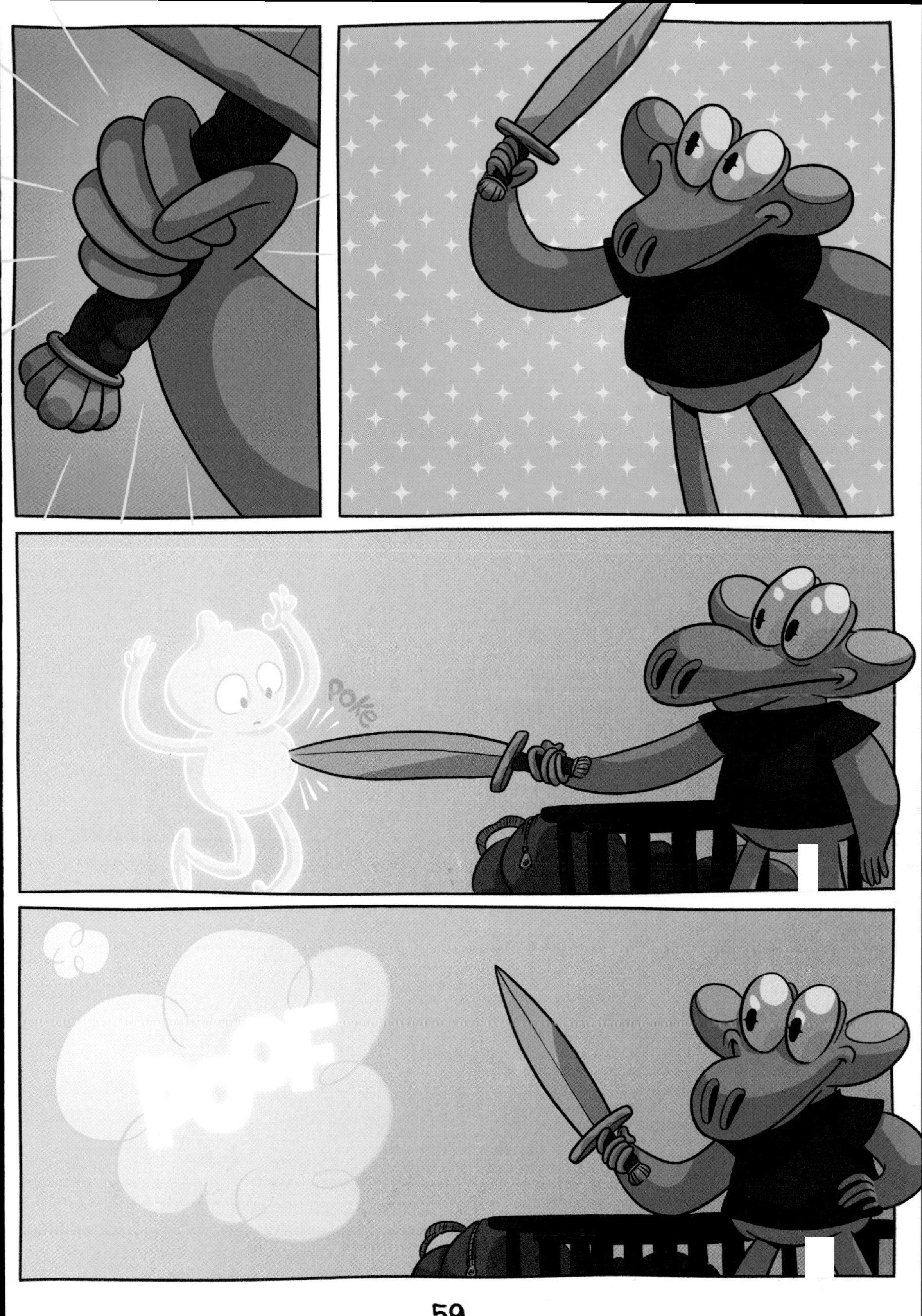
POKE
POOF

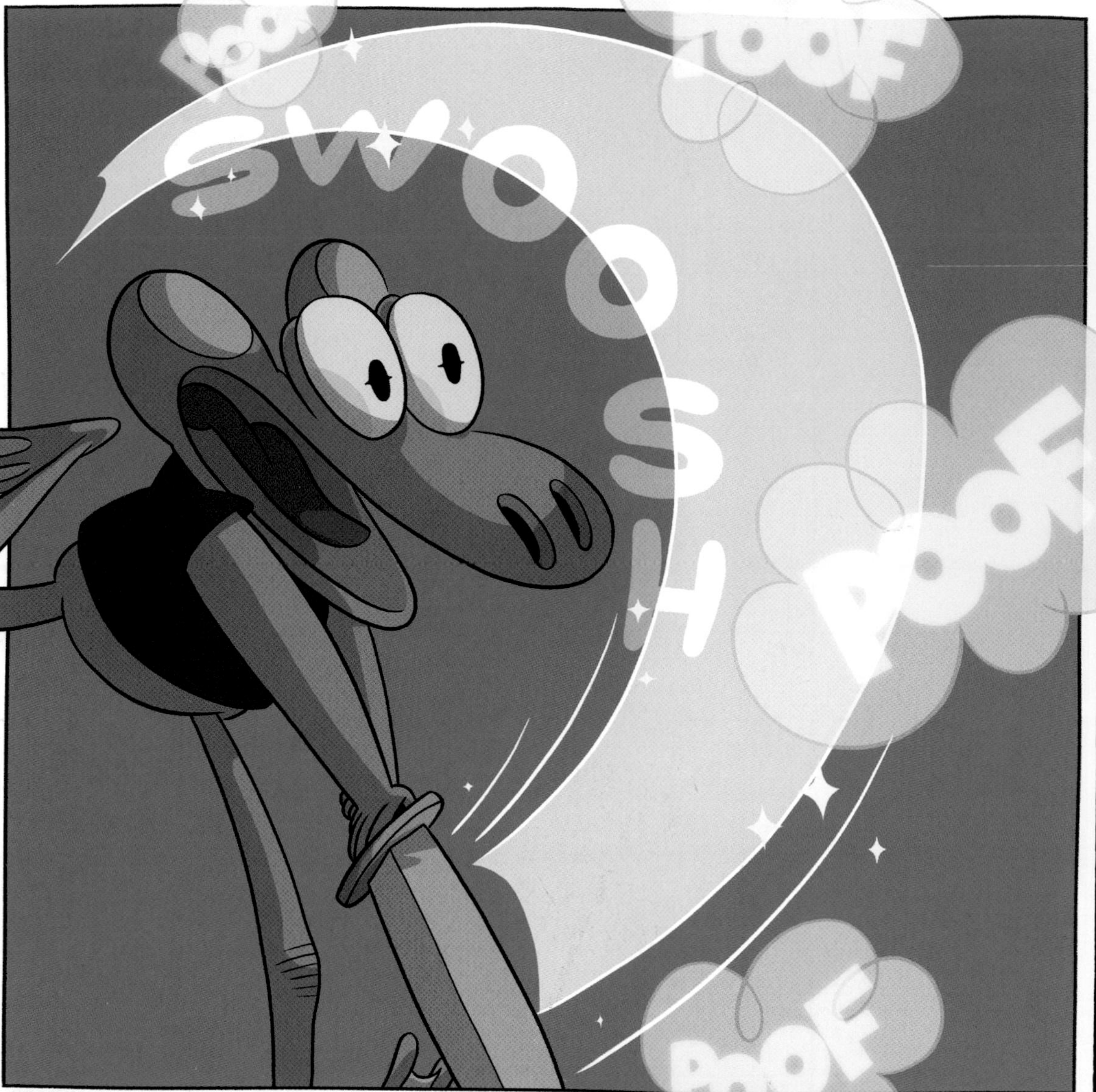
SWOOSH
POOF
POOF
POOF
POOF

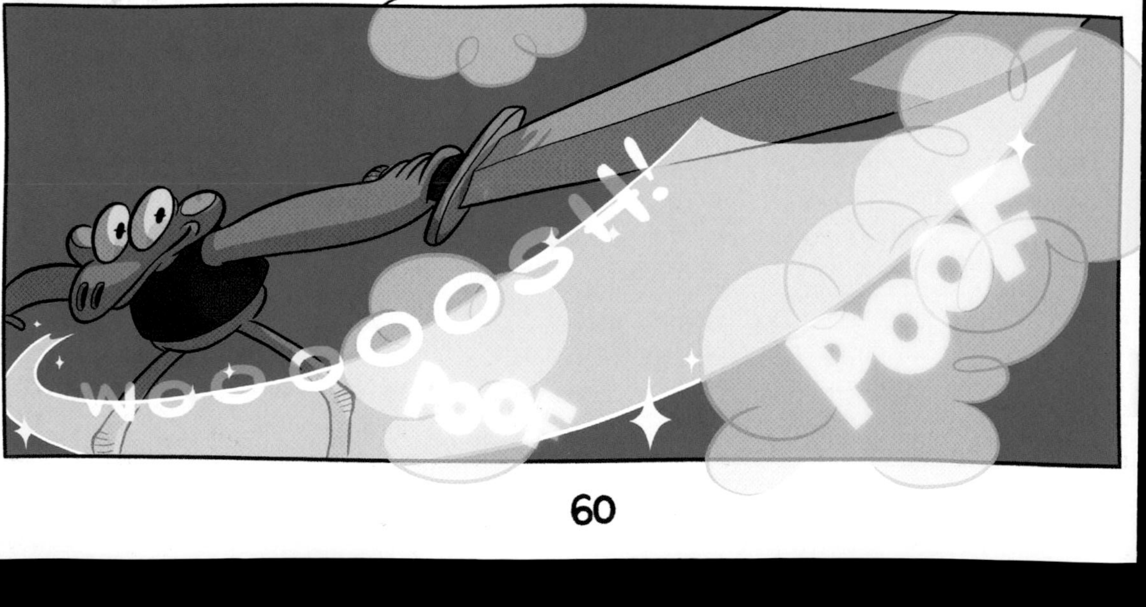
WOOOOOOOSH!
POOF
POOF

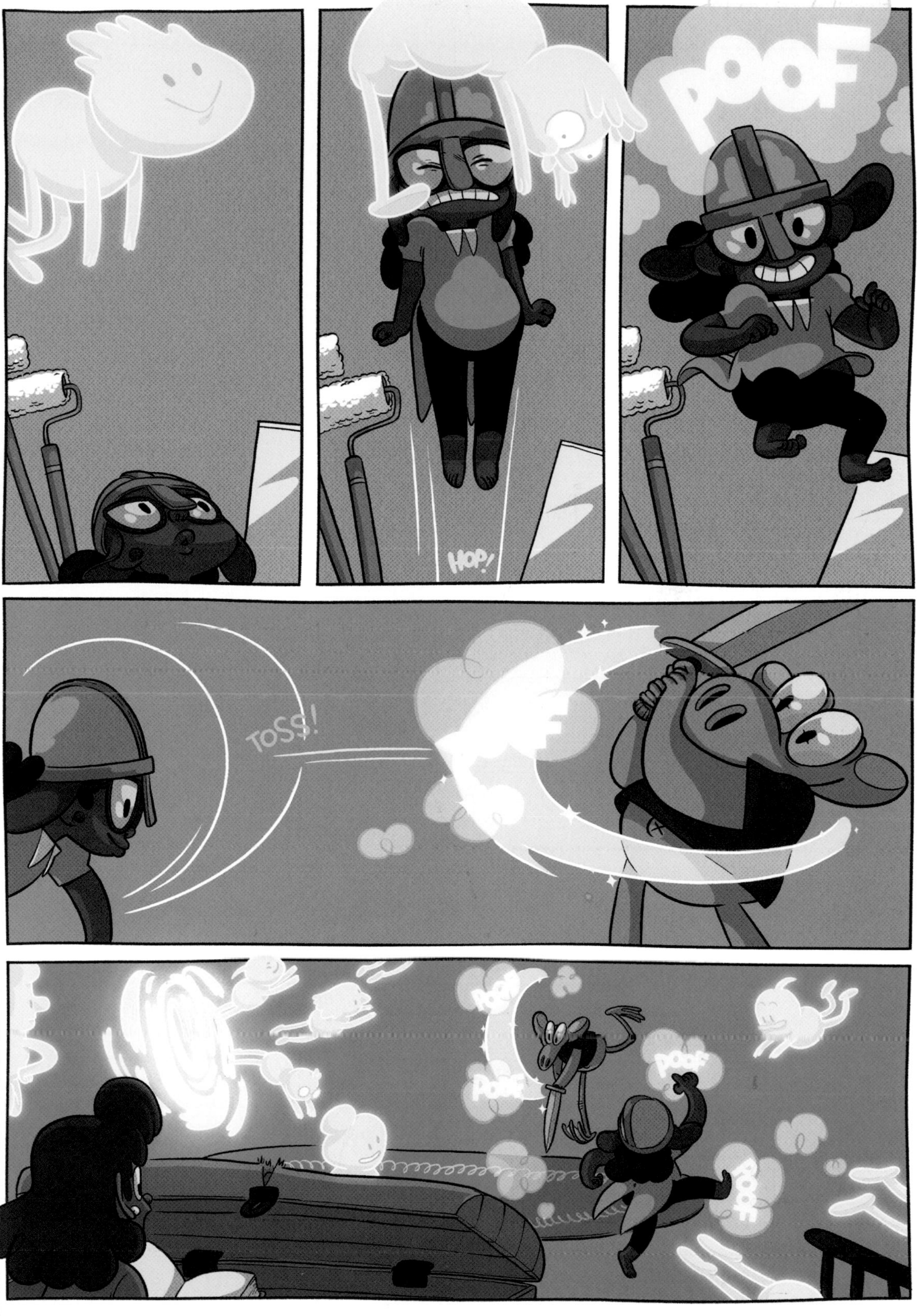
POOF
HOP!
TOSS!
POOF
POOF
POOF
POOF

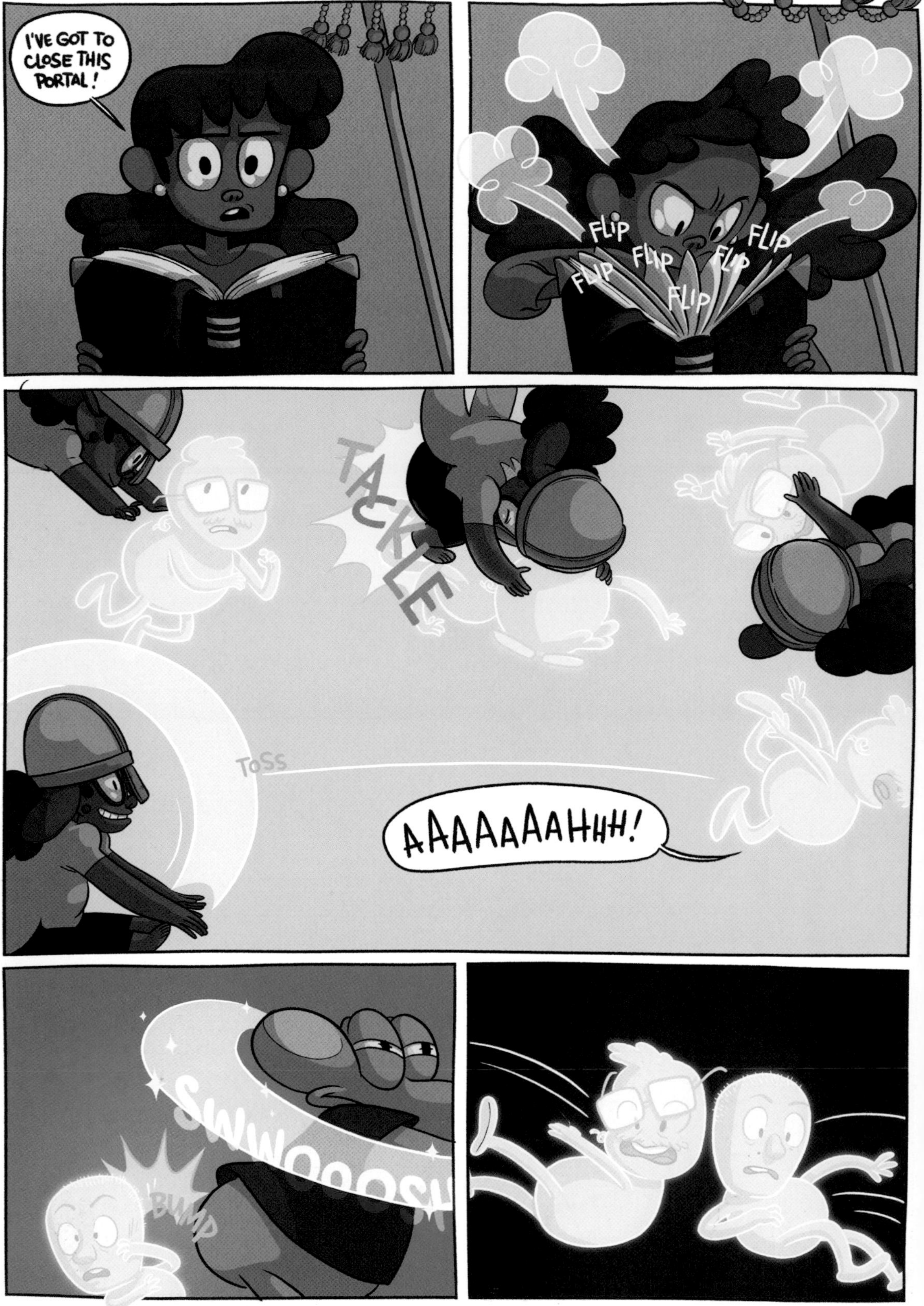

I'VE GOT TO CLOSE THIS PORTAL!
FLIP FLIP FLIP FLIP FLIP FLIP
TACKLE
TOSS
AAAAAAAHHH!
SWWOOOOSH
BUMP

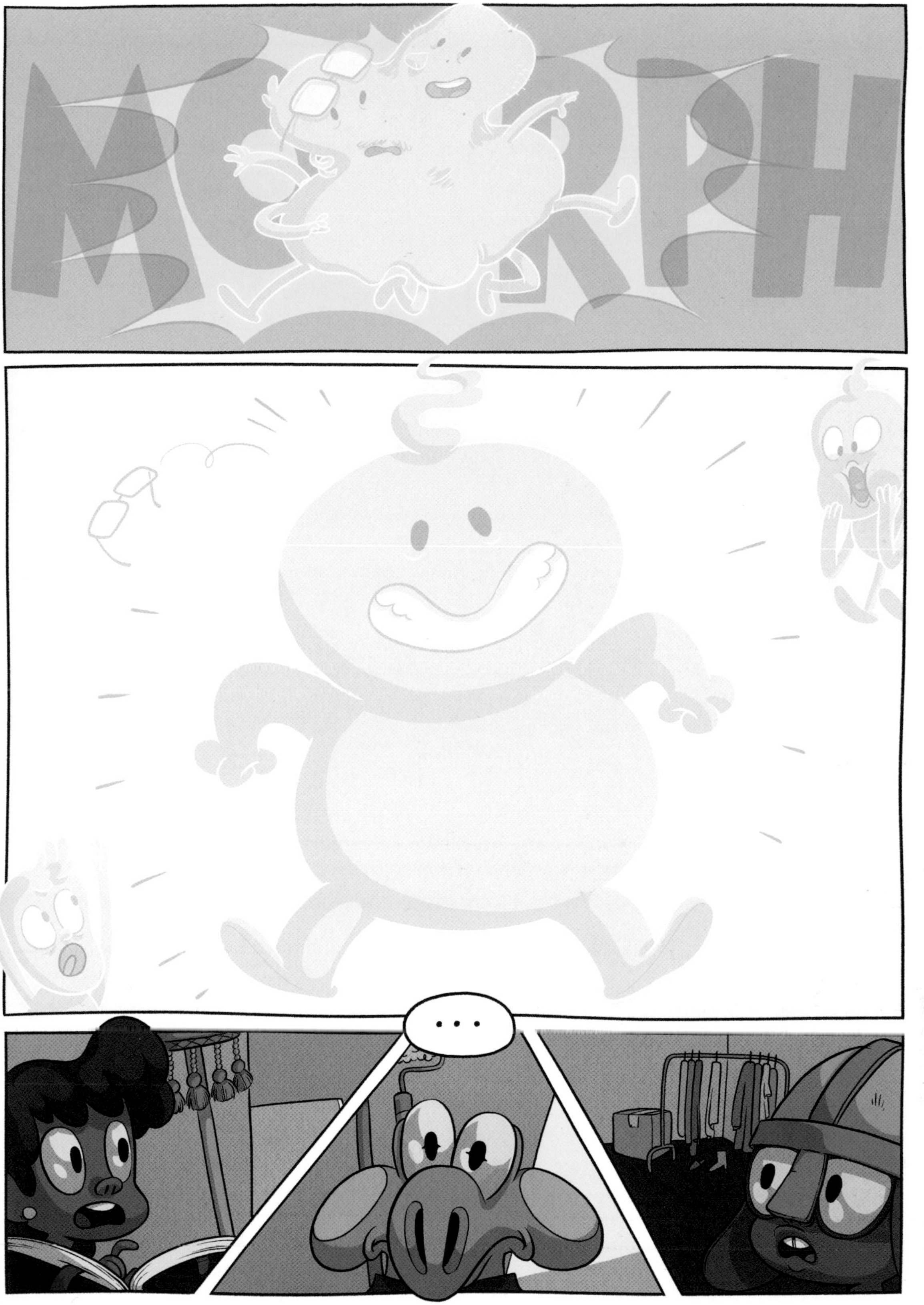
MORPH
...

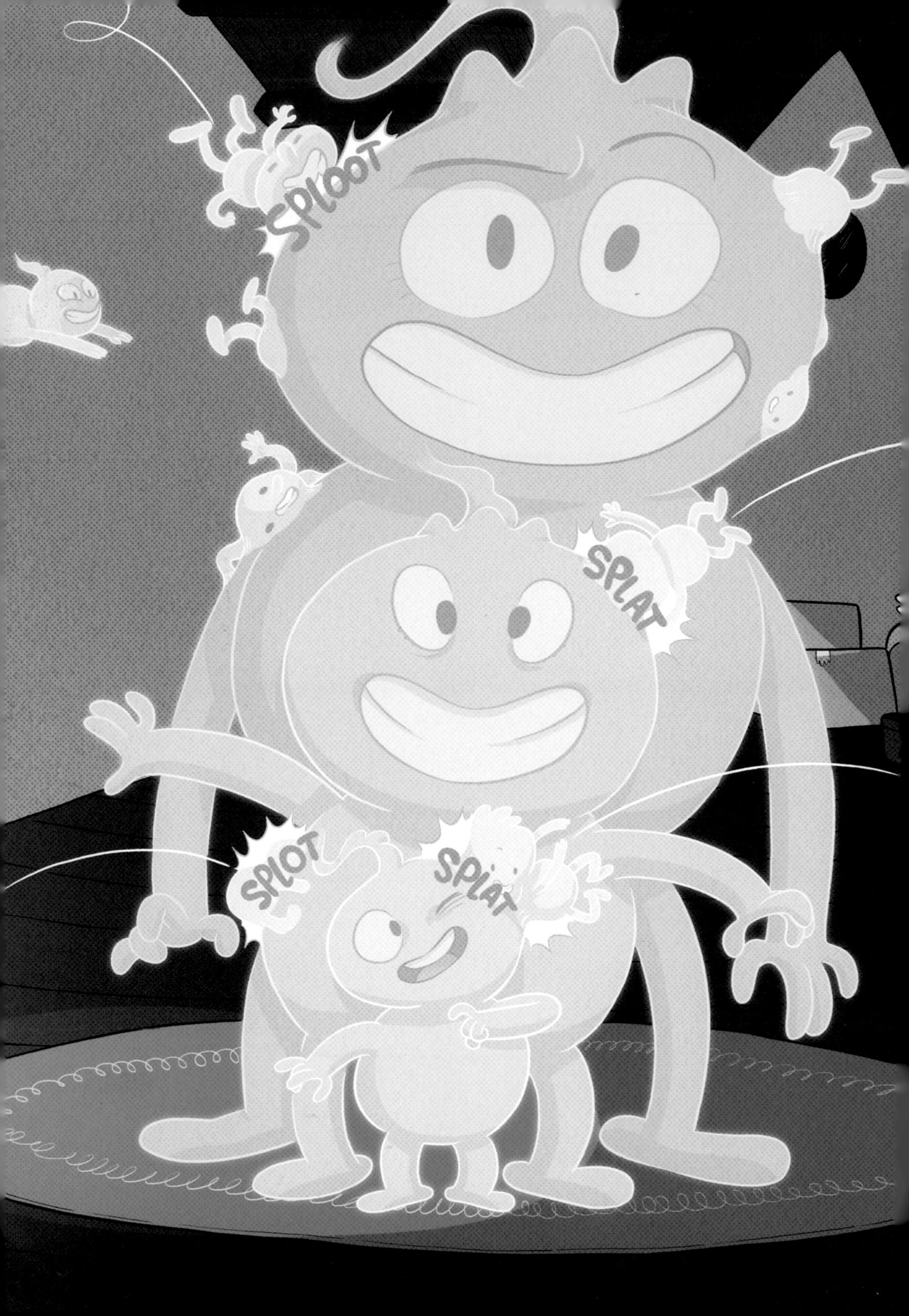
SPLOOT
SPLAT
SPLOT
SPLAT

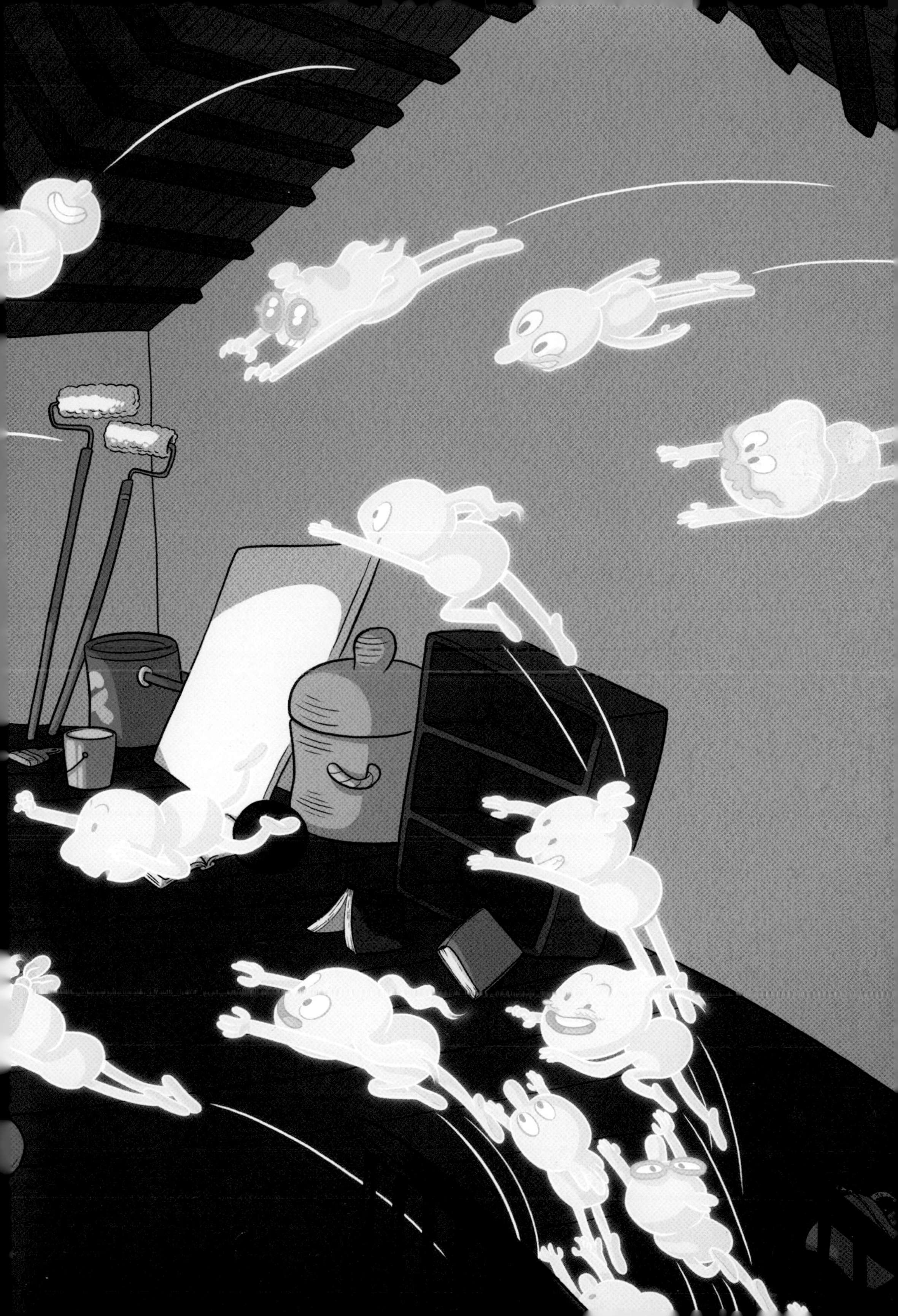

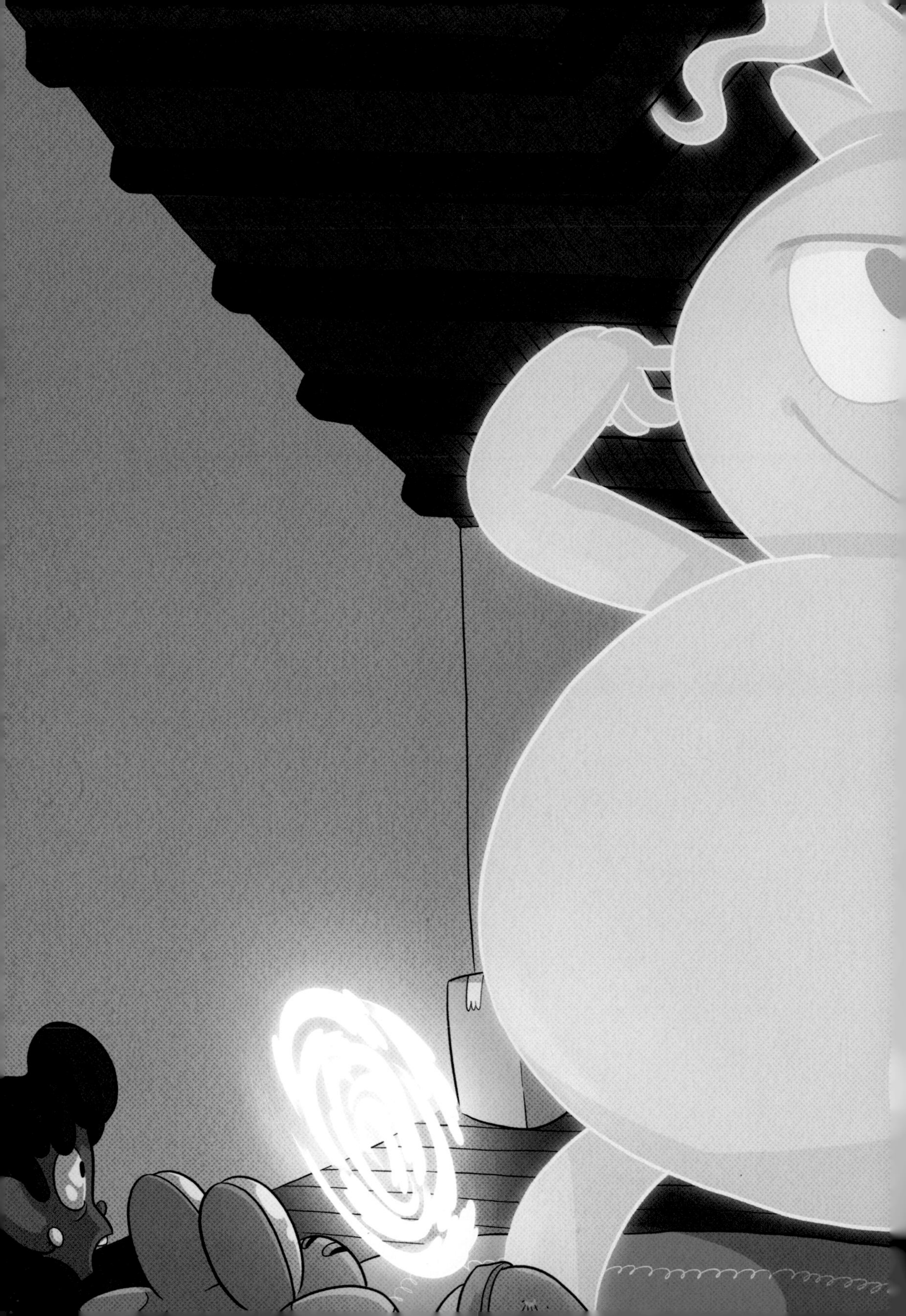

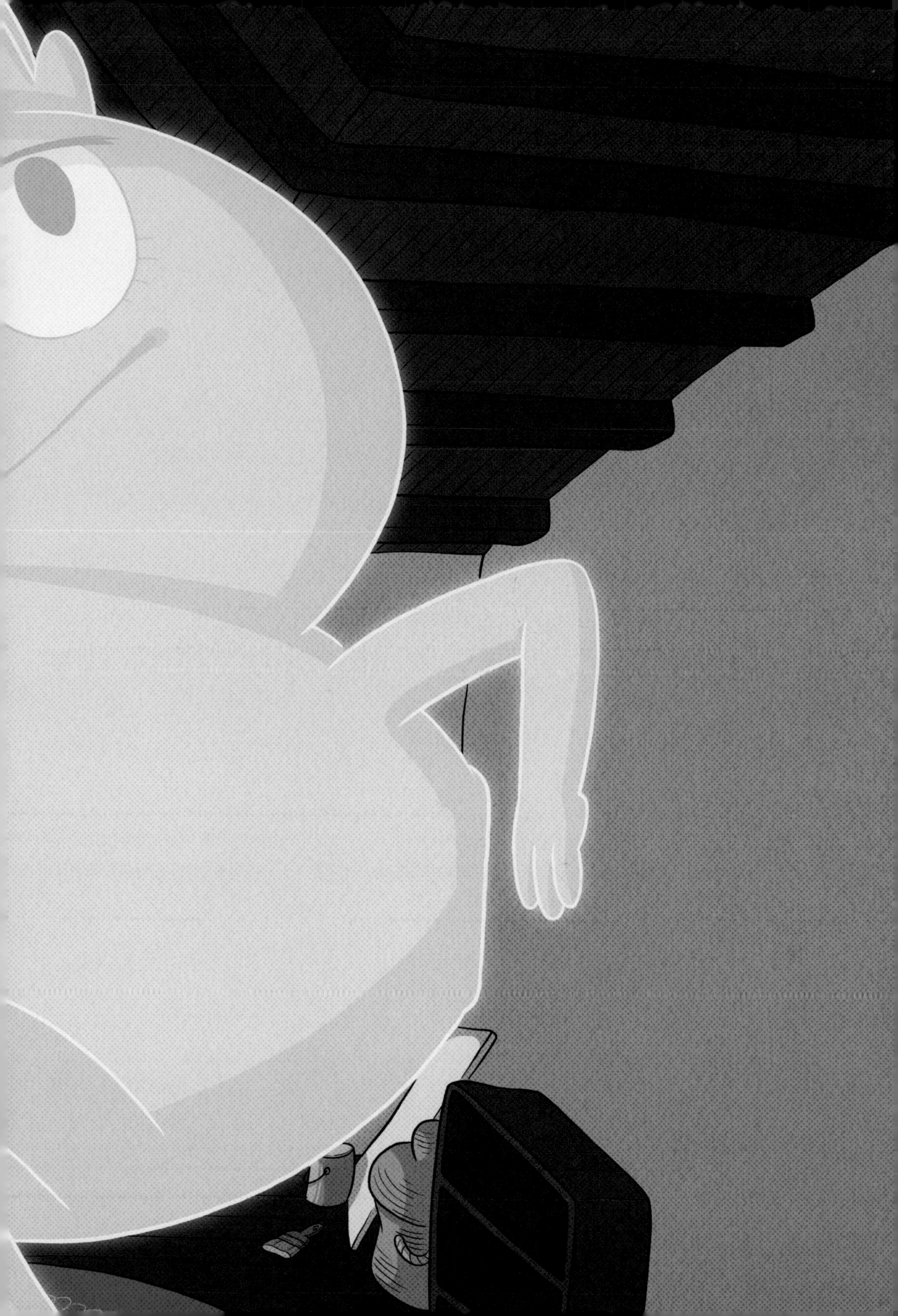

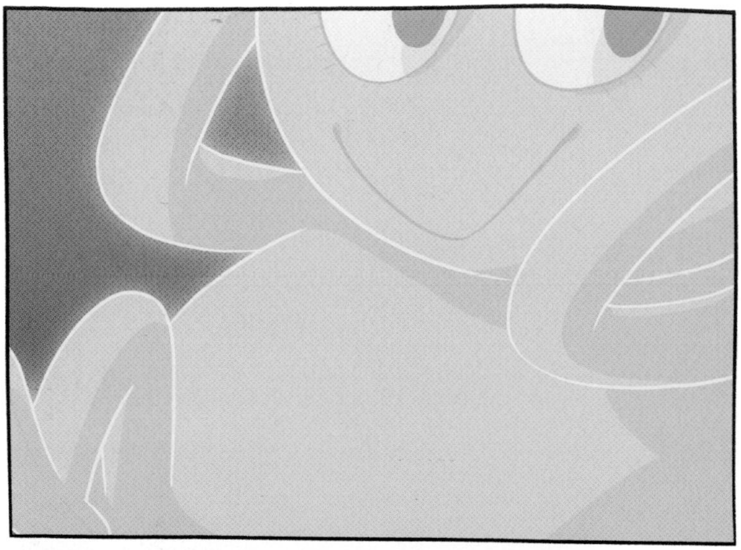
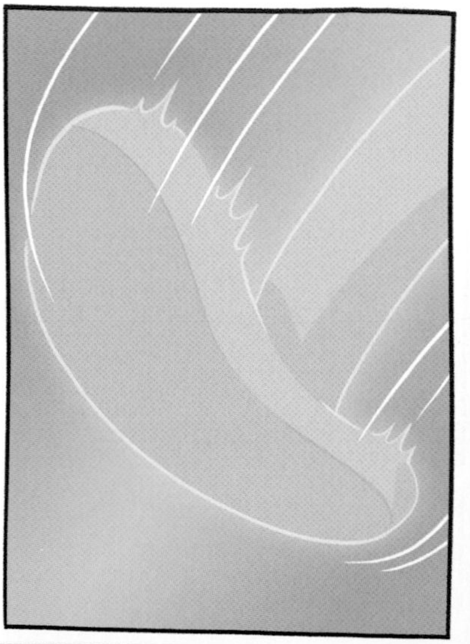
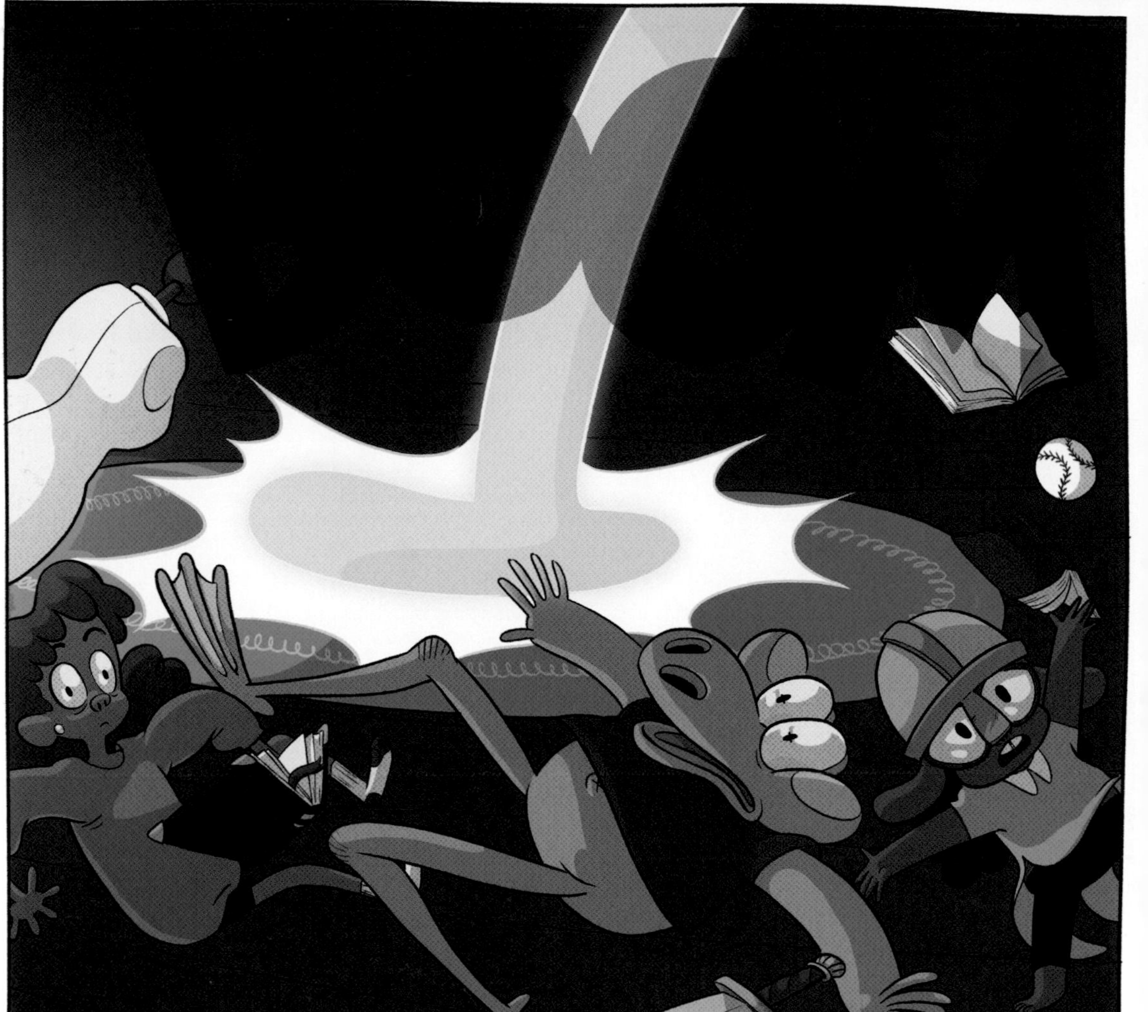

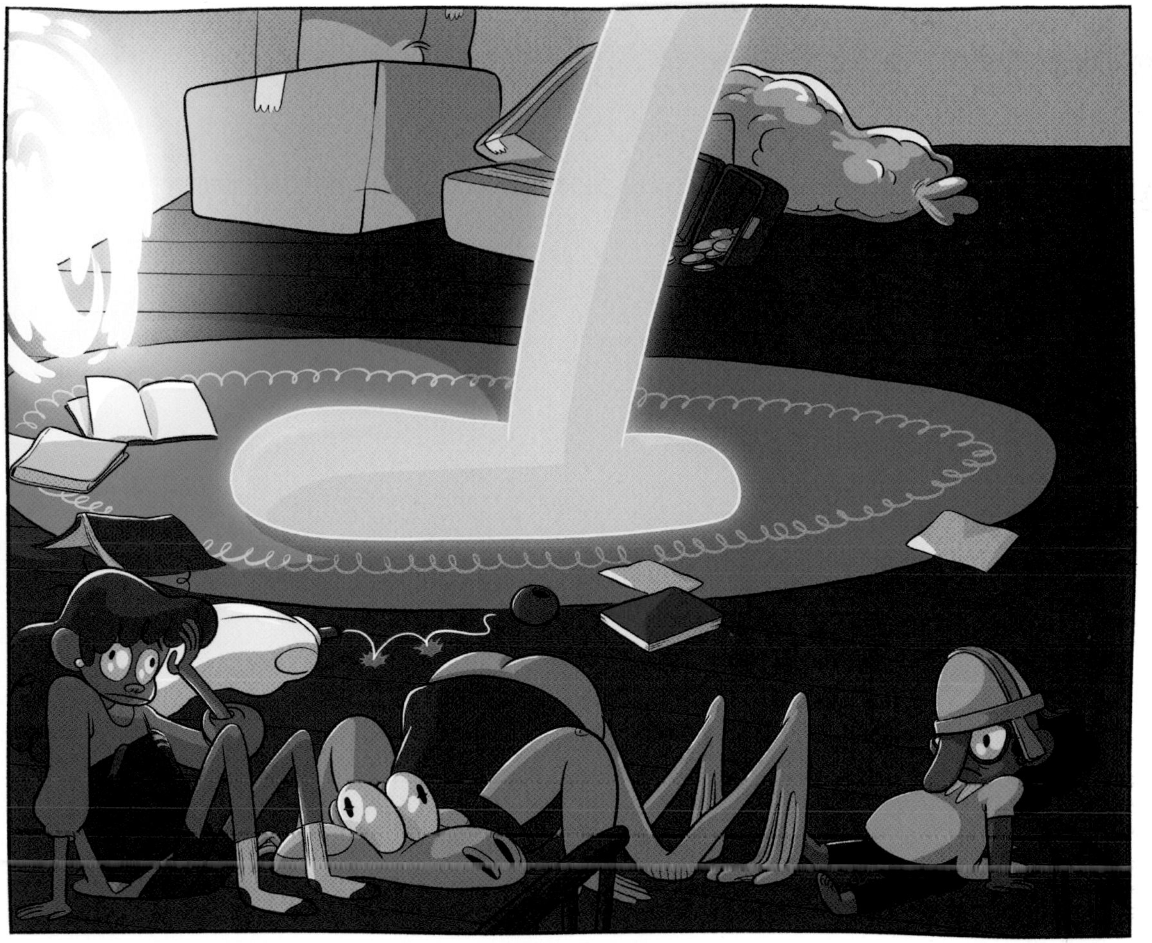

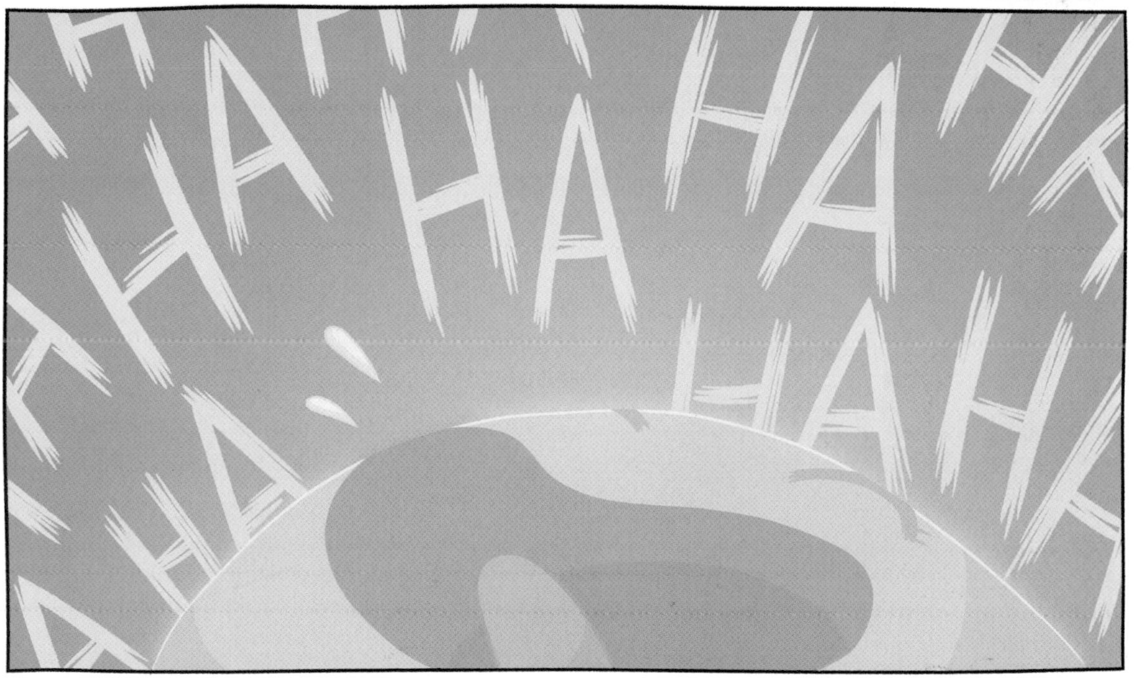
HA HA HA HA HA HA HA HA HA HA HA HA HA HA

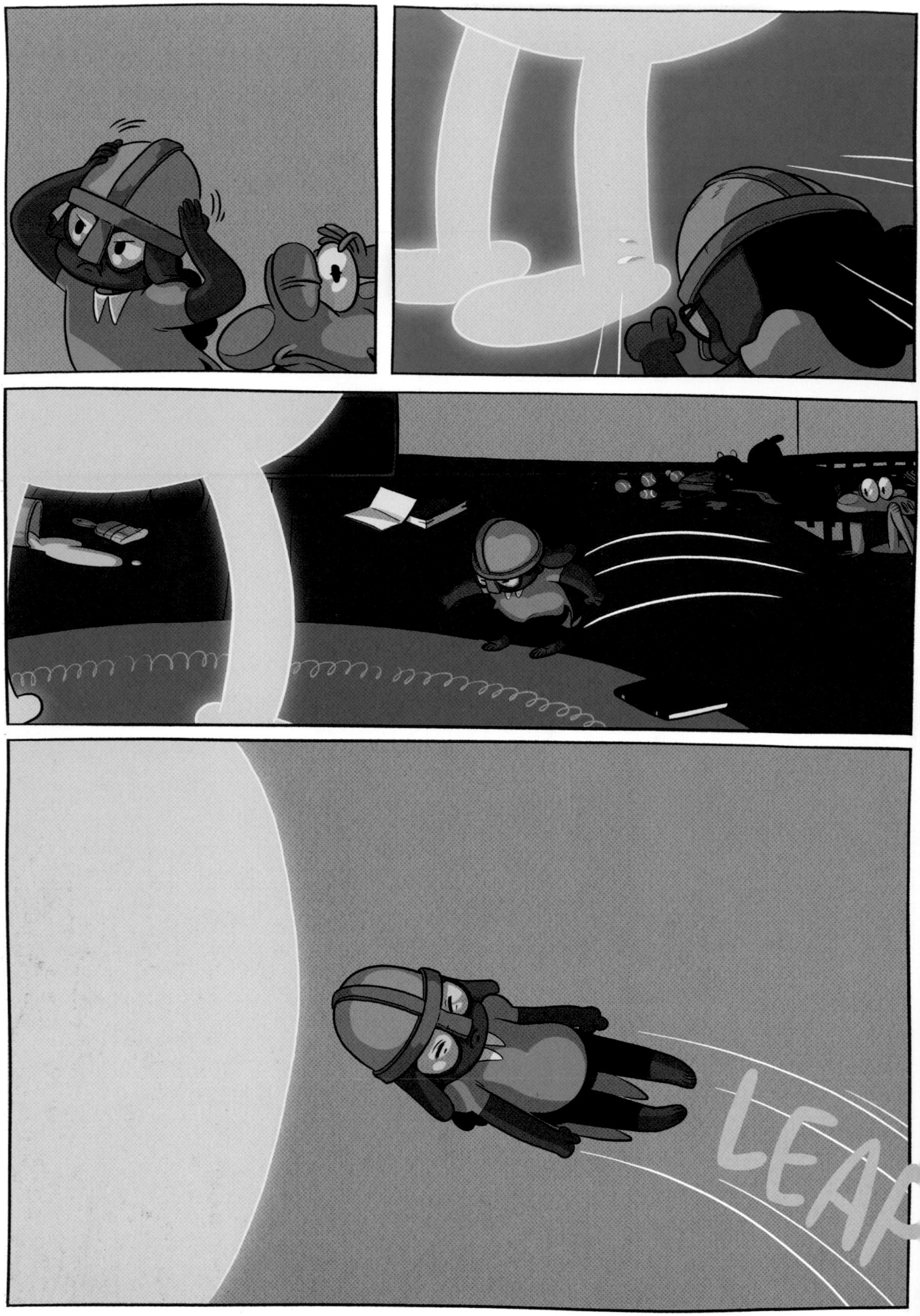
LEAP

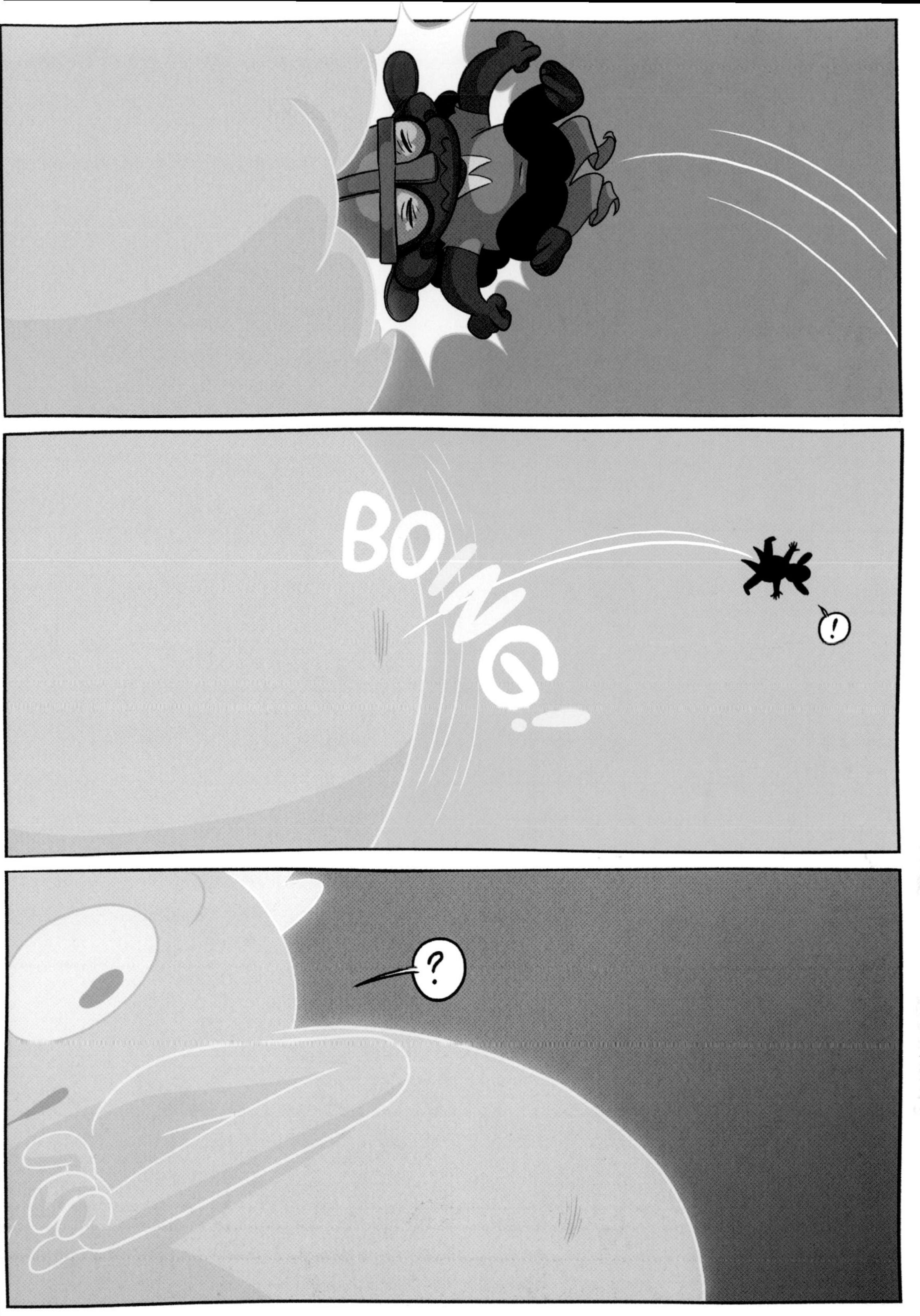
BOING!
!
?

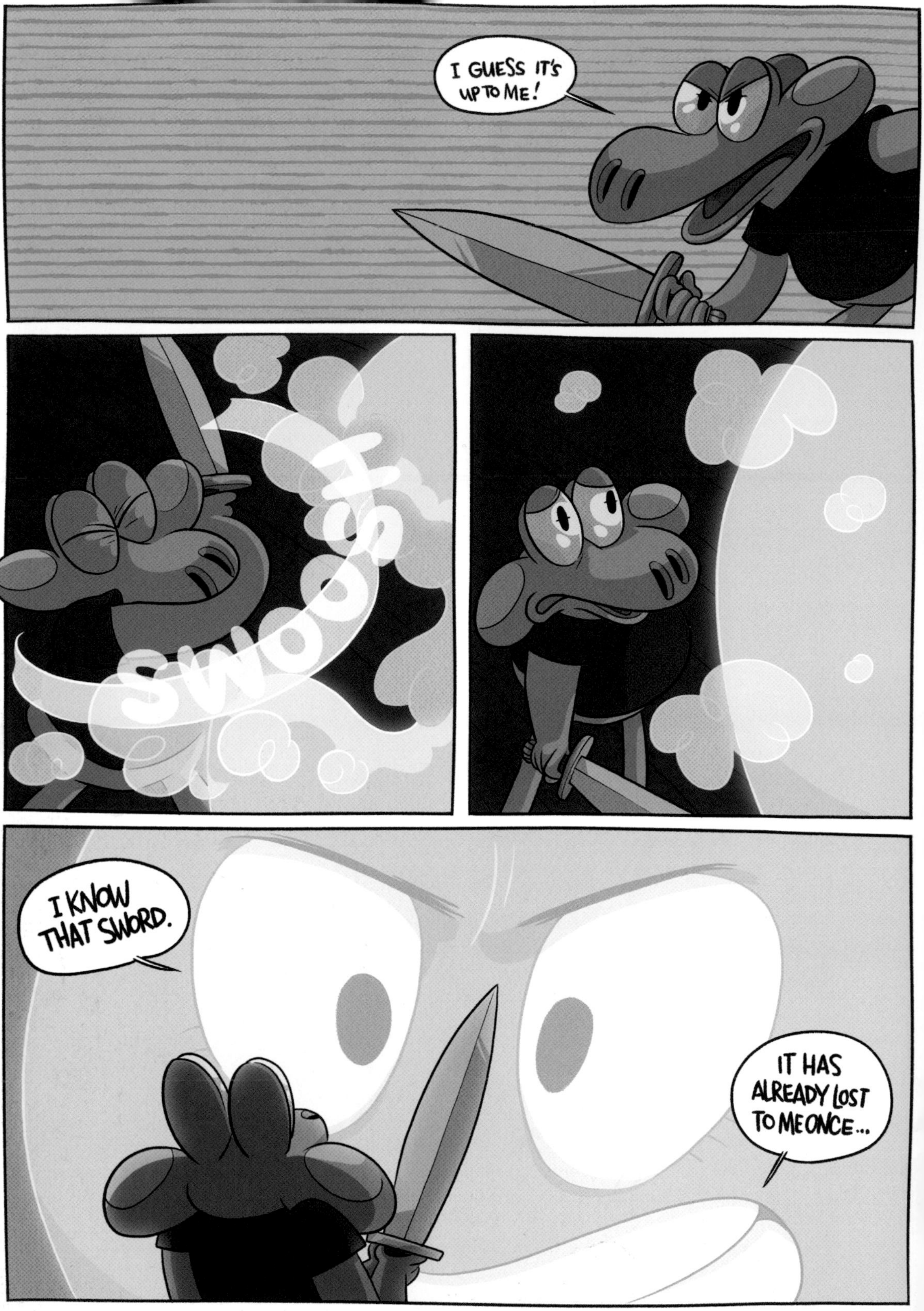
I GUESS IT'S UP TO ME!
SWOOSH
I KNOW THAT SWORD.
IT HAS ALREADY LOST TO ME ONCE...

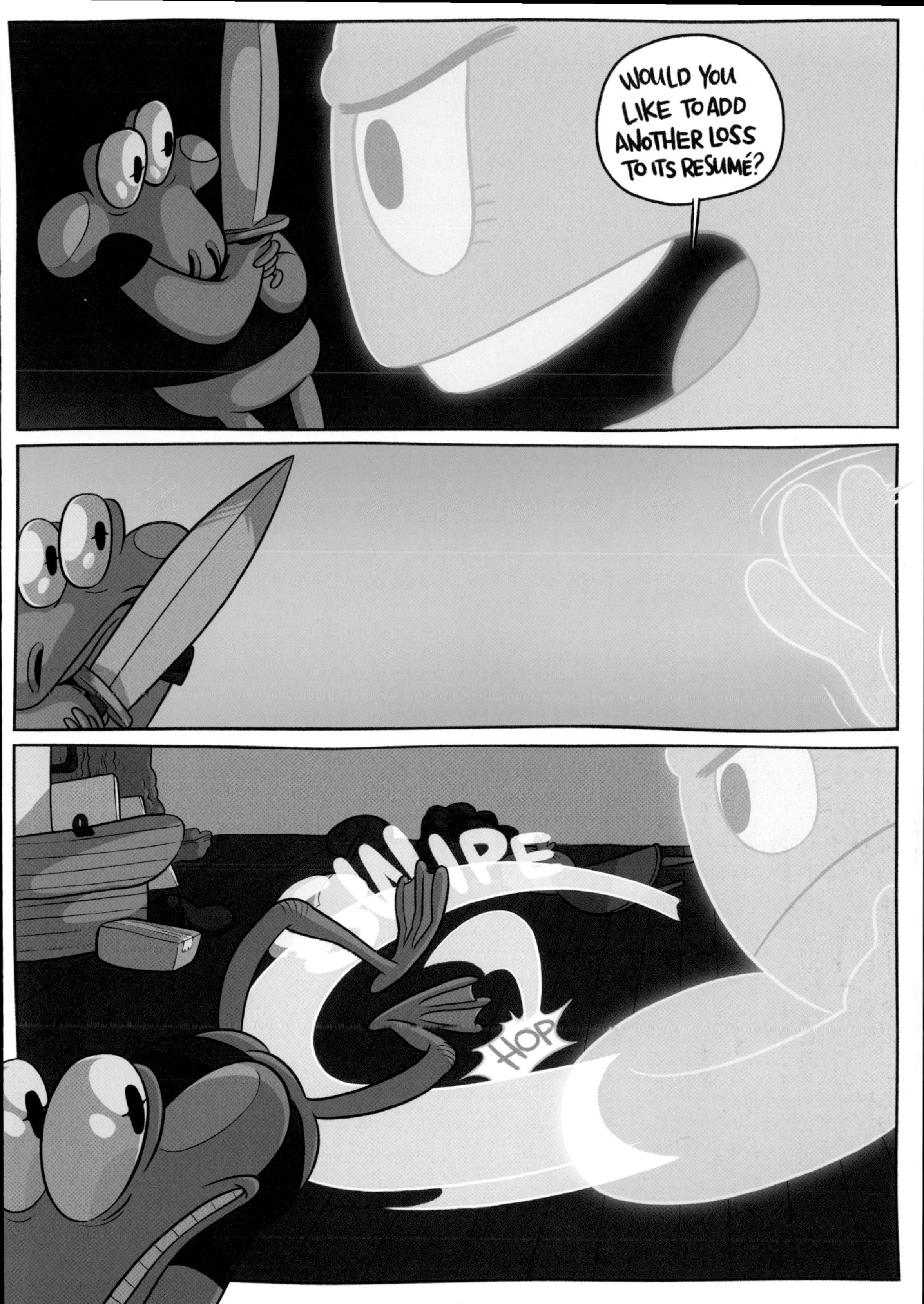
WOULD YOU LIKE TO ADD ANOTHER LOSS TO ITS RESUMÉ?
HOP

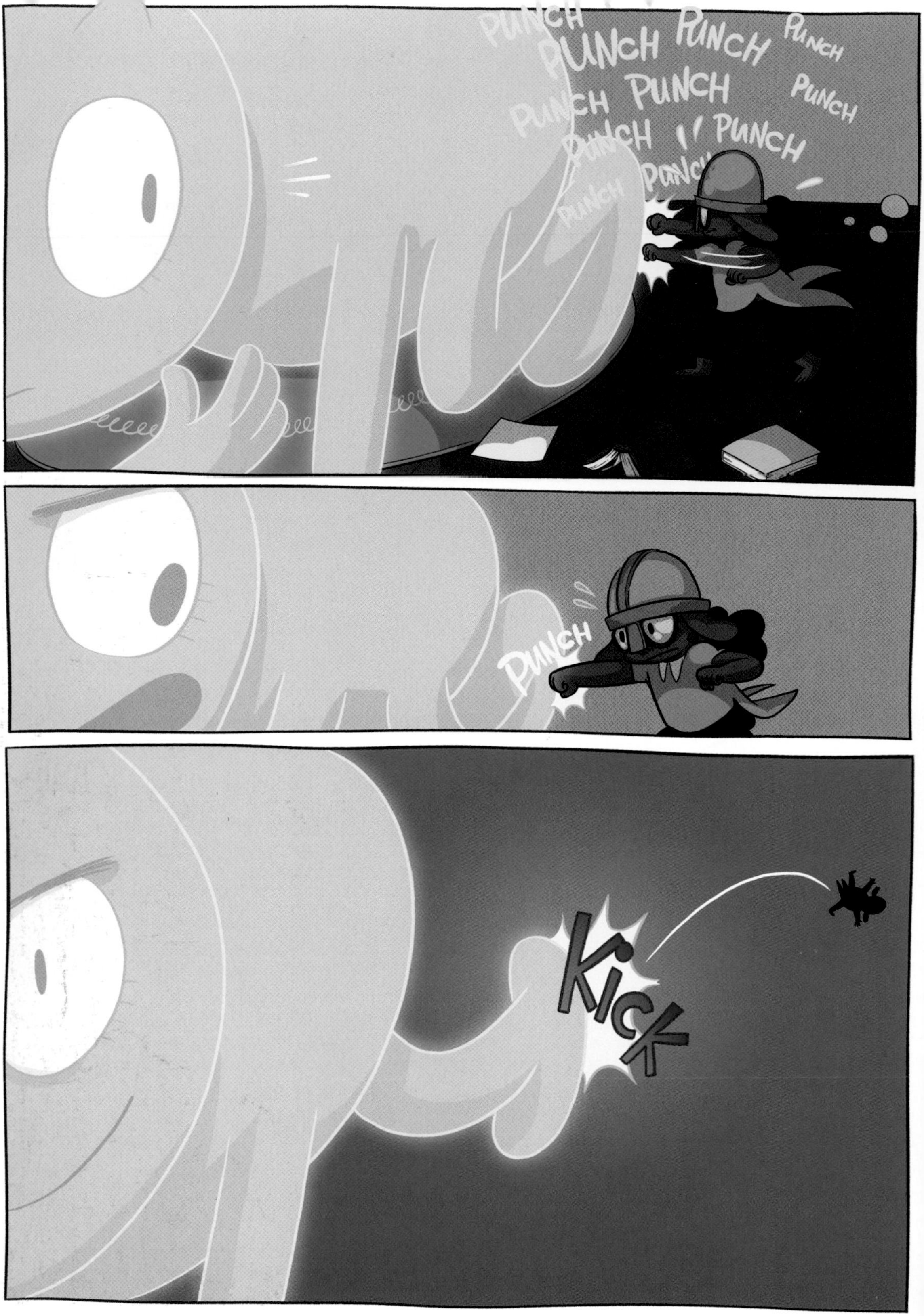
PUNCH
PUNCH PUNCH
PUNCH
PUNCH PUNCH
PUNCH
PUNCH PUNCH
PUNCH
PUNCH
PUNCH
PUNCH
KICK

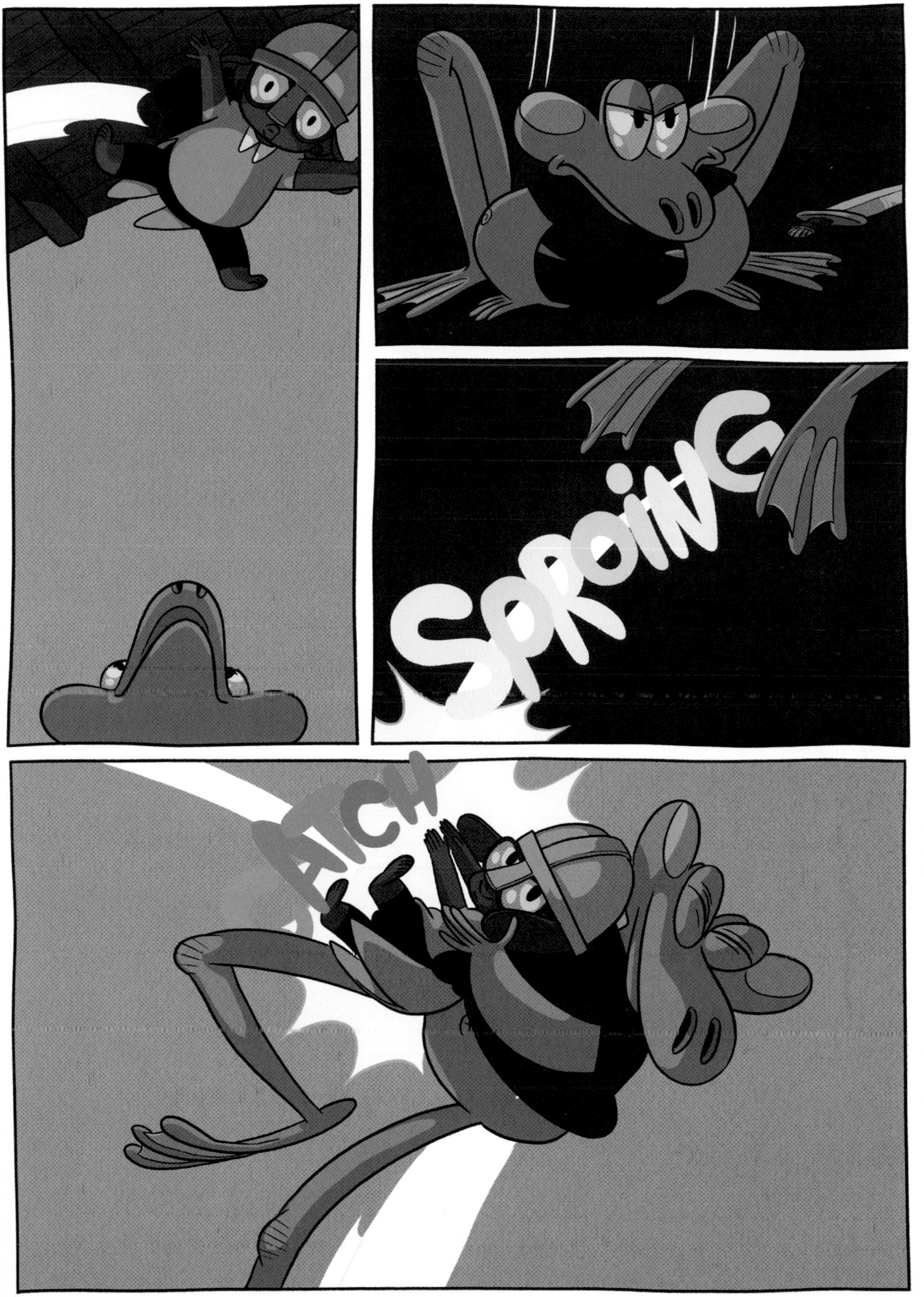
SPROING
ATCH

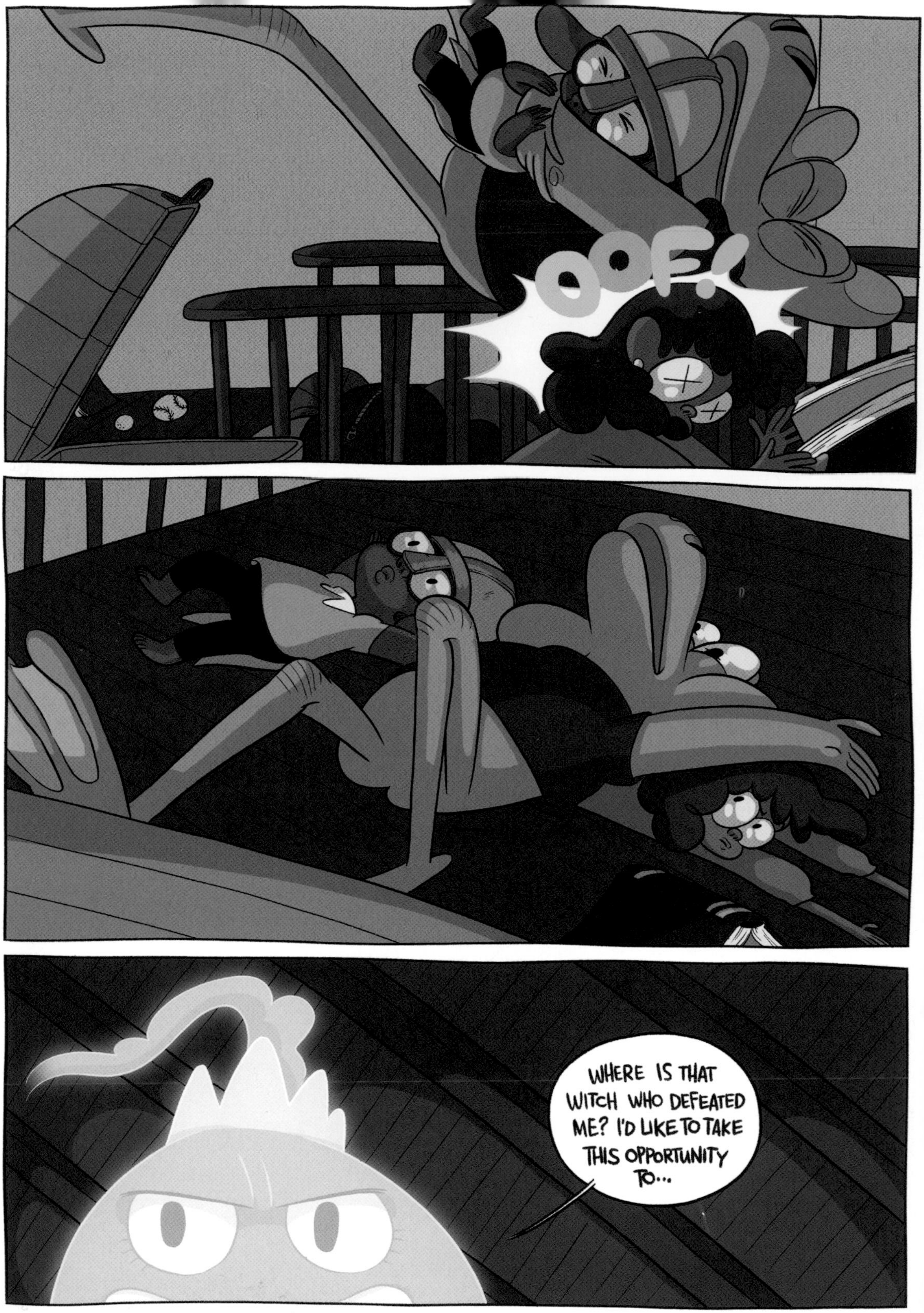
OOF!
WHERE IS THAT WITCH WHO DEFEATED ME? I'D LIKE TO TAKE THIS OPPORTUNITY TO...

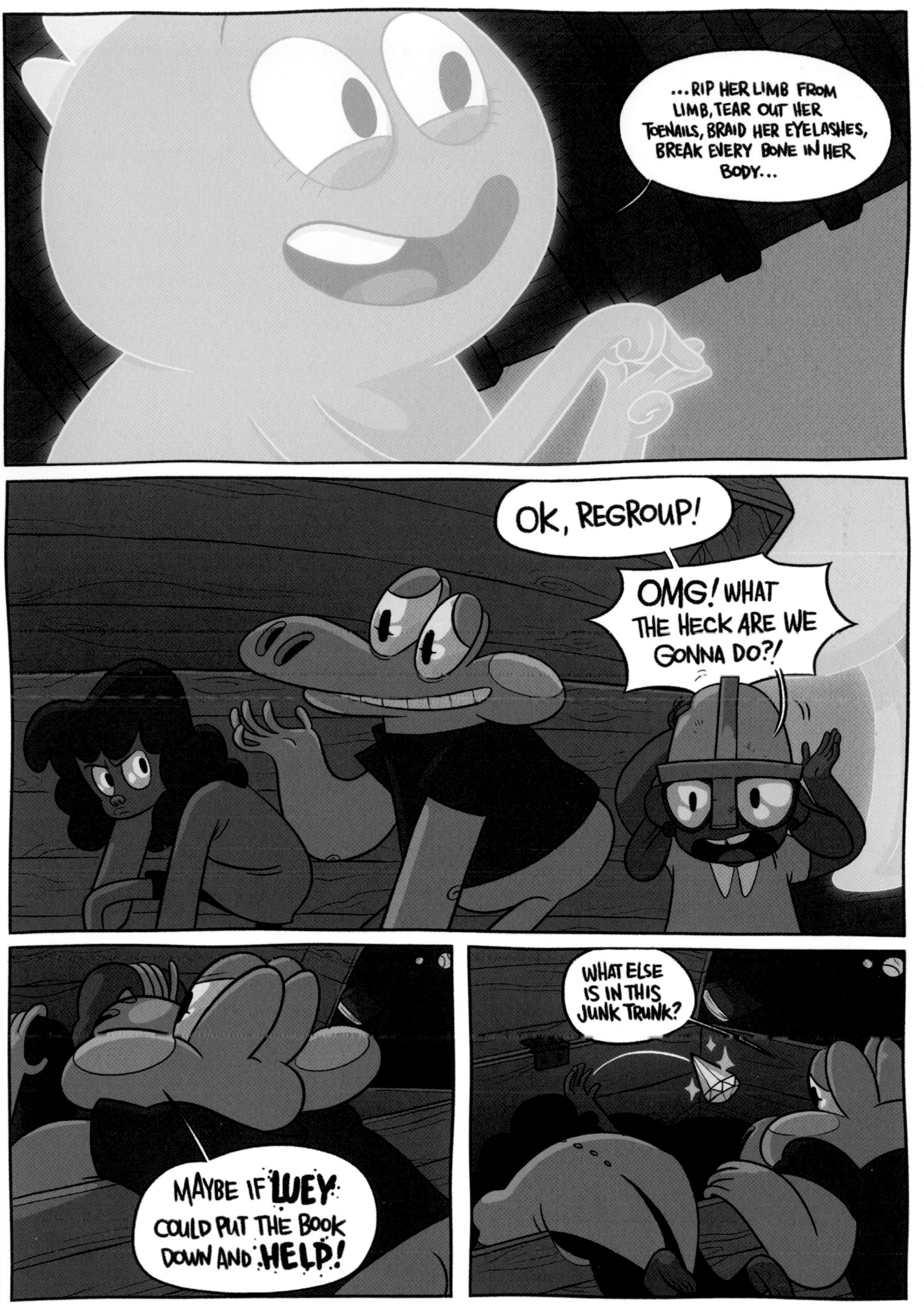
...RIP HER LIMB FROM LIMB, TEAR OUT HER TOENAILS, BRAID HER EYELASHES, BREAK EVERY BONE IN HER BODY...
OK, REGROUP!
OMG! WHAT THE HECK ARE WE GONNA DO?!
MAYBE IF LUCY COULD PUT THE BOOK DOWN AND HELP!
WHAT ELSE IS IN THIS JUNK TRUNK?

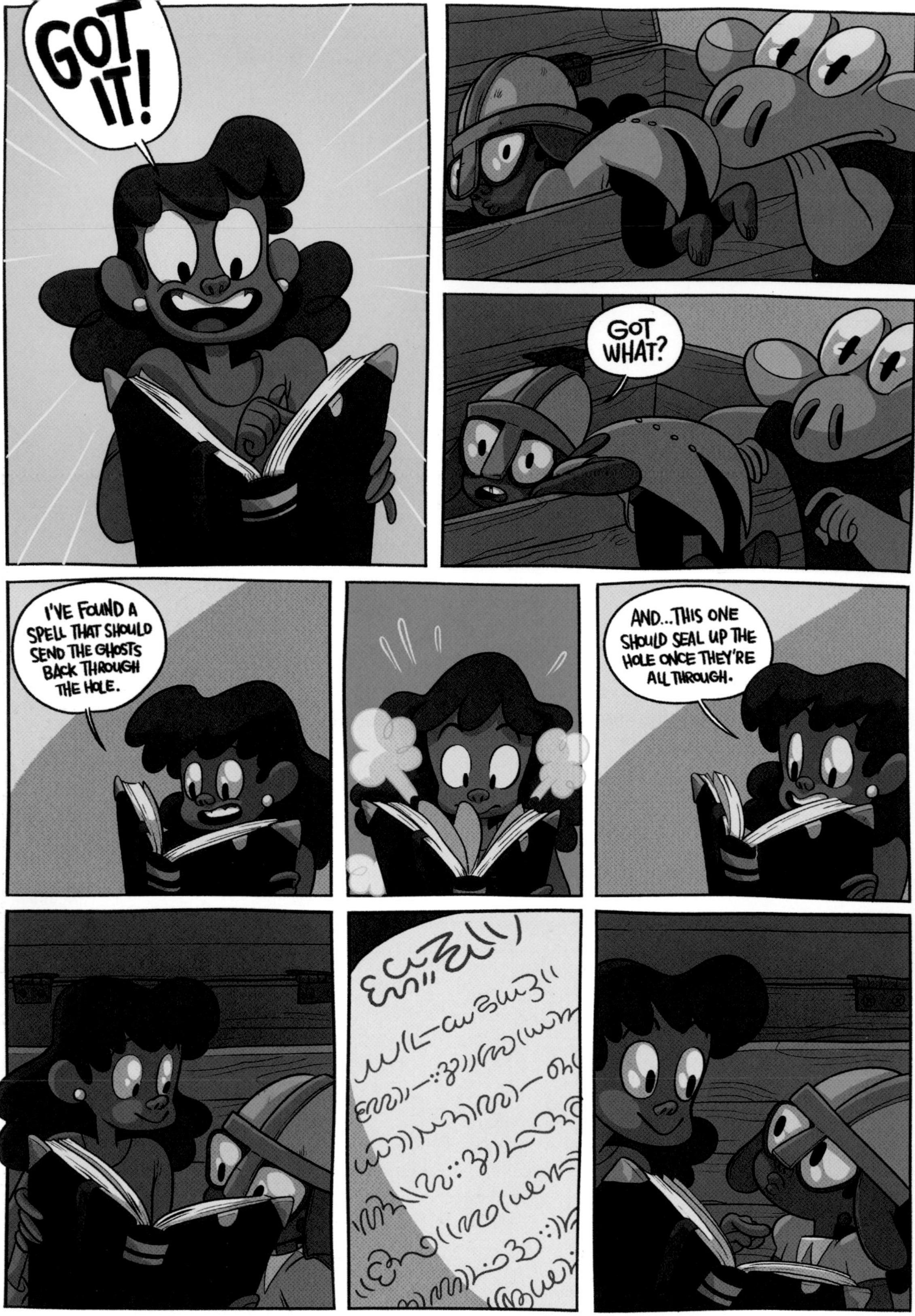
GOT IT!
GOT WHAT?
I'VE FOUND A SPELL THAT SHOULD SEND THE GHOSTS BACK THROUGH THE HOLE.
AND...THIS ONE SHOULD SEAL UP THE HOLE ONCE THEY'RE ALL THROUGH.

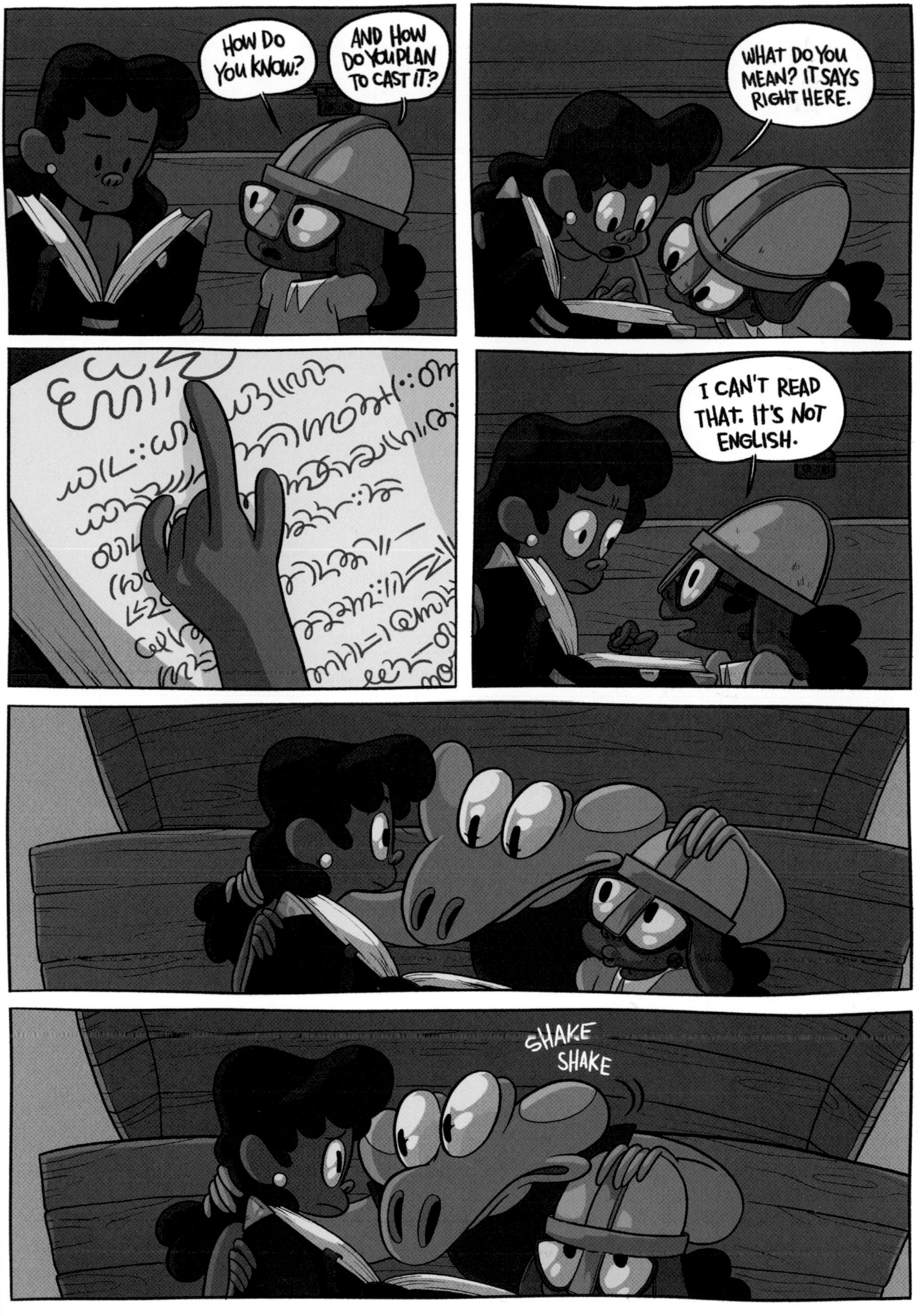
HOW DO YOU KNOW?
AND HOW DO YOU PLAN TO CAST IT?
WHAT DO YOU MEAN? IT SAYS RIGHT HERE.
I CAN'T READ THAT. IT'S NOT ENGLISH.
SHAKE SHAKE

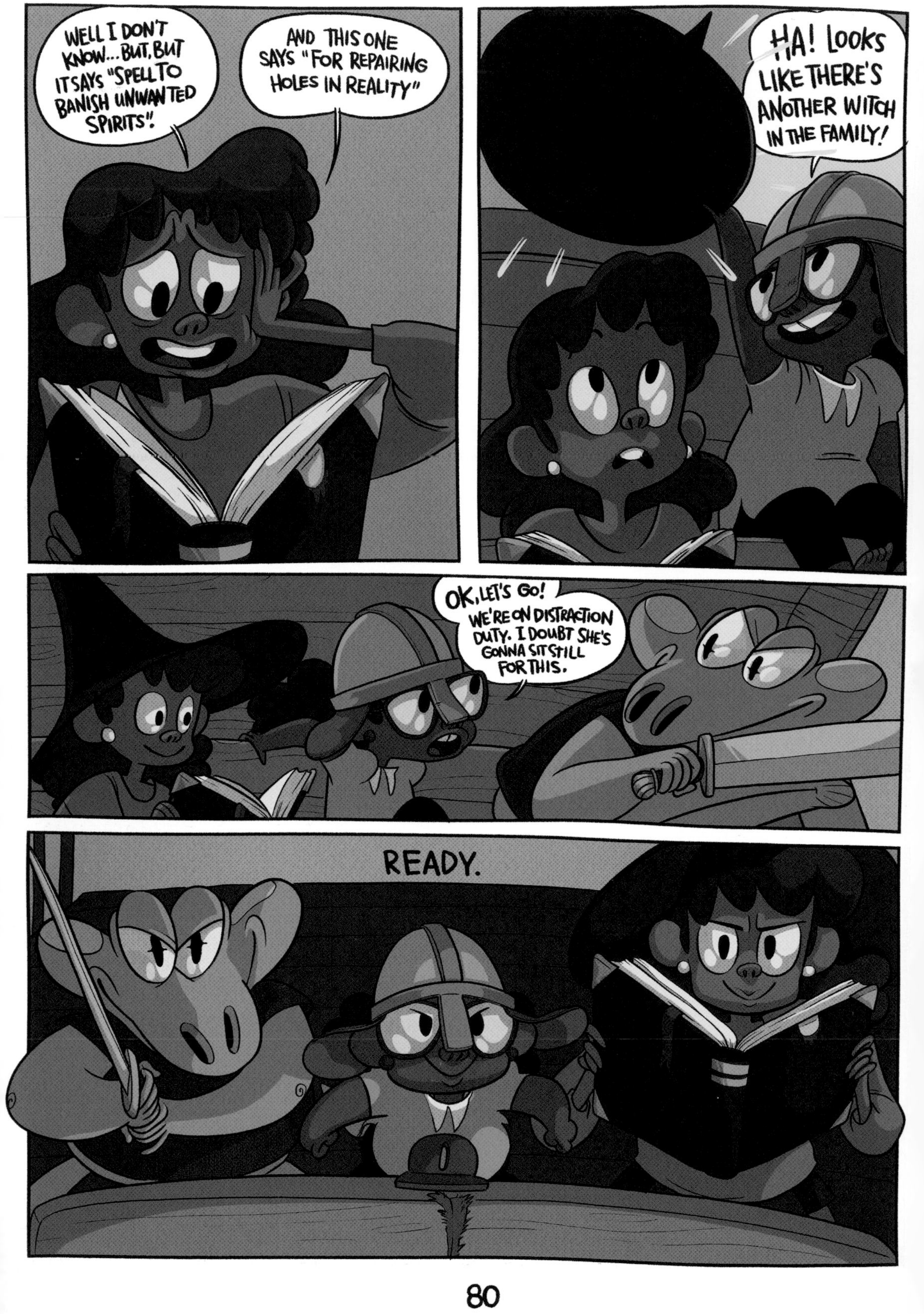
WELL I DON'T KNOW... BUT, BUT IT SAYS "SPELL TO BANISH UNWANTED SPIRITS"!
AND THIS ONE SAYS "FOR REPAIRING HOLES IN REALITY"
HA! LOOKS LIKE THERE'S ANOTHER WITCH IN THE FAMILY!
OK, LET'S GO! WE'RE ON DISTRACTION DUTY. I DOUBT SHE'S GONNA SIT STILL FOR THIS.
READY.

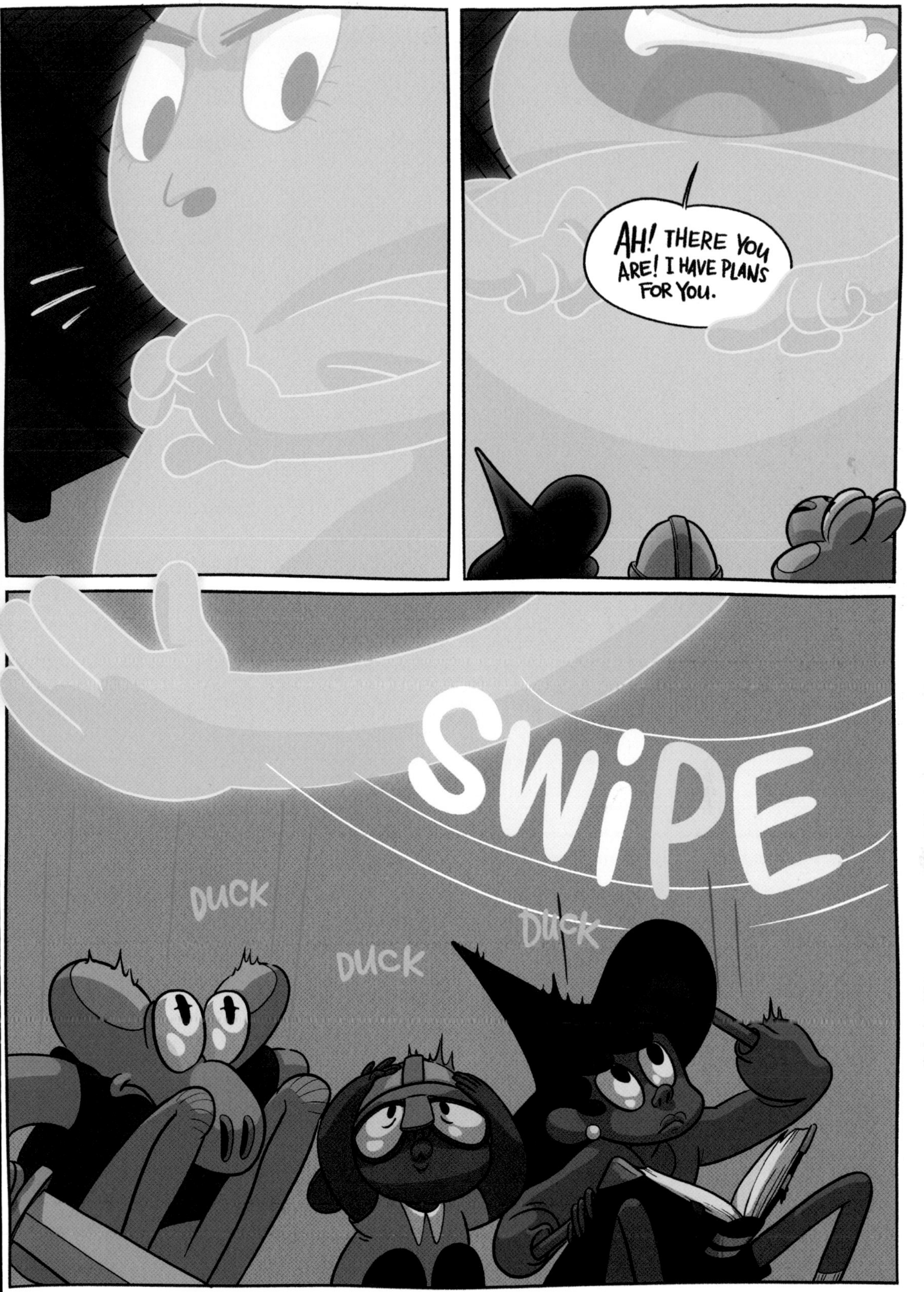
AH! THERE YOU ARE! I HAVE PLANS FOR YOU.
SWIPE
DUCK
DUCK
DUCK

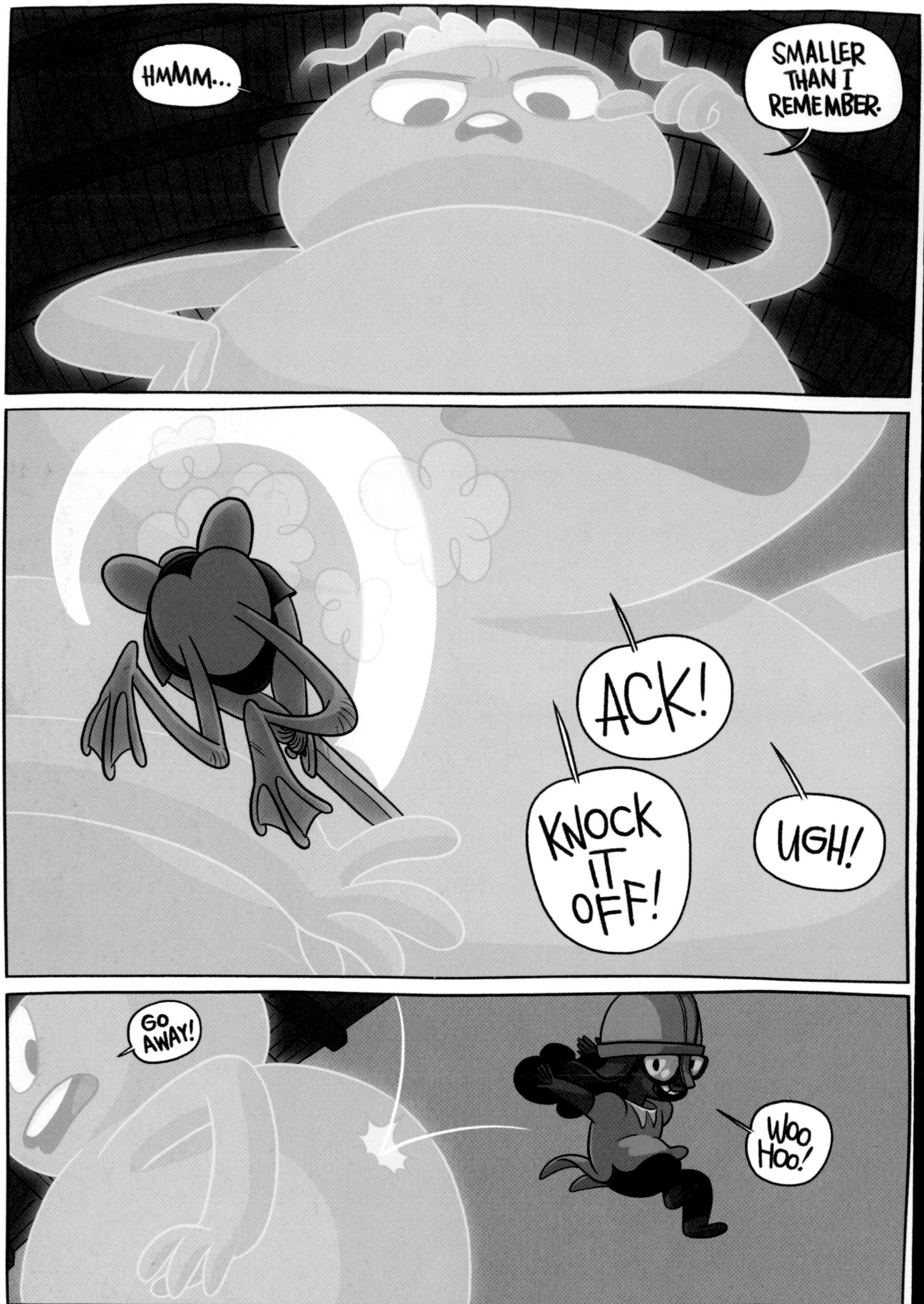
HMMM...
SMALLER THAN I REMEMBER.
ACK!
KNOCK IT OFF!
UGH!
GO AWAY!
WOO HOO!

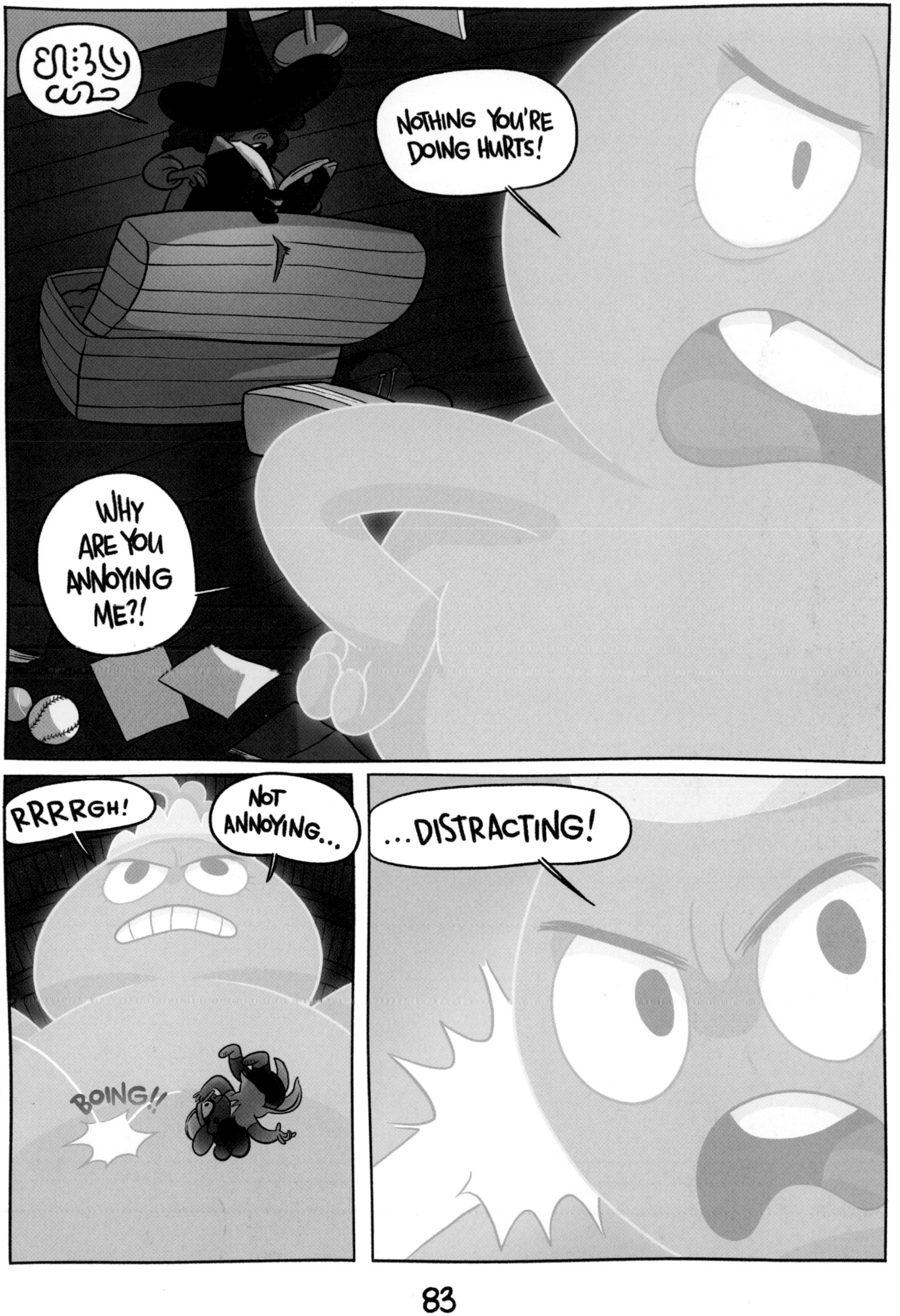
NOTHING YOU'RE DOING HURTS!
WHY ARE YOU ANNOYING ME?!
RRRRGH!
NOT ANNOYING...
BOING!!
...DISTRACTING!

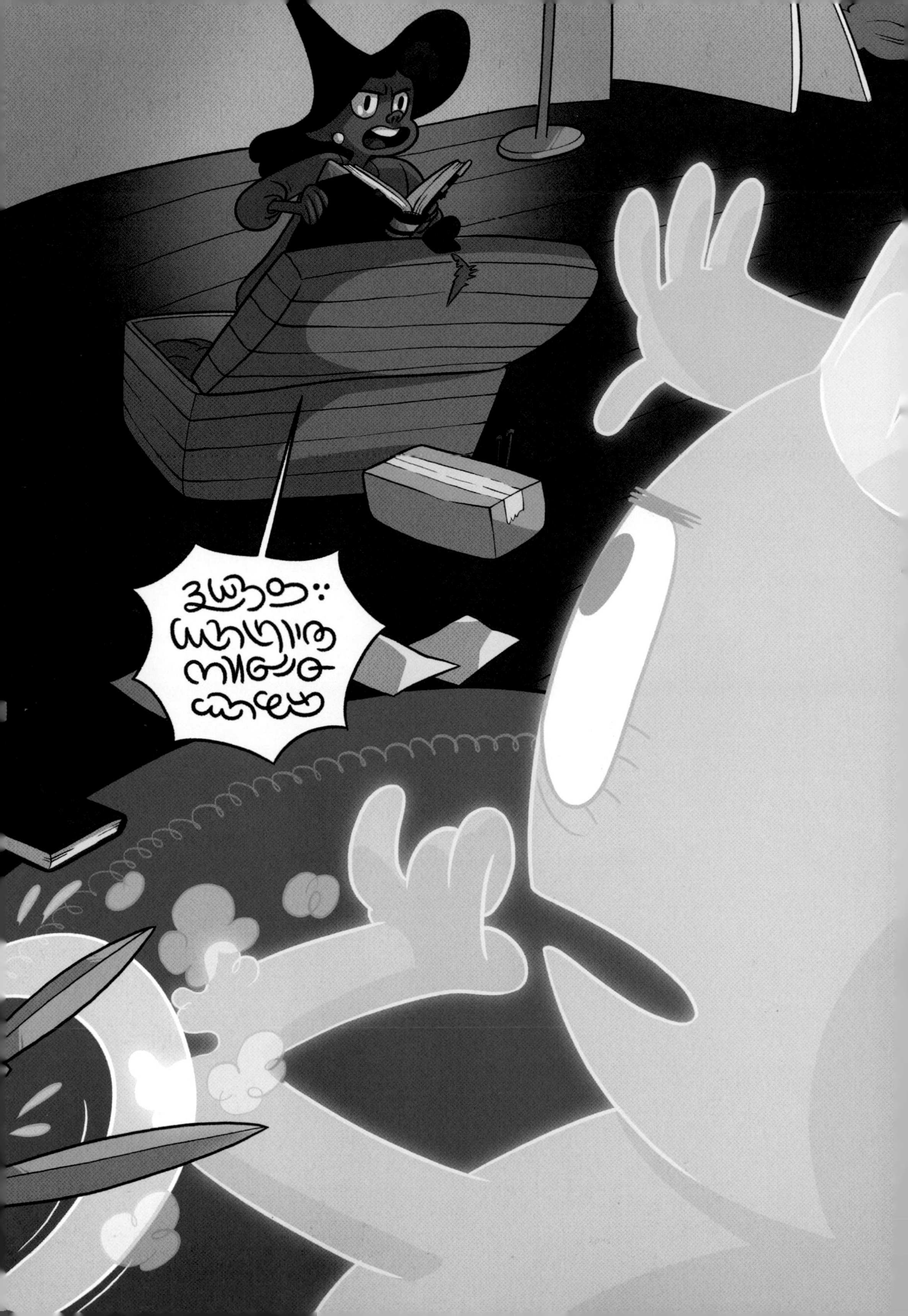

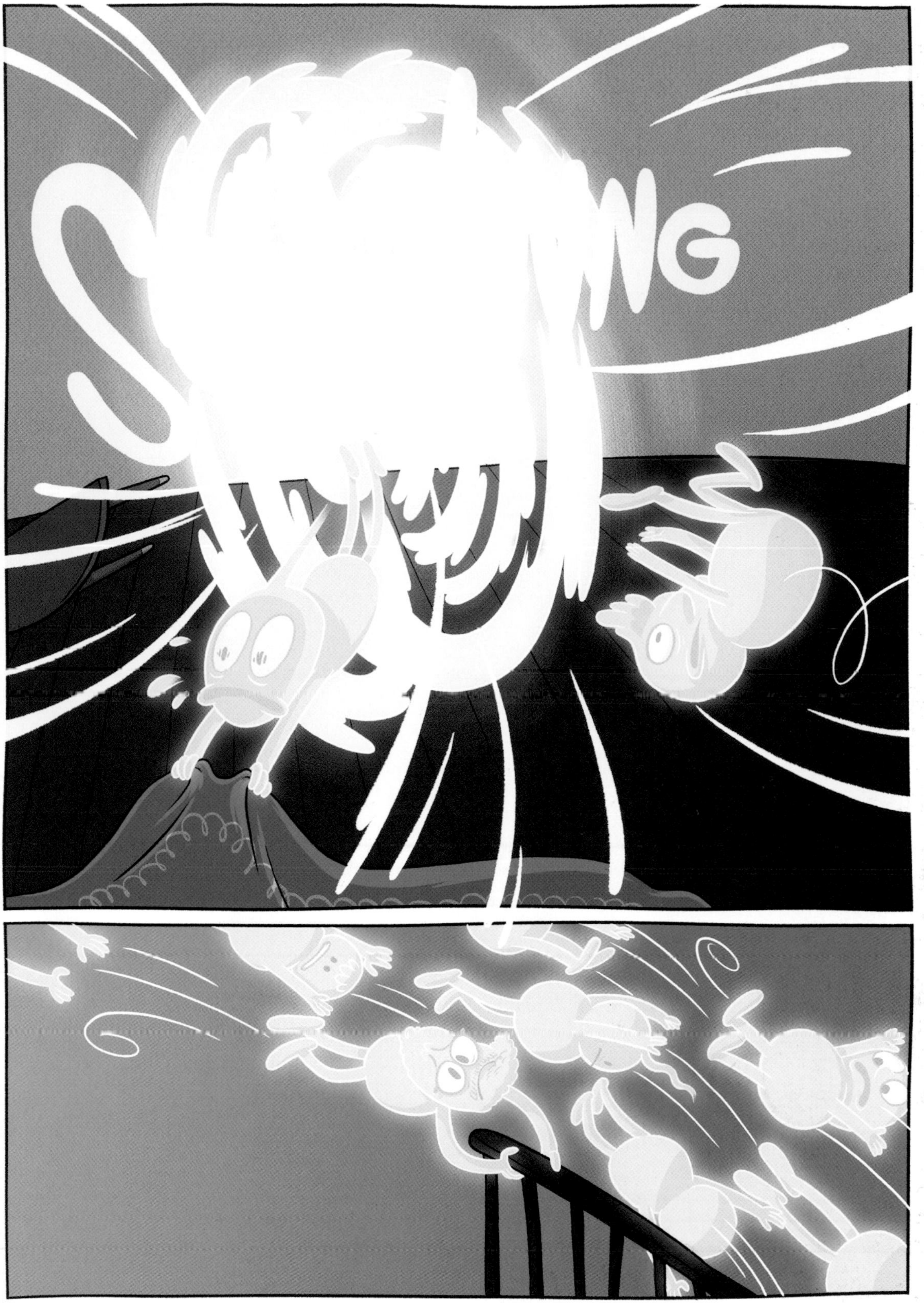

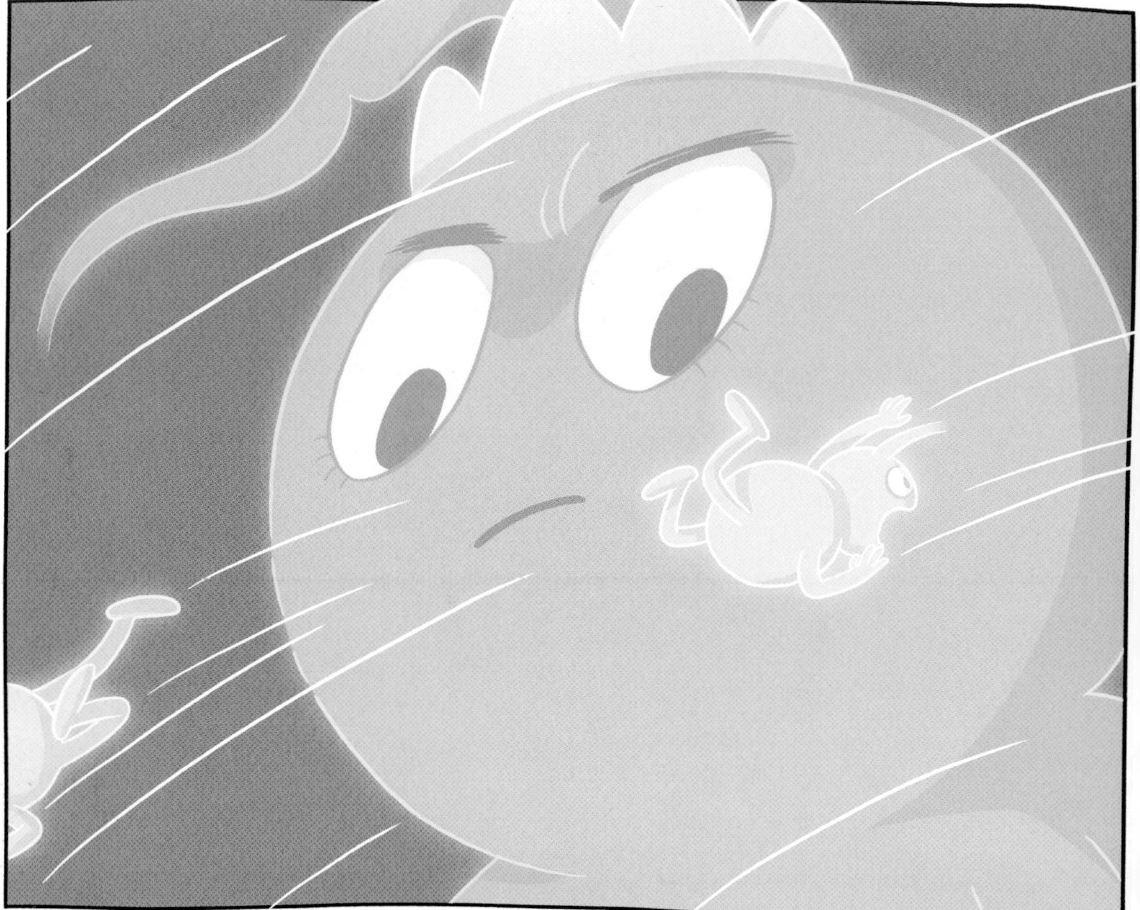

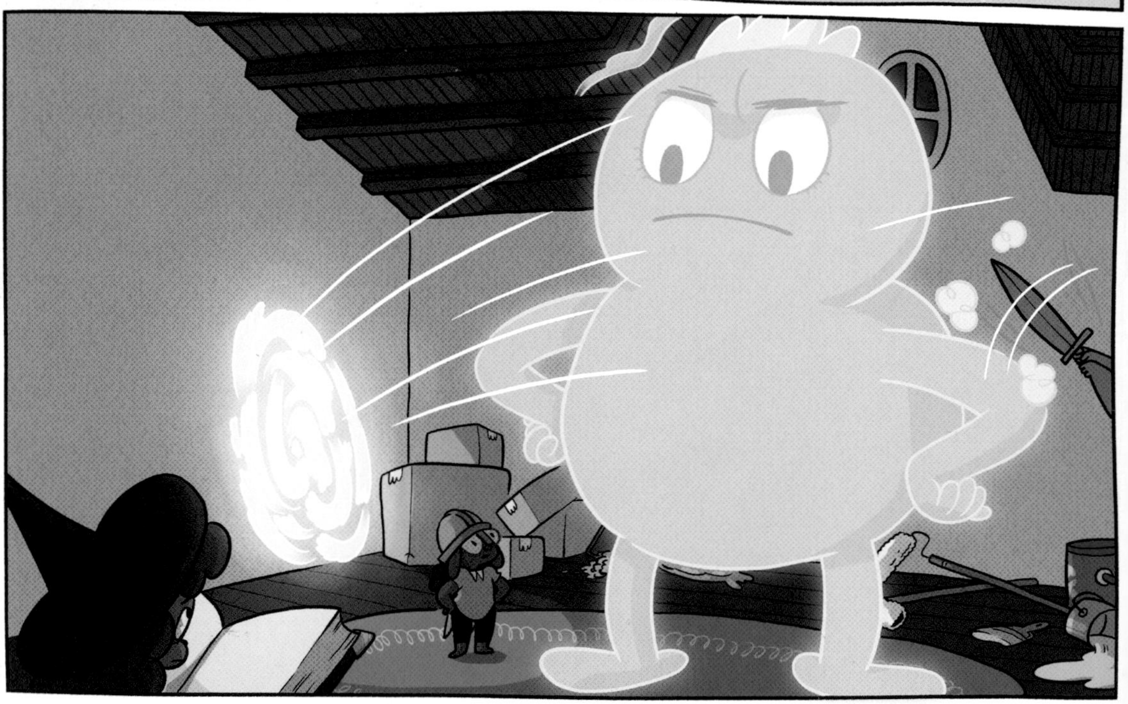

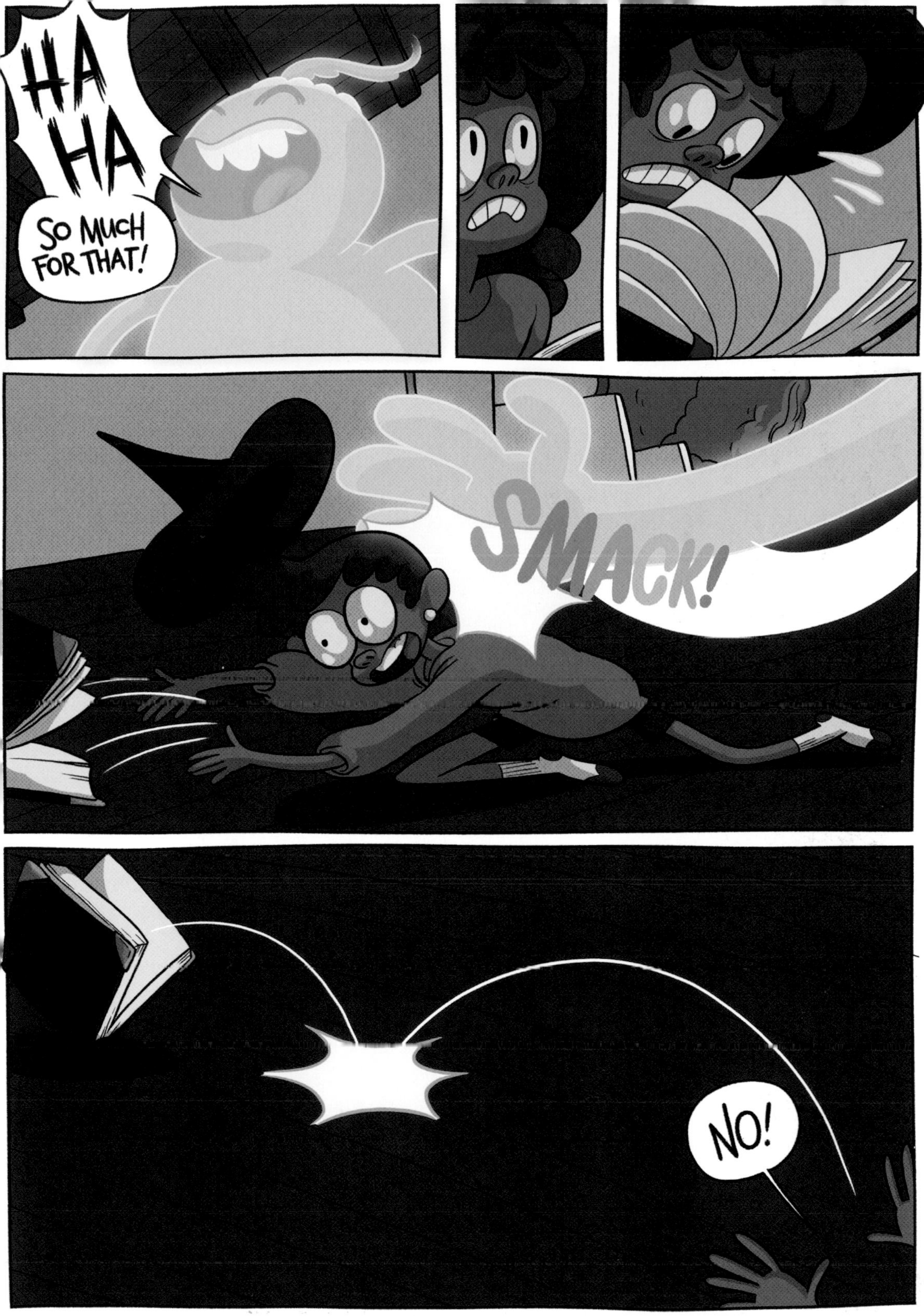
HA HA
SO MUCH FOR THAT!
SMACK!
NO!

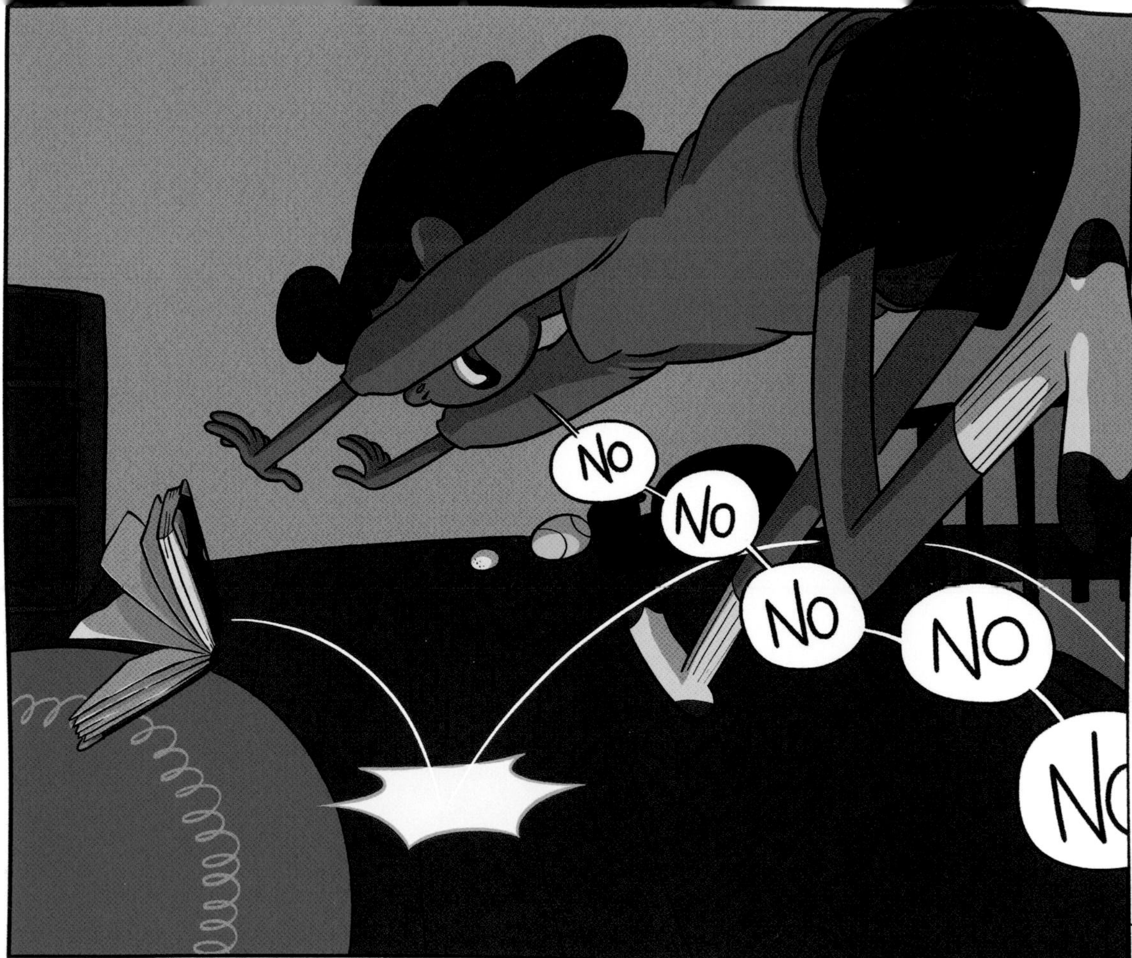
No
No
No
NO
NO

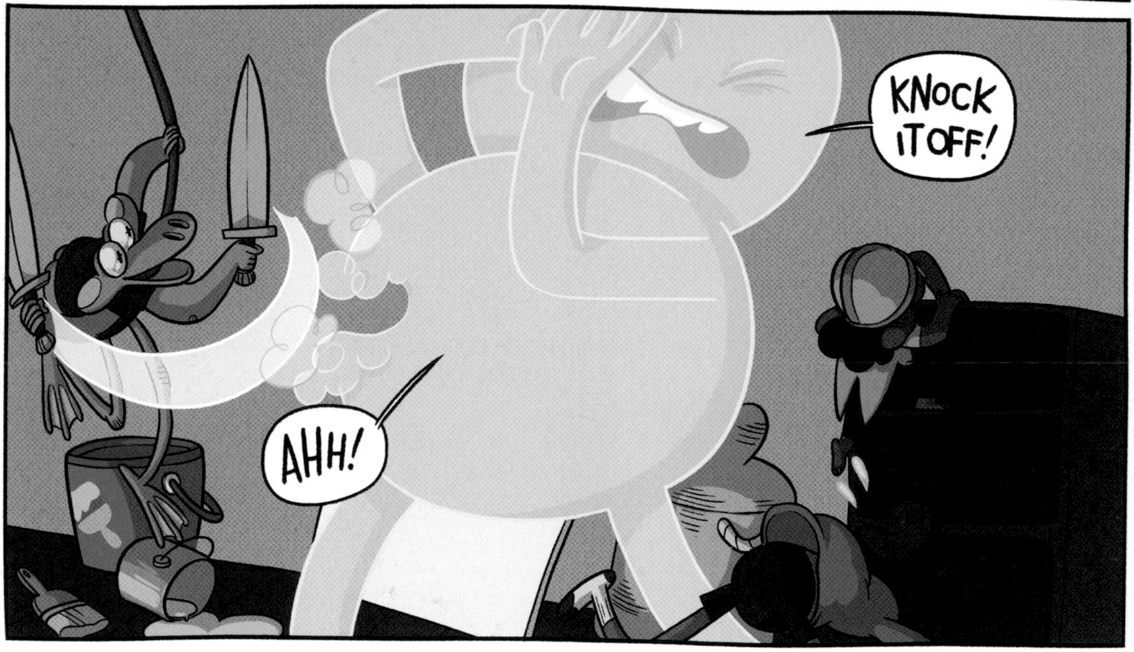
KNOCK IT OFF!
AHH!

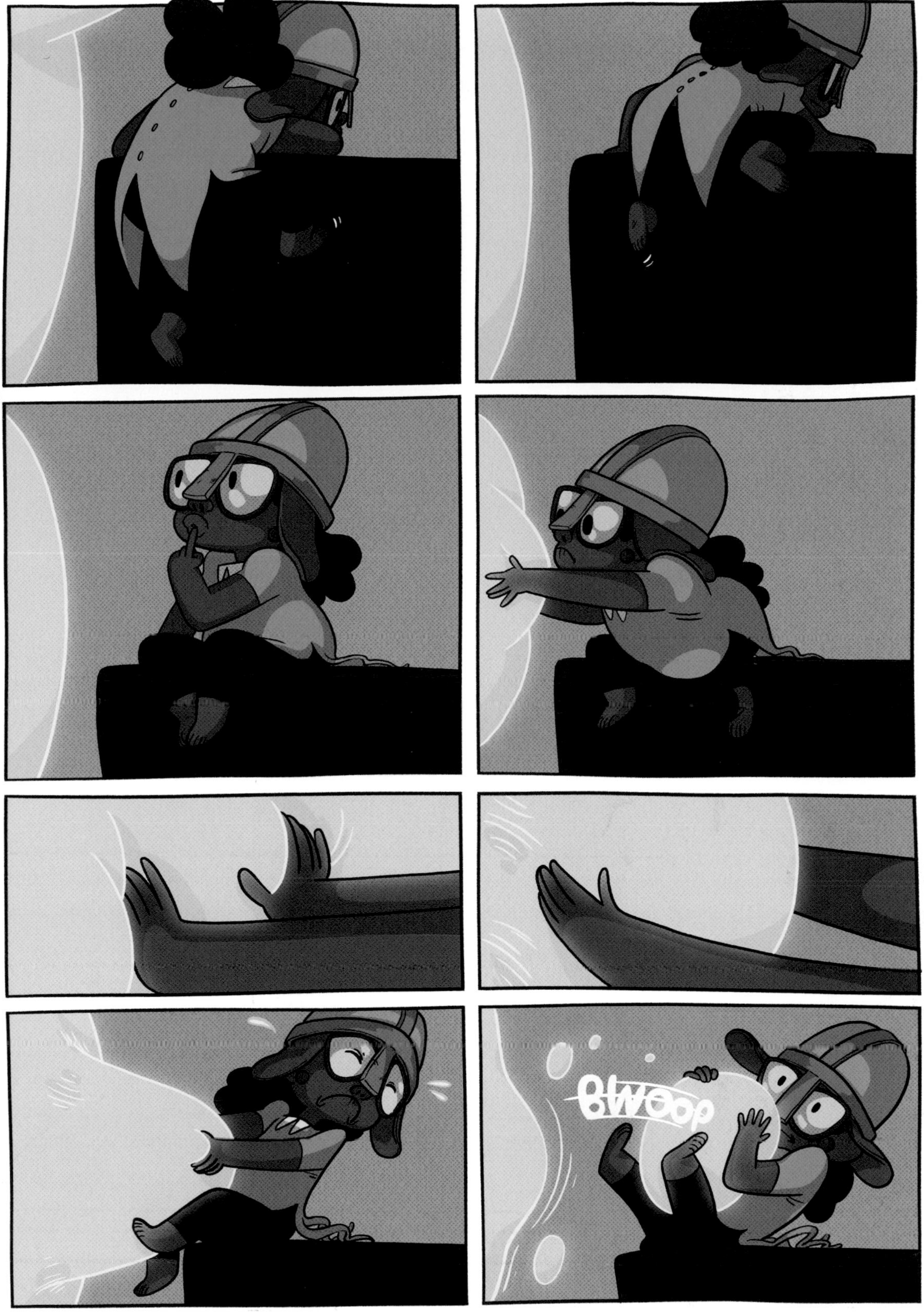
BWOOP

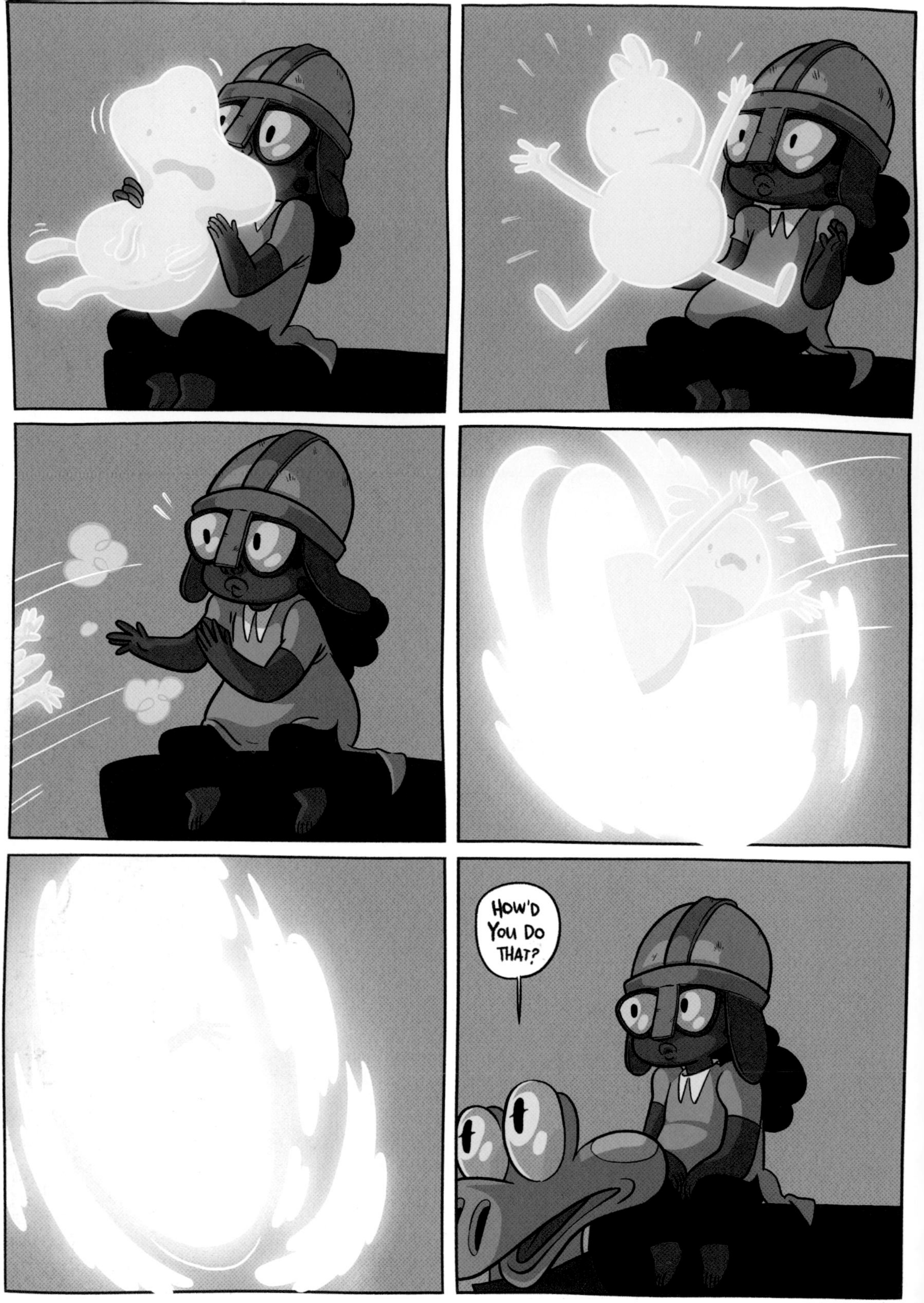
HOW'D YOU DO THAT?

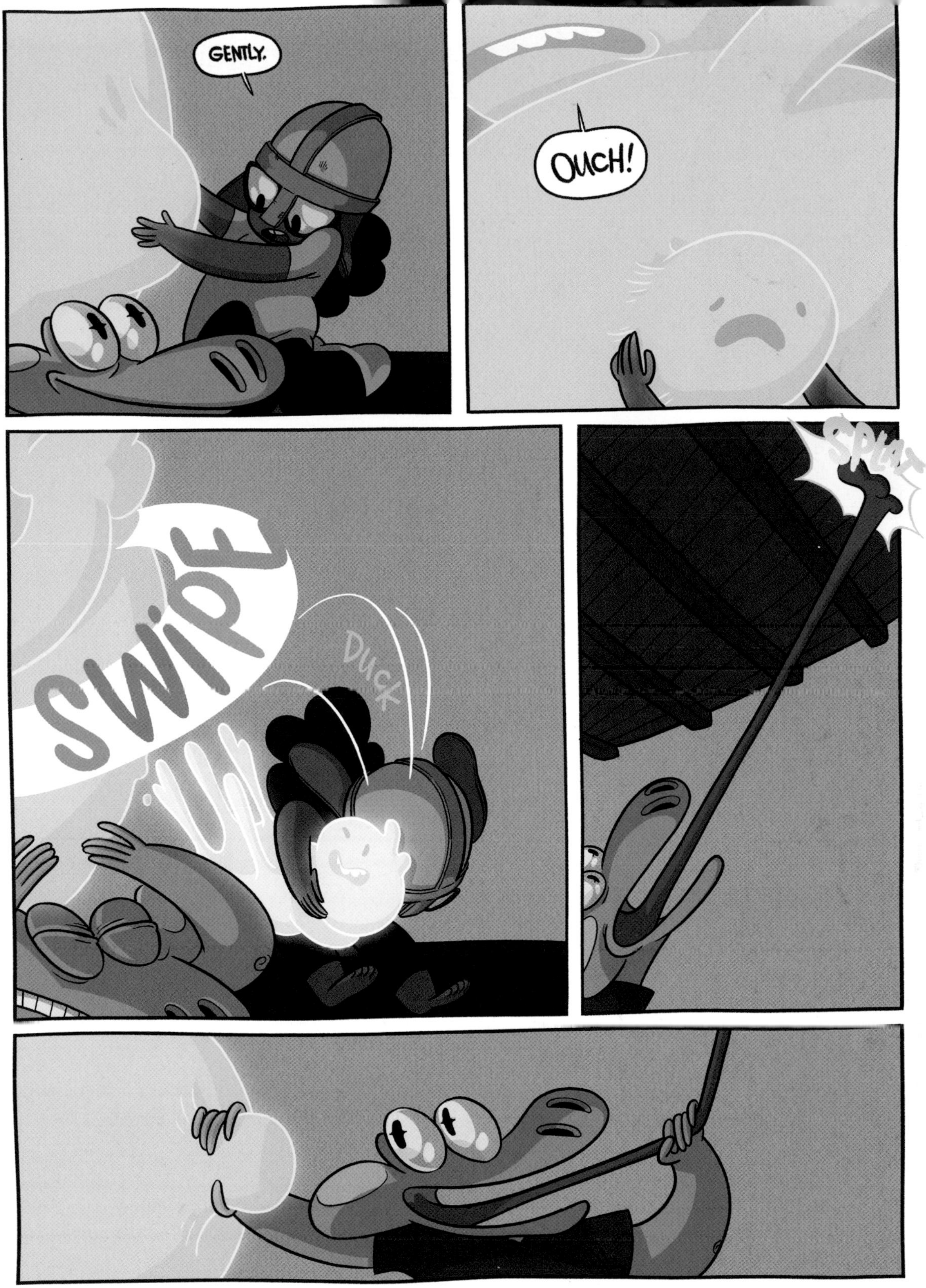

GENTLY.
OUCH!
SWIPE
DUCK
SPLAT

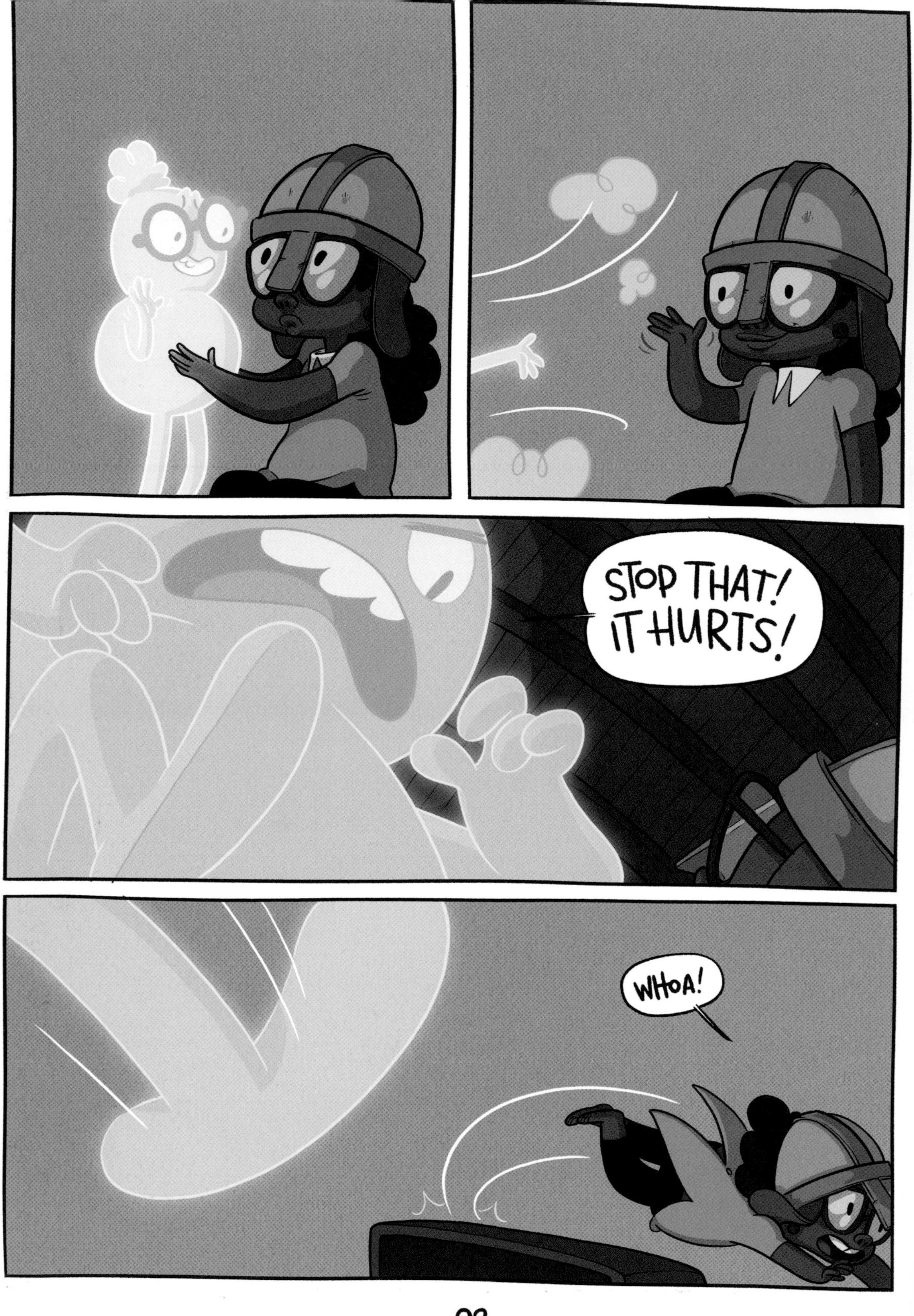
STOP THAT! IT HURTS!
WHOA!

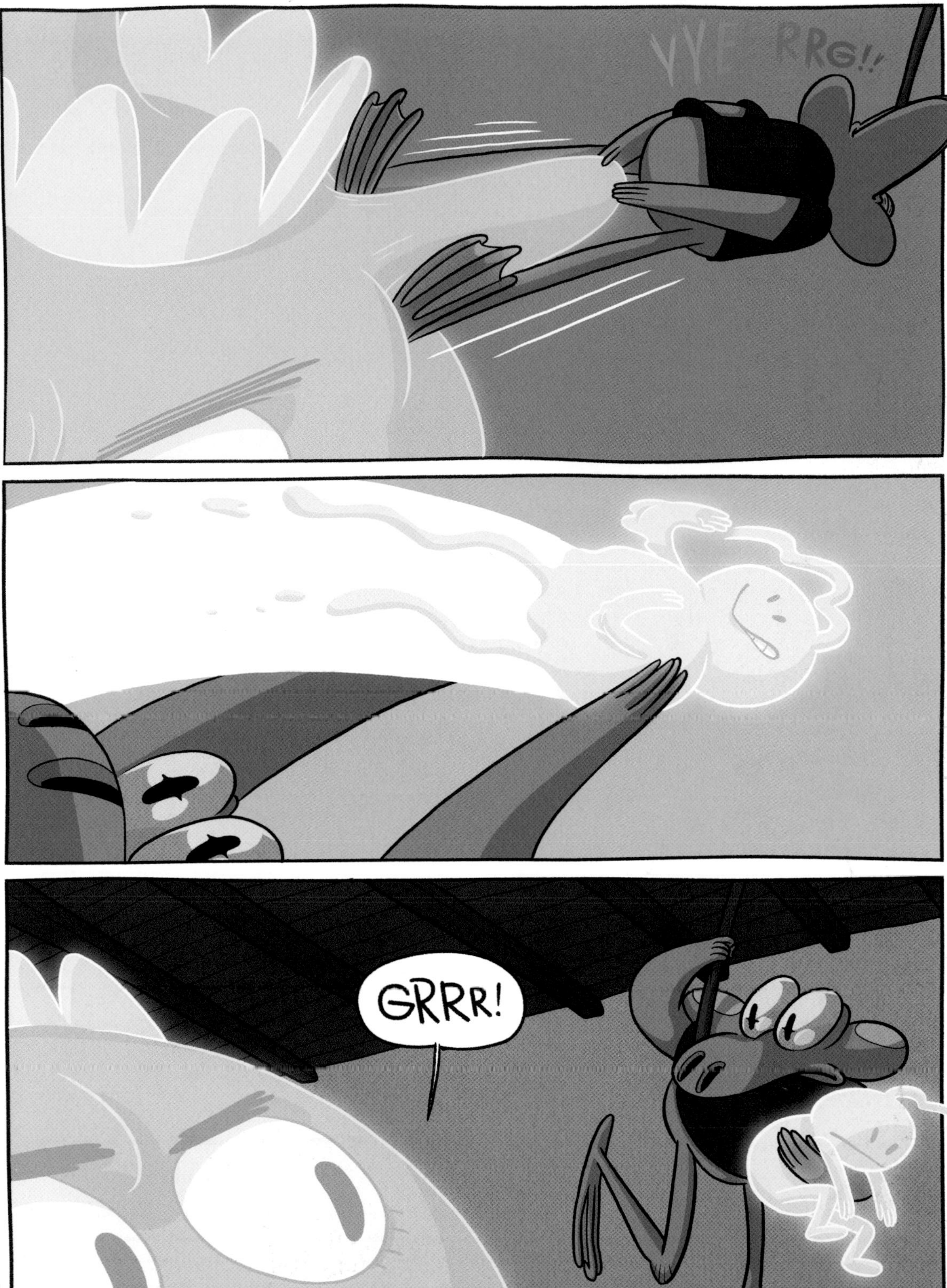
YYE RRG!!
GRRR!

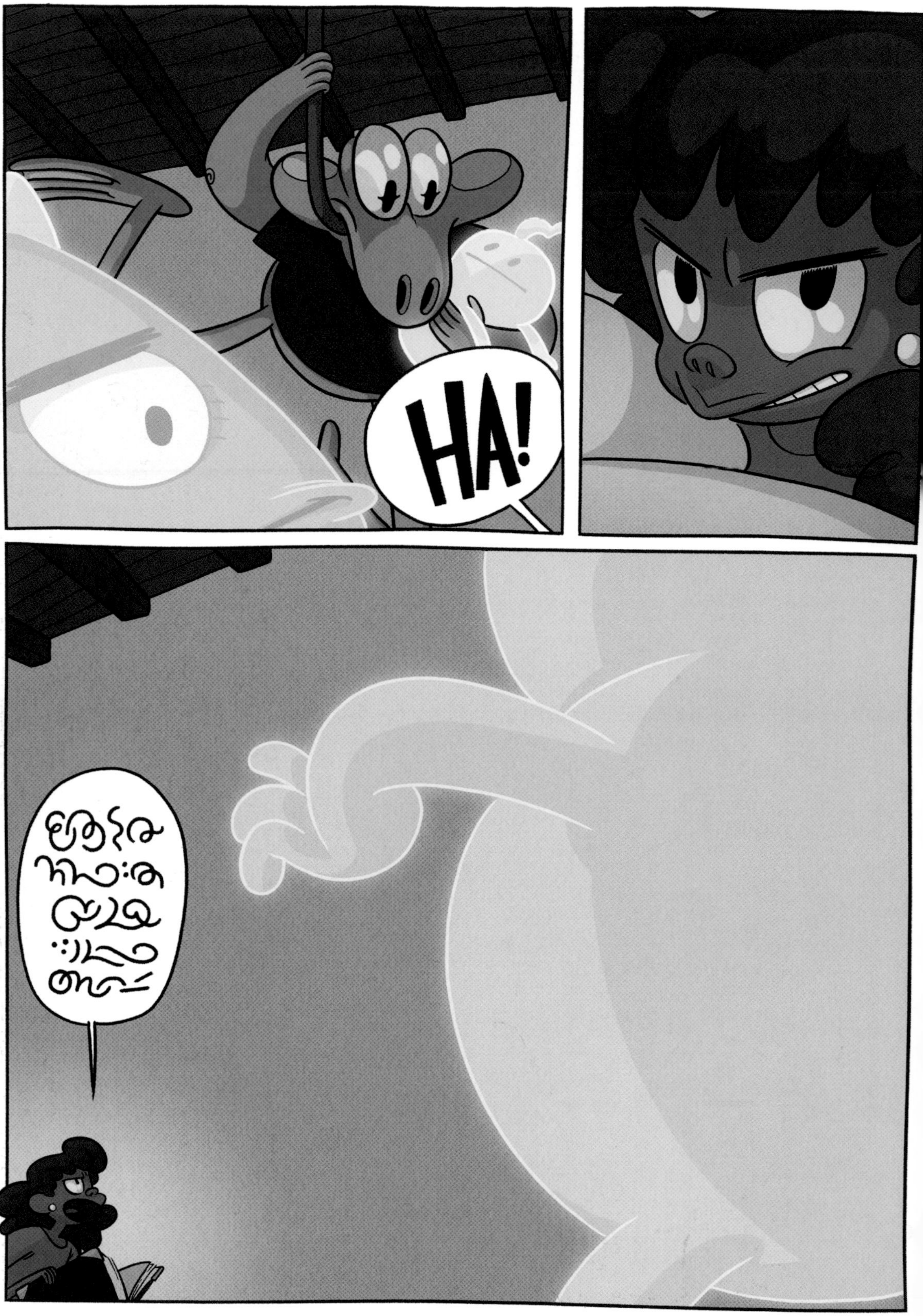
HA!

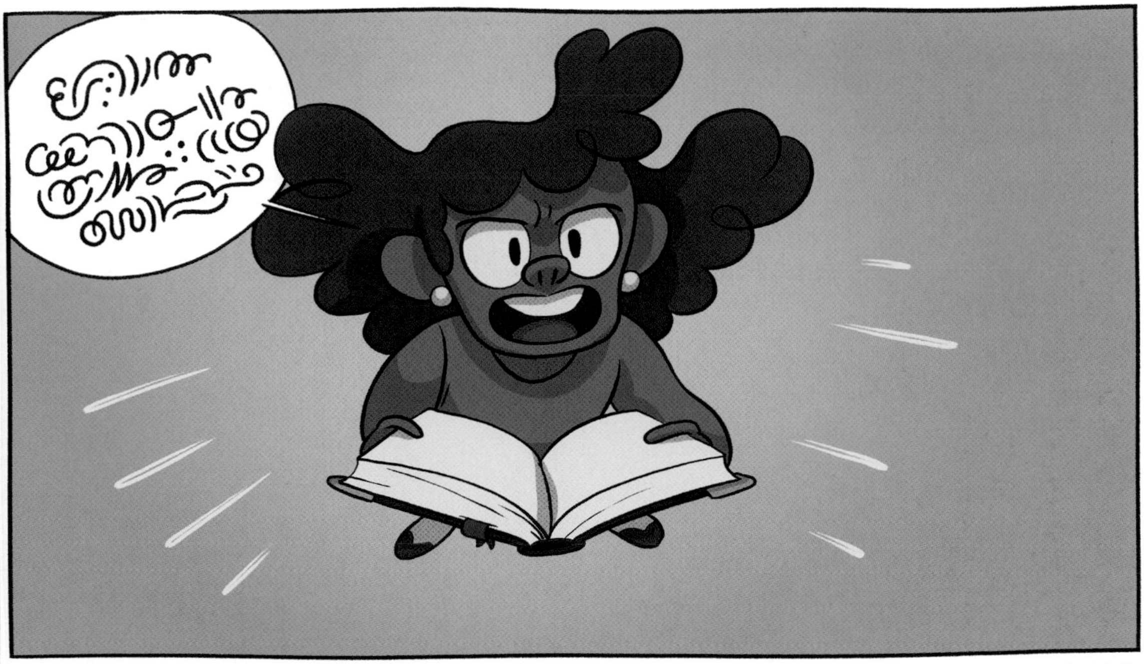

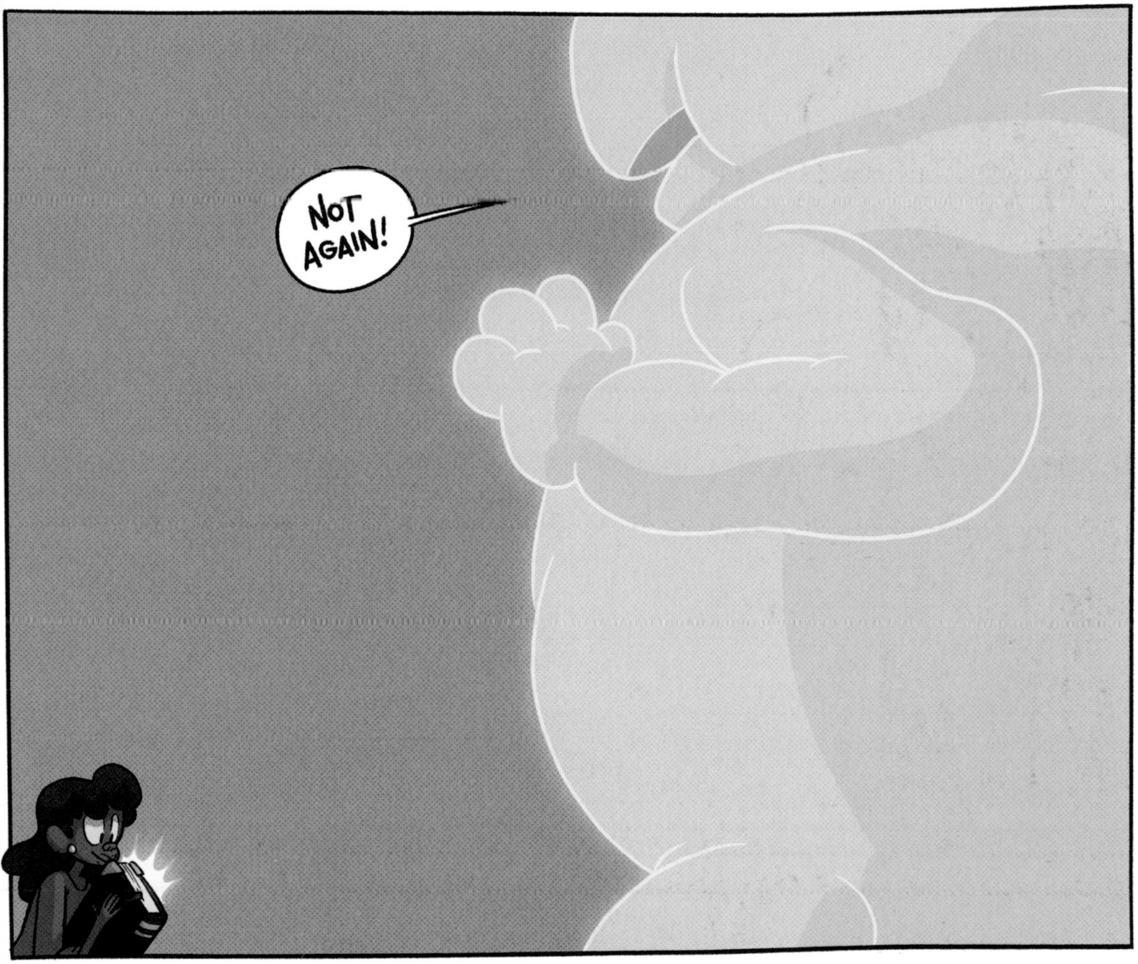
NOT AGAIN!

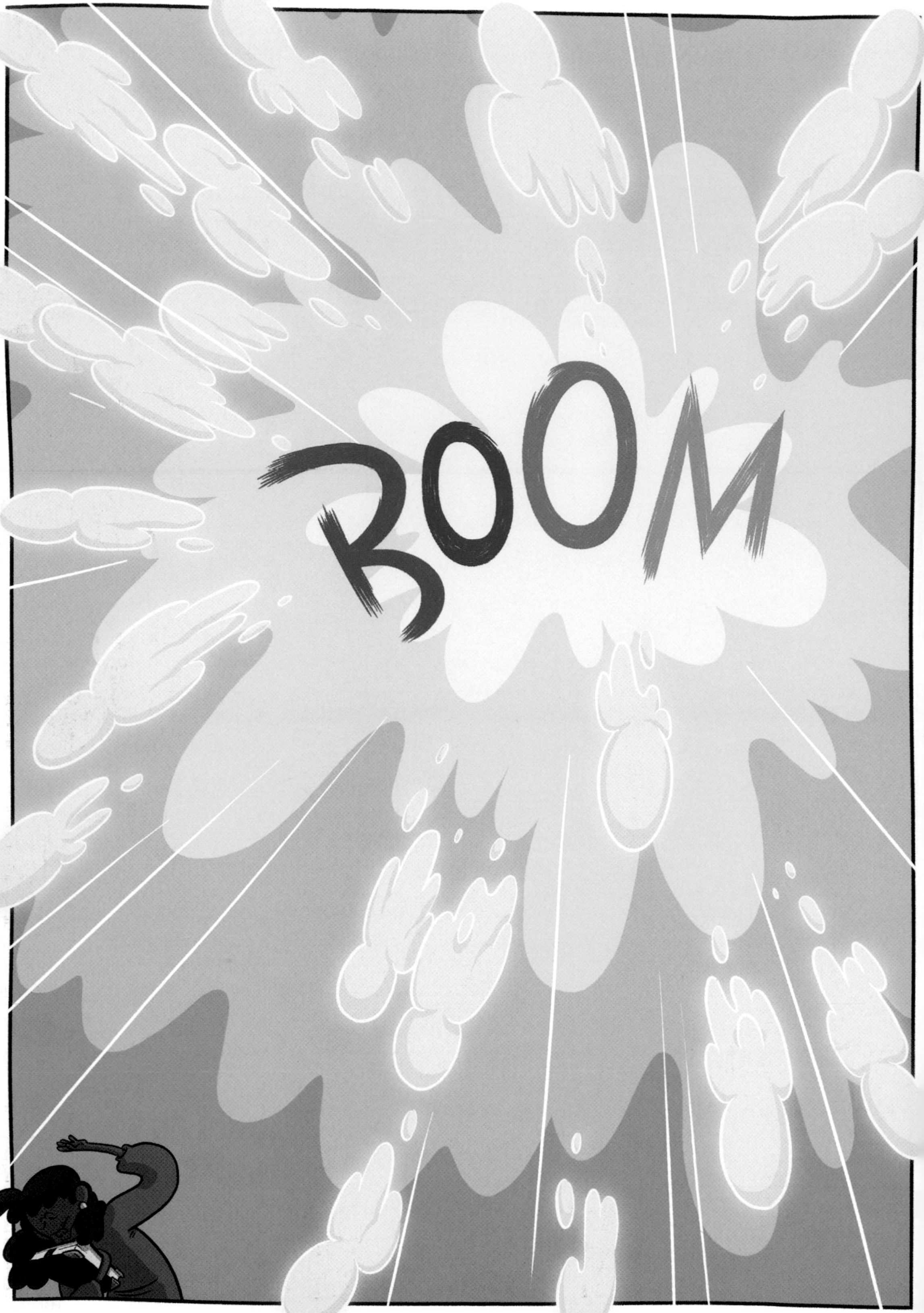
BOOM

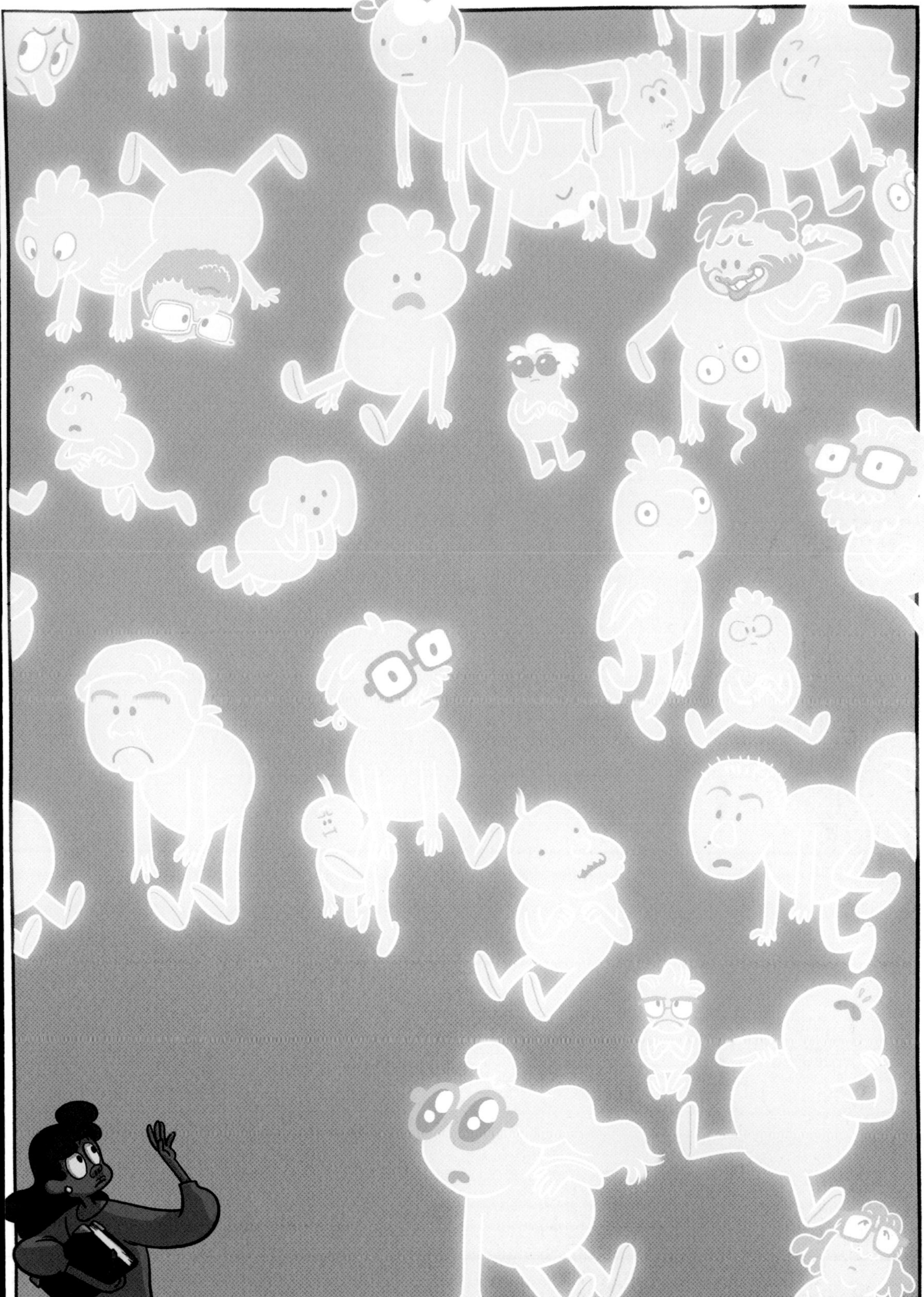

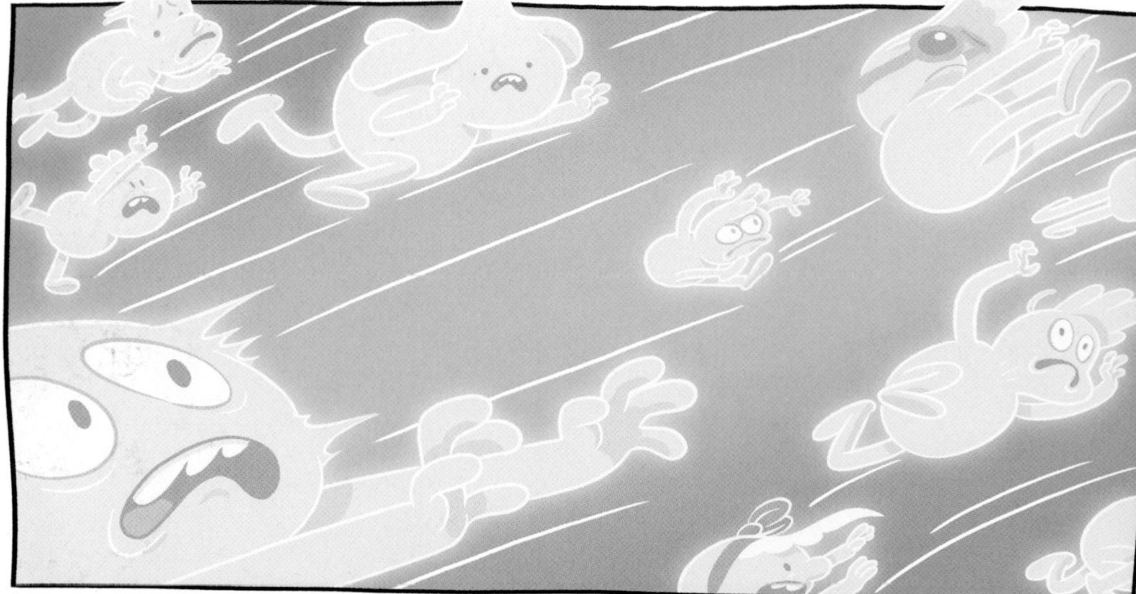

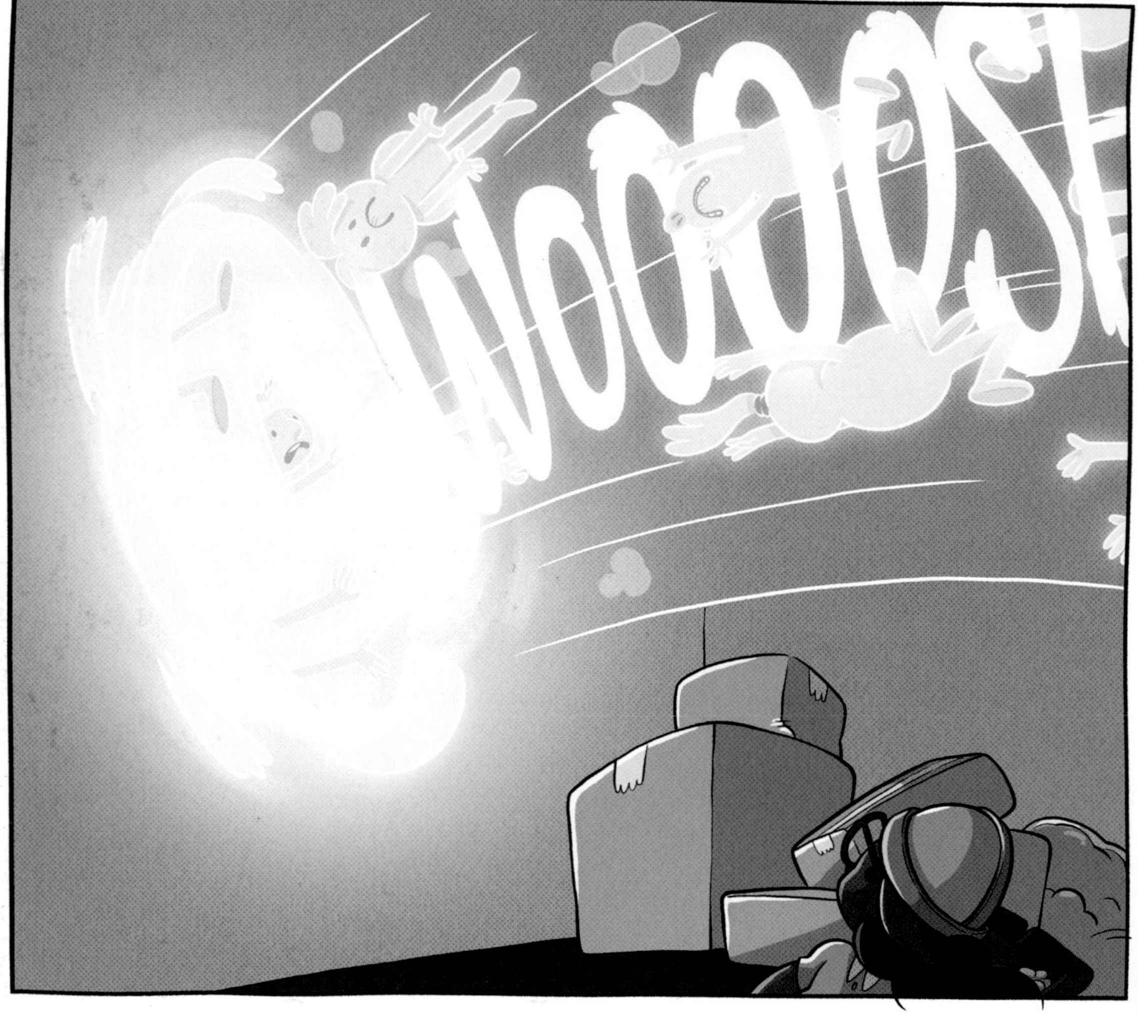
WOOOOOSH

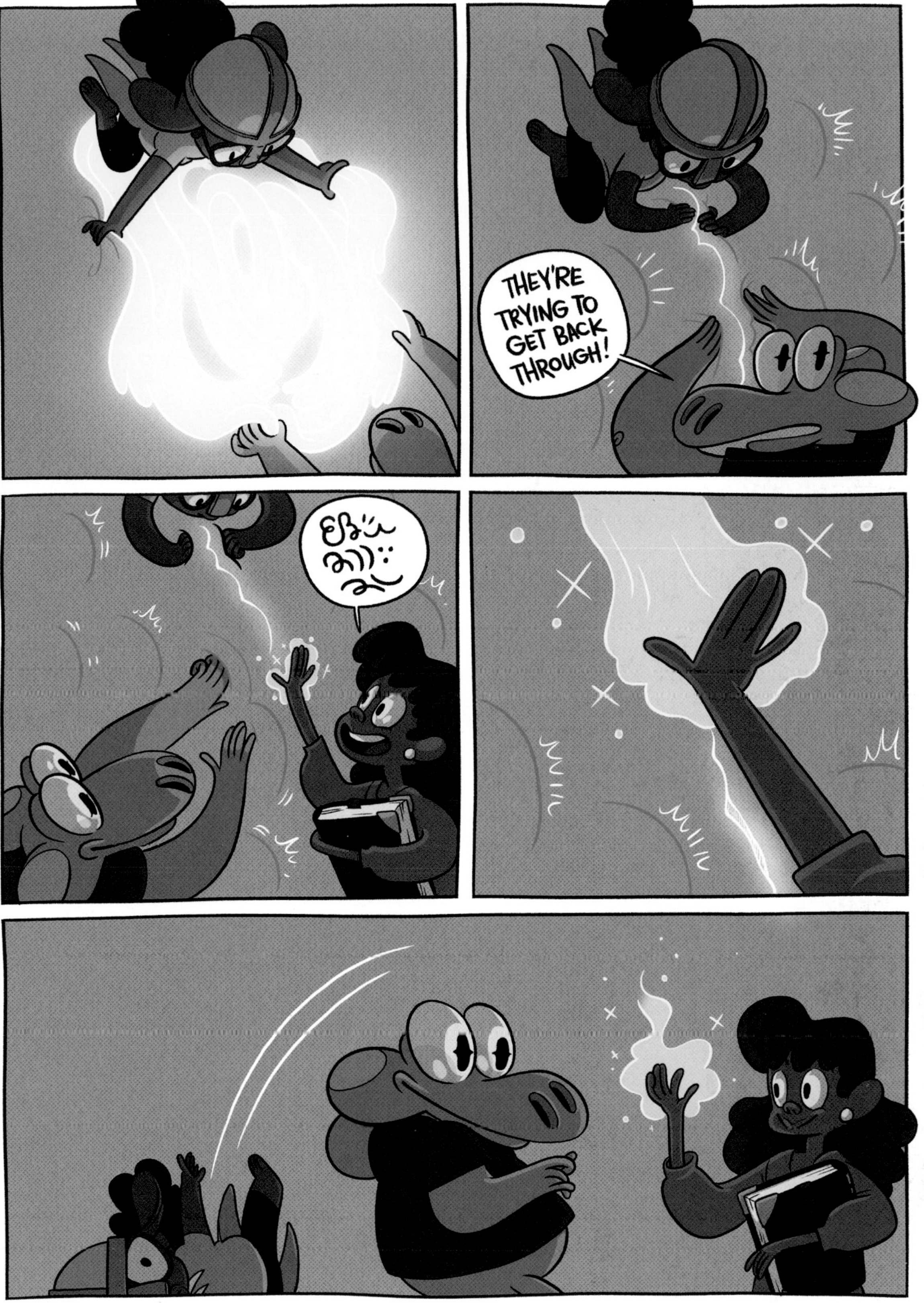
THEY'RE TRYING TO GET BACK THROUGH!

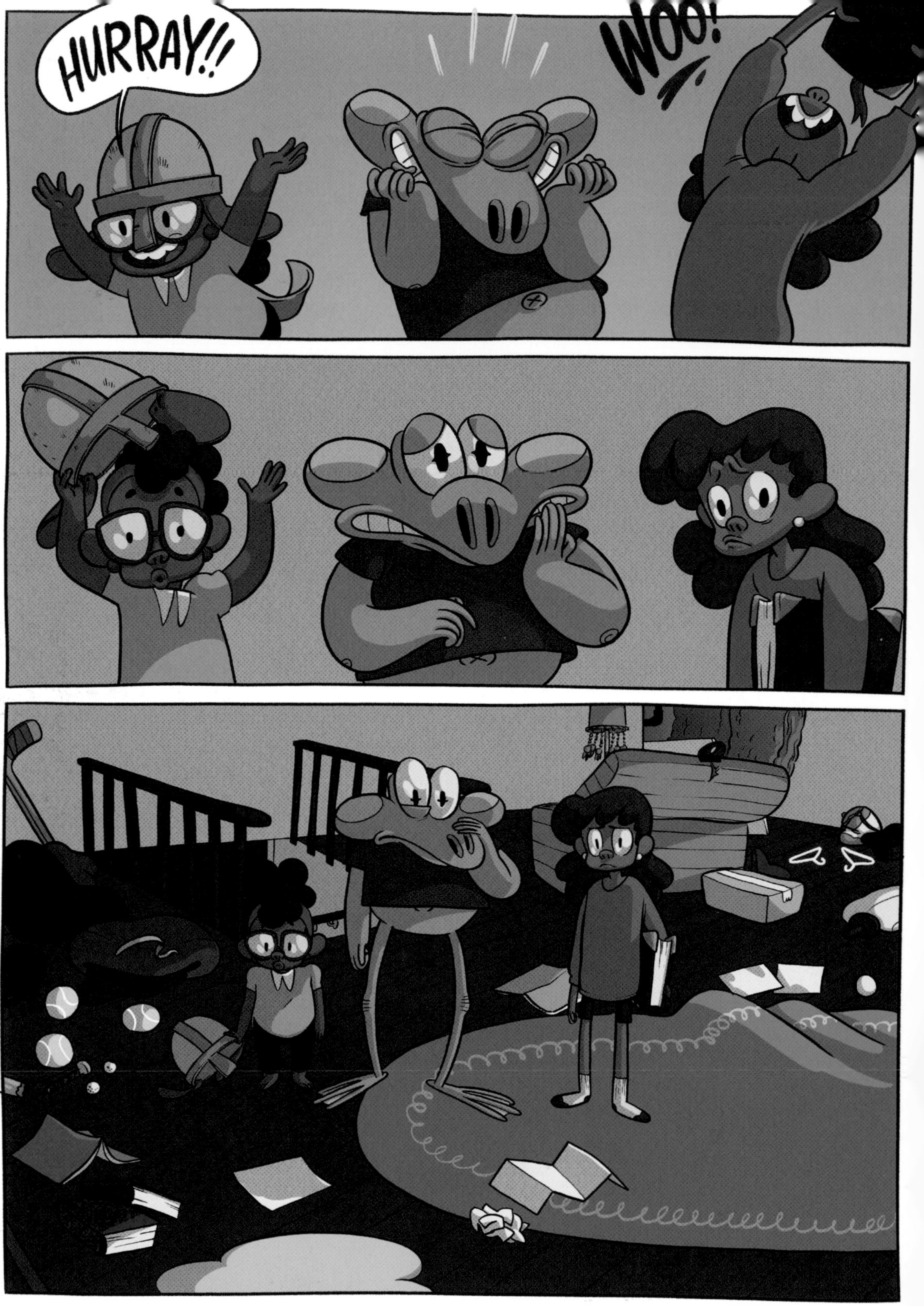
HURRAY!!
WOO!

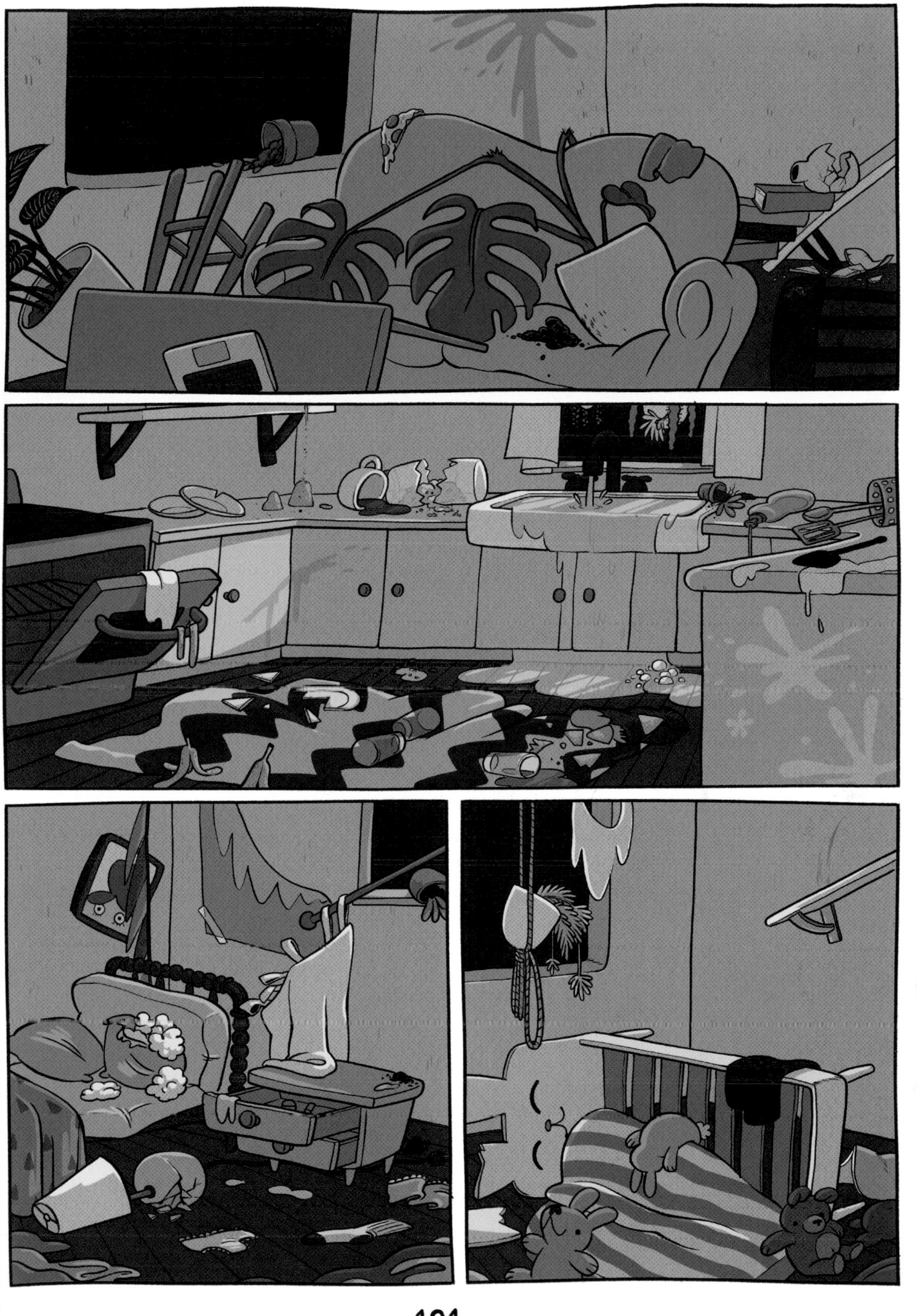

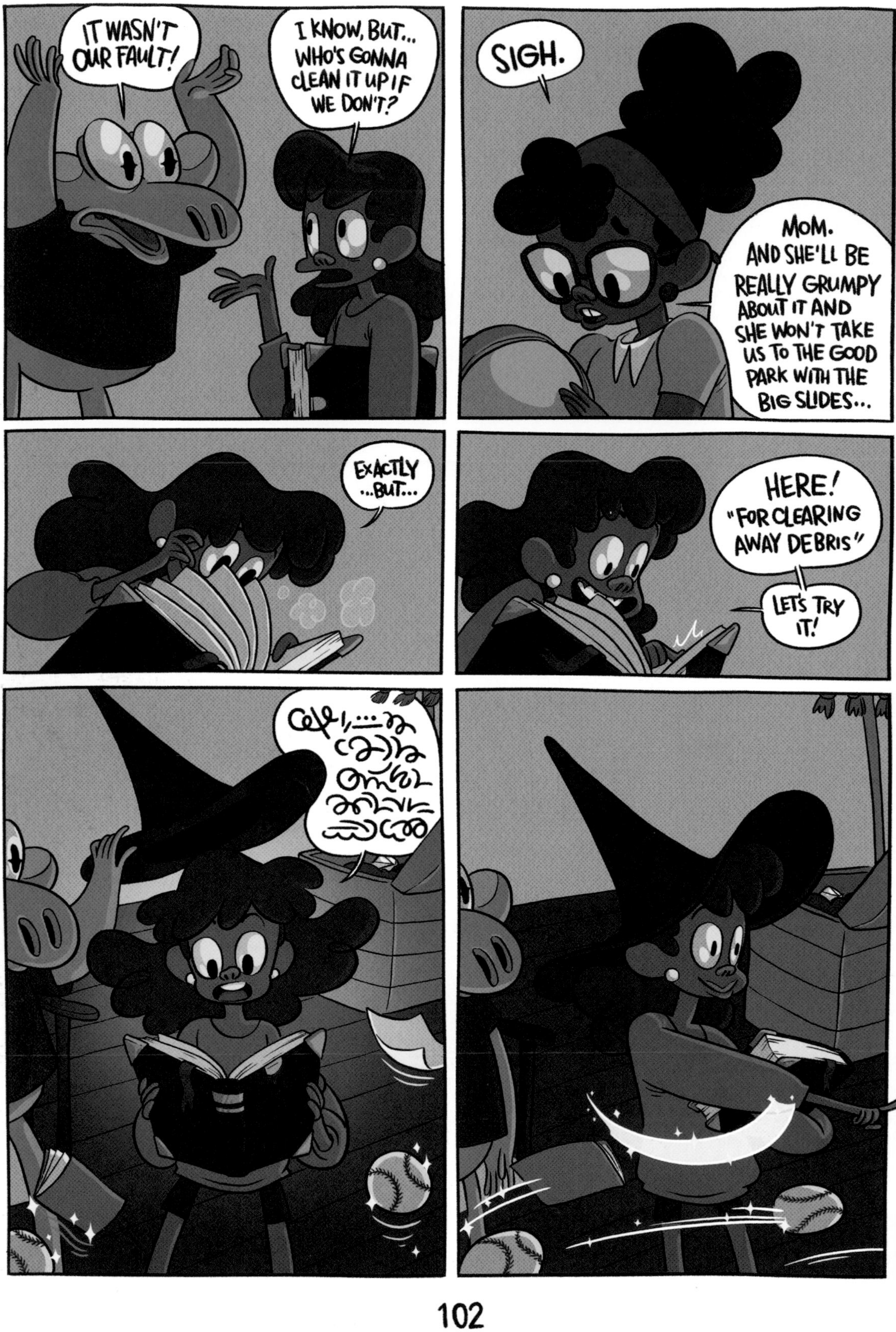
IT WASN'T OUR FAULT!
I KNOW, BUT... WHO'S GONNA CLEAN IT UP IF WE DON'T?
SIGH.
MOM. AND SHE'LL BE REALLY GRUMPY ABOUT IT AND SHE WON'T TAKE US TO THE GOOD PARK WITH THE BIG SLIDES...
EXACTLY ...BUT...
HERE! "FOR CLEARING AWAY DEBRIS"
LET'S TRY IT!

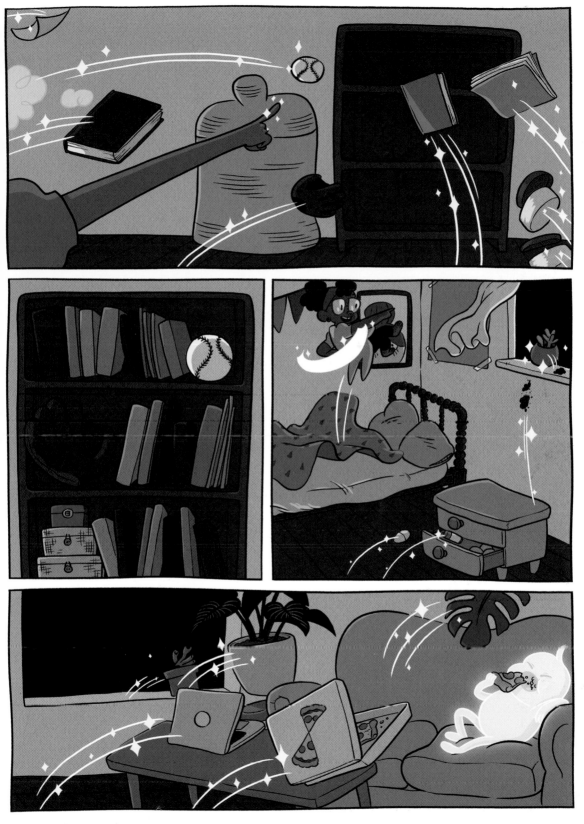

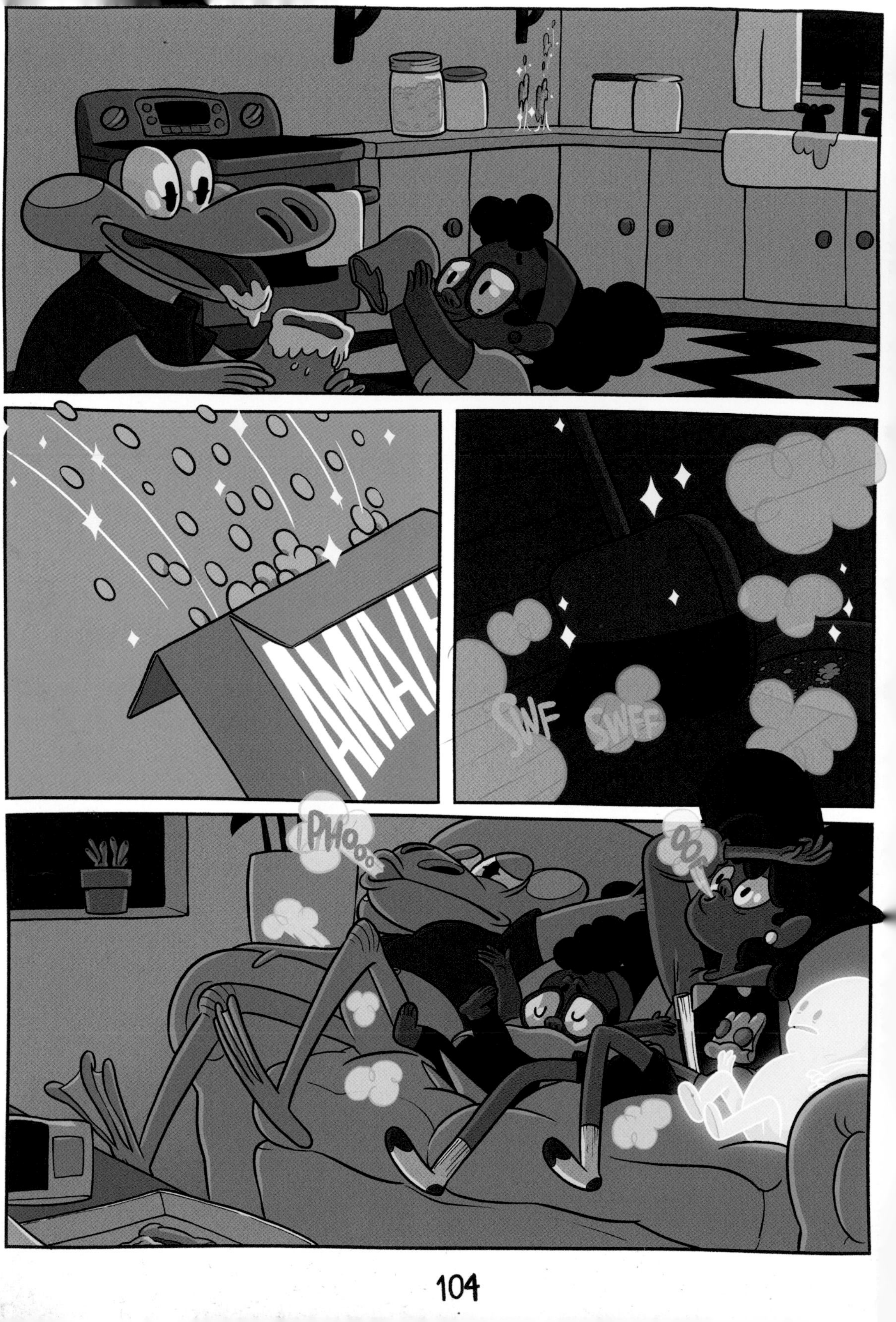
SWF
SWEF
PHOooo
OOF

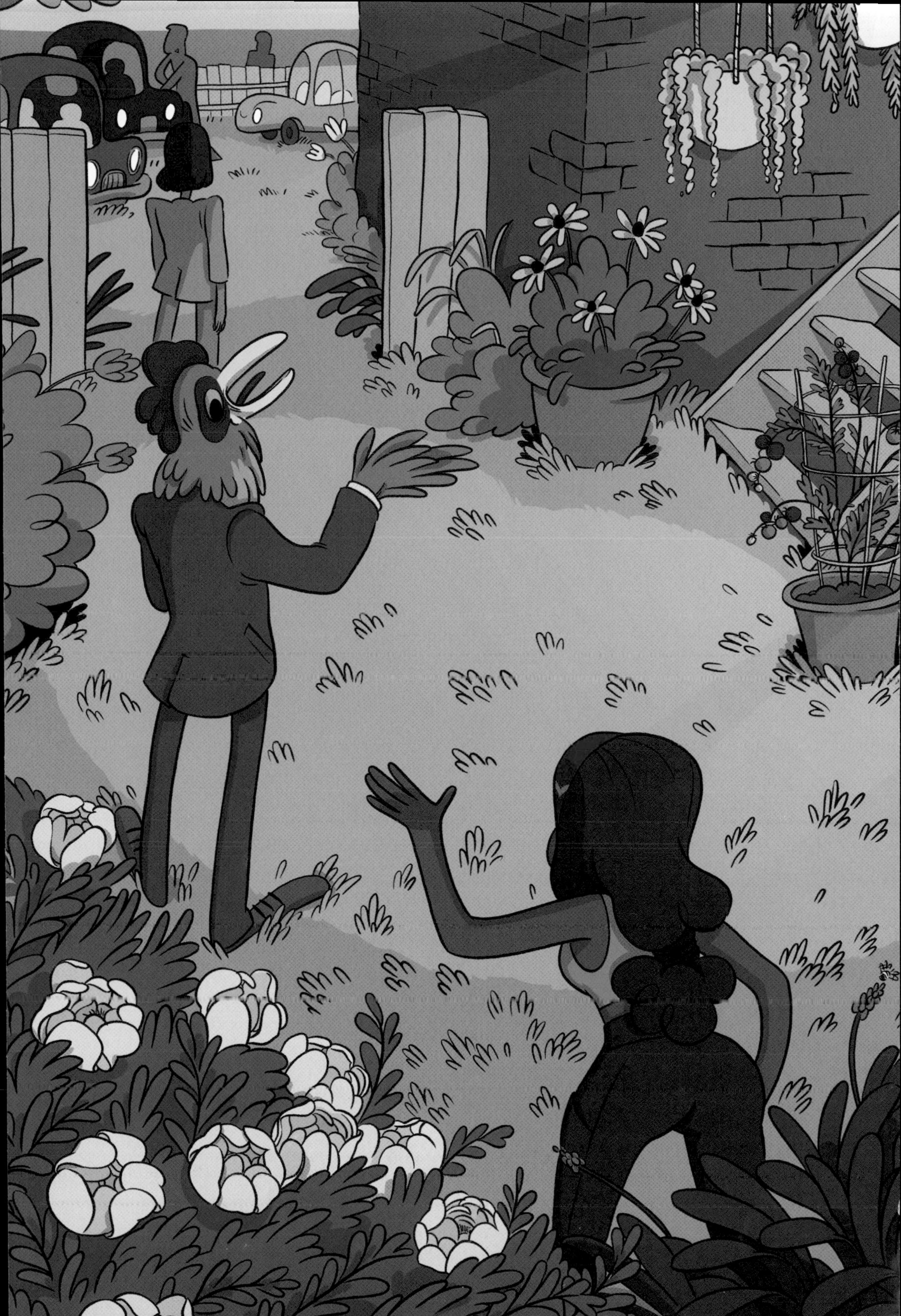

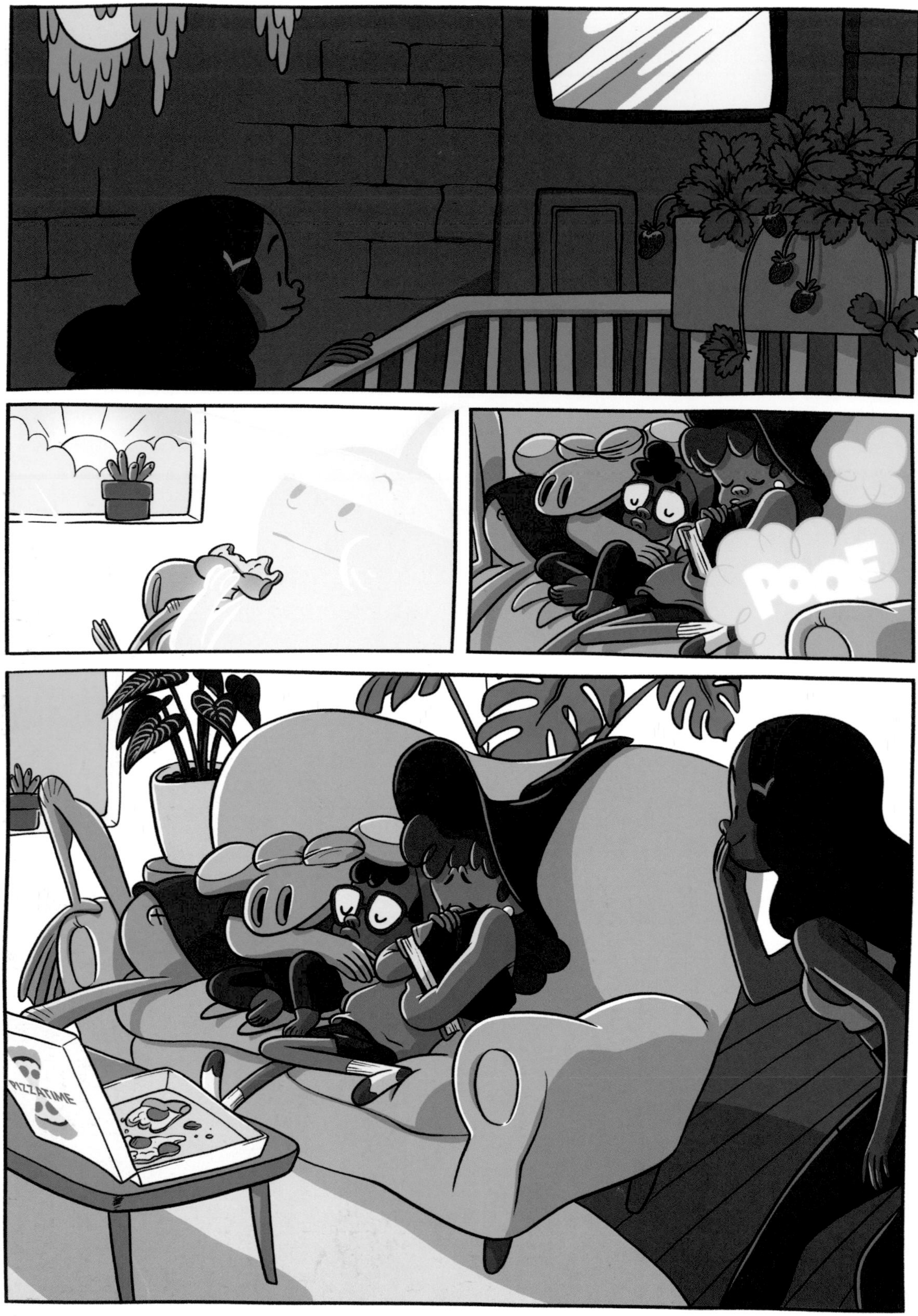
POOF
PIZZATIME

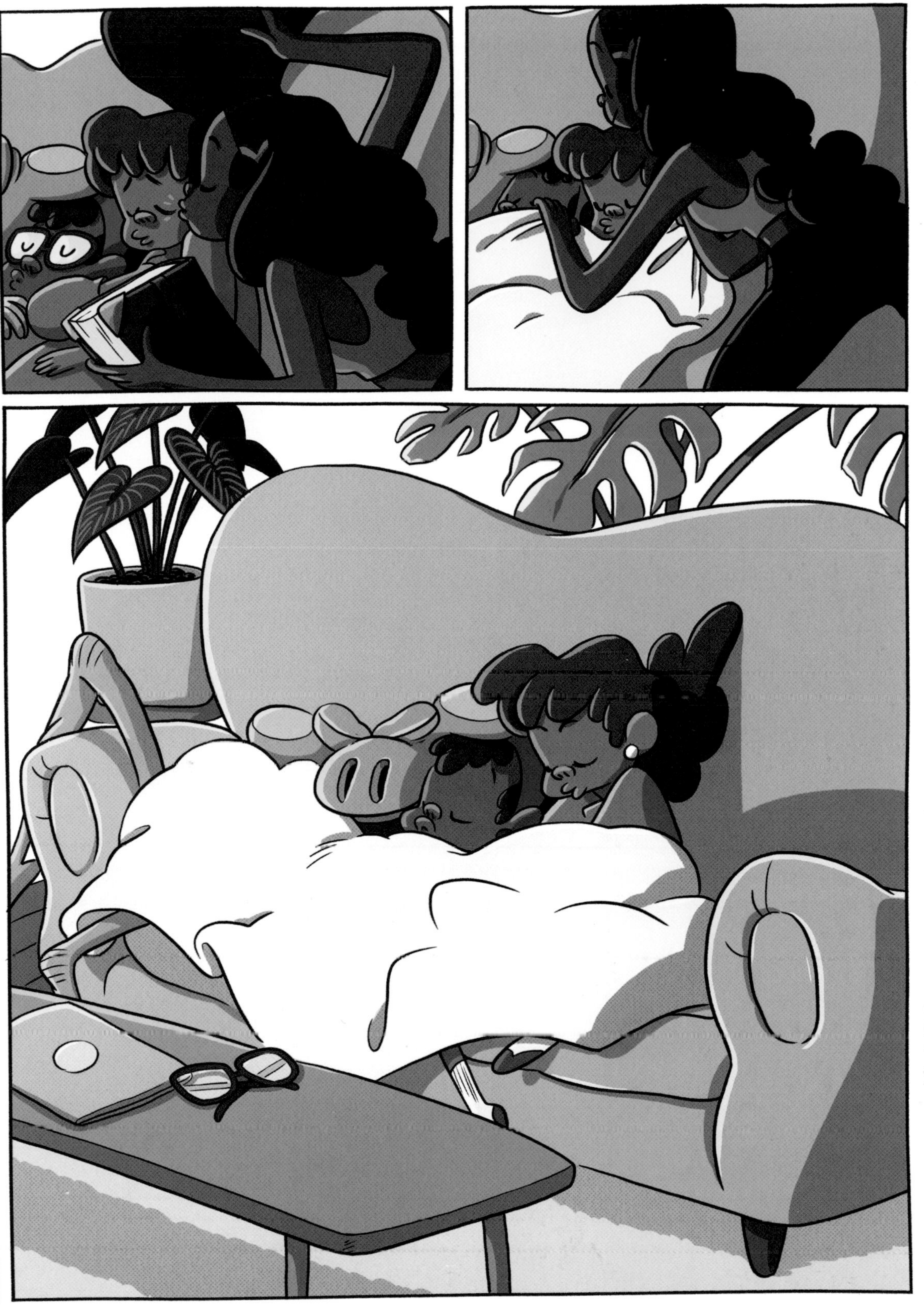

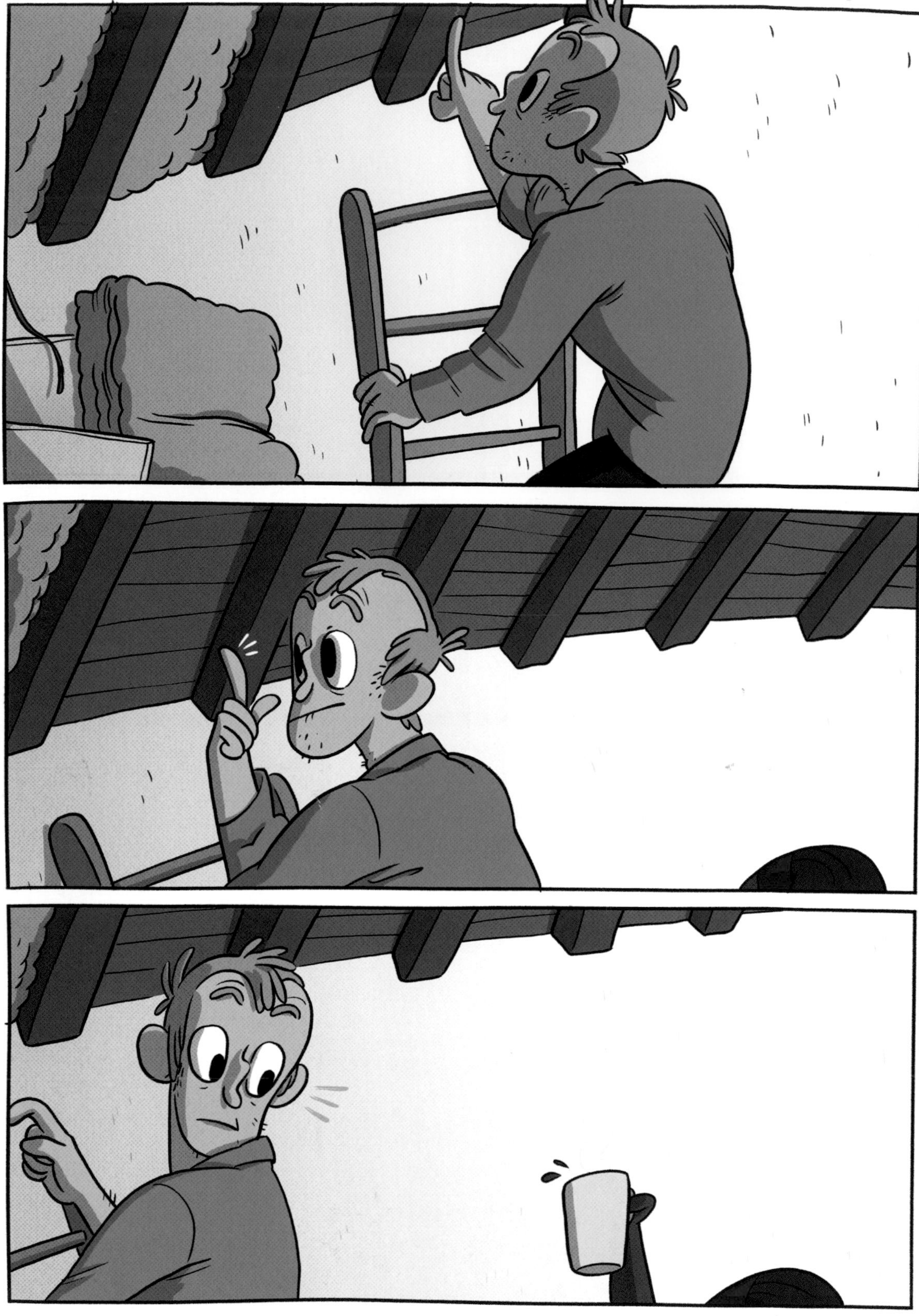

YOU DID A GREAT JOB, HON! I CAN'T SEE ANY DAMAGE AT ALL!
OF COURSE I DID! IF I CAN BANISH A 10th LEVEL GHOST QUEEN, I CAN FIX A LEAK.

THE END.

Britt Wilson is a Desk Troll. A creature known for its hunchback, pasty complexion, grubby attire and generally grouchy demeanour. Desk Trolls rarely leave the chaotic near vicinity of their desks, mostly because they've accidentally barricaded themselves in with detritus. Britt's desk is located in a house in Toronto, Ontario, that it shares with two cats, a pitiable man who made a silly decision to marry a Desk Troll seemingly of his own volition, and a (mostly) cheerful small child. The Desk Troll loves her large metal behemoth work surface, despite the ugly brown paint job and musty smelling linoleum top with the proliferation of somewhat empty coffee cups and dried out markers that litter its surface.

A MESSAGE FROM THE TROLL:

THANK YOU, AVIV, MY IDEA MAN, MY LATE NIGHT SNACK GOFER, MY PARTNER IN PARENTING. ALISE, FOR HER INDISPENSIBLE HELP FLATTING. MY MOM, NANCY, WHO FLATTED ROUGHLY ⅔ OF THIS BOOK, AND WITH DAD, BABYSAT, RAN ERRANDS, GAVE MORAL SUPPORT. WITHOUT THEM, THIS BOOK SIMPLY WOULDN'T EXIST. ANNIE, AND HER IMMENSE PATIENCE. HELEN + ED FOR ALL THEIR ENTHUSIASM, HELEN, I OWE YOU A TOKEN! MY IN-LAWS, (I REALLY LUCKED OUT) WHO SUPPORT US IN SO MANY WAYS WITHOUT EVEN NEEDING TO BE ASKED. MY PATREON PATRONS, WHO NOT ONLY AIDED FINANCIALLY, BUT LEANT THEIR LIKENESSES TOO!

LASTLY, THE CANADA COUNCIL FOR THE ARTS.

I'M SURROUNDED BY INCREDIBLE PEOPLE. THANK YOU.

Published by Koyama Press
koyamapress.com

First edition: September 2018
ISBN: 978-1-927668-61-0
Printed in China

Koyama Press gratefully acknowledges the Canada Council for the Arts
and the Ontario Arts Council for their support of our publishing program.

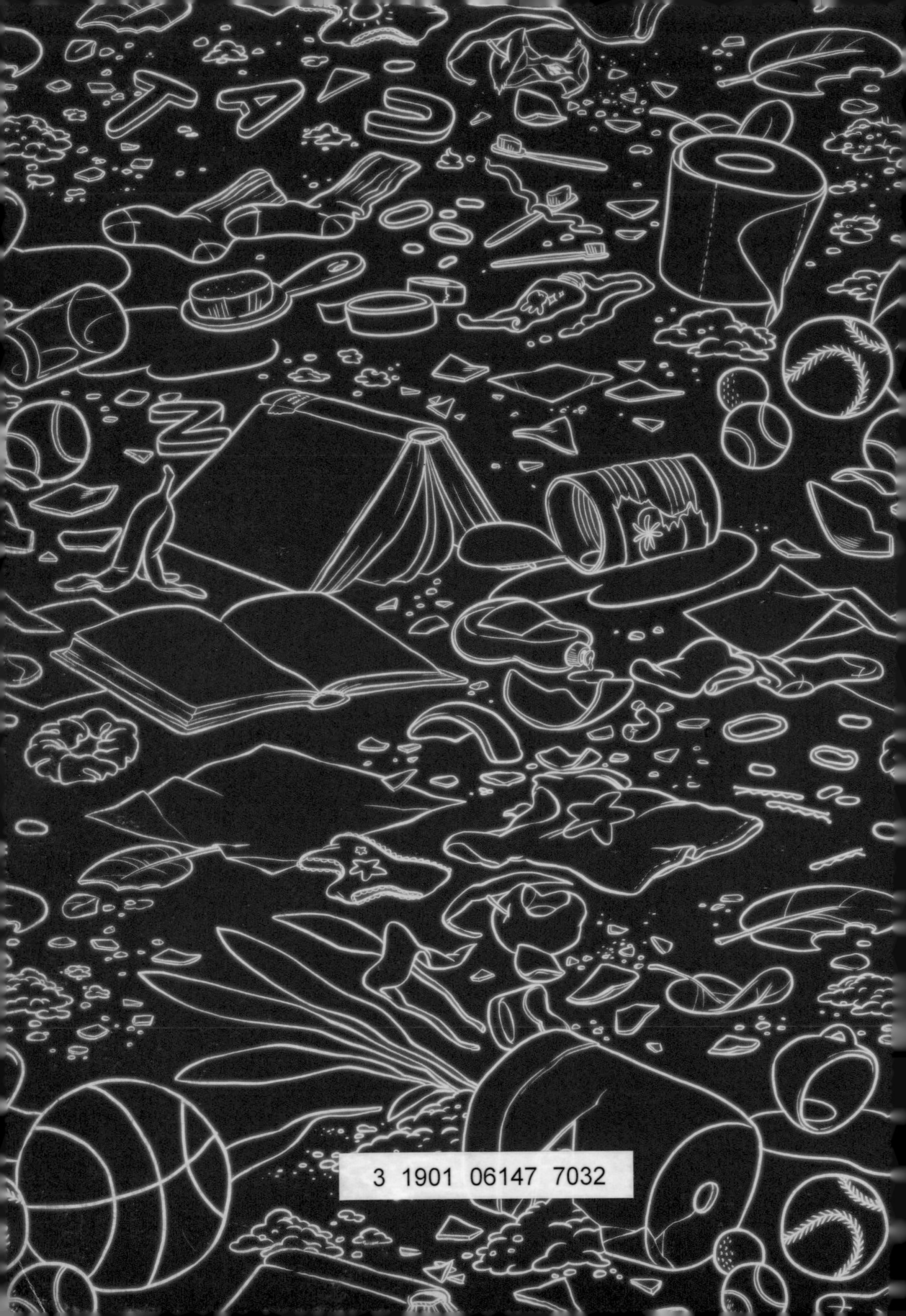